The Unruly Heart of Miss Darcy

Erin Edwards

LITTLE, BROWN AND COMPANY
LARGE PRINT EDITION

This book is a work of fiction. Names, characters, places, and incidents are the product of the author's imagination or are used fictitiously. Any resemblance to actual events, locales, or persons, living or dead, is coincidental.

Copyright © 2026 by Erin Edwards

Ornaments © CoffeeTime/Shutterstock.com

Cover art copyright © 2026 by Bijou Karman. Cover design by Karina Granda.
Cover copyright © 2026 by Hachette Book Group, Inc.
Interior design by Carla Weise.

Hachette Book Group supports the right to free expression and the value of copyright. The purpose of copyright is to encourage writers and artists to produce the creative works that enrich our culture.

The scanning, uploading, and distribution of this book without permission is a theft of the author's intellectual property. If you would like permission to use material from the book (other than for review purposes), please contact permissions@hbgusa.com. Thank you for your support of the author's rights.

Little, Brown and Company
Hachette Book Group
1290 Avenue of the Americas, New York, NY 10104
Visit us at LBYR.com

First Edition: April 2026

Little, Brown and Company is a division of Hachette Book Group, Inc.
The Little, Brown name and logo are registered trademarks
of Hachette Book Group, Inc.

The publisher is not responsible for websites (or their content)
that are not owned by the publisher.

Little, Brown and Company books may be purchased in bulk for business, educational, or promotional use. For information, please contact your local bookseller or the Hachette Book Group Special Markets Department at special.markets@hbgusa.com.

Library of Congress Cataloging-in-Publication Data
Names: Edwards, Erin author
Title: The unruly heart of Miss Darcy / Erin Edwards.
Description: First edition. | New York : Little, Brown and Company, 2026. | Audience term: Teenagers | Audience: Ages 12 and up. | Summary: "Directly after the events of *Pride and Prejudice*, Georgiana Darcy falls in love with one of the Bennet sisters in this queer historical romance." —Provided by publisher.
Identifiers: LCCN 2025005392 | ISBN 9780316591003 hardcover |
ISBN 9780316591133 ebook
Subjects: CYAC: Romance stories | Great Britain—History—Regency, 1811–1820—Fiction | Characters in literature—Fiction. | LGBTQ+ people—Fiction | LCGFT: Romance fiction | Queer fiction | Historical fiction | Novels
Classification: LCC PZ7.1.E2925 Un 2026 | DDC [Fic]—dc23
LC record available at https://lccn.loc.gov/2025005392

ISBNs: 978-0-316-59100-3 (hardcover), 978-0-316-59113-3 (ebook),
978-0-316-61049-0 (large print)

To Mum and Dad, who have always given me everything

Chapter One

The gingerbread at Pemberley was the one thing in my life that had never changed. I had a plate of it resting beside the piano, warm and spiced enough to make my tongue tingle. All these years later it was identical to my first taste of it, when my baby teeth had been too sensitive for the hard biscuits so I'd sucked on them until they dissolved in my mouth. I had lost my mother, then my father and then almost lost my reputation, but Ruth still made the gingerbread the exact same.

For every page of music I successfully played,

I rewarded myself with a bite, cleaning my fingers on the hem of my petticoat to ensure I didn't get grease on the keys.

I fought my way through a particularly complicated section, one I'd been struggling to get right for weeks. My brother and Elizabeth both insisted it sounded perfectly lovely whenever they heard it, but I knew what it was supposed to sound like. The notes in my head never corresponded to the ones my hands were playing. I'd tried it first on the harp and now on the piano—my last attempt to breathe some life into the melody in my mind. Otherwise I was going to need to learn to play some new instruments.

It still wasn't right. My fingers flew over the keys as fast as I could make them go, but they tripped over one another and the notes weren't crisp enough. The song came to an end, and a silence settled over the room, broken only by my sigh. I didn't reach for a gingerbread round. I didn't deserve one. Soft applause from the doorway interrupted my despondency.

"That was beautiful," Elizabeth said, stepping into the room. "Is it finished?"

"No," I said. "It still doesn't sound like I need it to."

"Well, it's as good as anything I've heard in a music hall," she promised, reaching out to steal a piece of gingerbread.

She looked very well considering the late hour she'd likely seen the night before. Pemberley's monthly ball was one its revellers were never keen to quit early. The house was too vast for the noise to reach my apartments, but the staff grumbled to one another about the sleep of which they'd been robbed when they thought I couldn't hear them.

Elizabeth sank into her usual chair by the window and took a moment to observe the view, golden in the last of the day's light, before she focused her attention back on me. This wasn't a casual visit to my drawing room.

"Your absence was noted at the ball last night, particularly since it was the second since your return from London and you have been seen at neither," she began, her voice gentle.

My cheeks coloured. Neither she nor my brother had ever encouraged me to attend social events if I preferred the company of books and instruments, and I always preferred the company of books and instruments. The very reason I had been sent to London was to be tutored in proper social etiquette, and yet all it had instilled in me was a deep desire to avoid every social engagement that consisted of more than half a dozen people.

I was no good in large crowds, particularly when half the room was looking at me as a freshly instructed potential wife. In truth, I had no desire to ever find a husband. My interests lay elsewhere, but that was nothing I could ever tell Elizabeth.

Tucking my hands into my lap, I avoided Elizabeth's eyes. I didn't want to bring rumour and disapproval to Pemberley's door. Before I could apologise, she continued.

"Word was you are in a delicate condition and have hidden yourself away in the country for the duration, or perhaps some travesty overcame you in London and left you quite disfigured." Her words were musical, threaded with laughter she tried to suppress as she teased me. "Or, the most fanciful of all, that you met an untimely death in the city and are not here at all."

I couldn't help but pull a face. Finding myself the centre of conversation was little better than finding myself the centre of attention. At least if I was in the room, speculation was restrained.

"Am I truly all they have to talk about?" I said with a sigh. "Surely there is something more interesting, some real scandal."

"Those who meet you, you intrigue, and those who don't are left all the more curious for it," Elizabeth said, getting up to rest her hand on my shoulder and squeeze it reassuringly. "You have your brother's way of commanding attention, I fear. I tried my best to divert conversation elsewhere but with limited success. I would not make you do something you'd rather not, but perhaps show your face at the ball next month to assure people you are not dead, maimed, or with child?"

She went quiet for a moment, and I thought perhaps she was finished, but when she added a final point it was with a new air of solemnity.

"I heard your name mentioned alongside that of George Wickham. In the interest of preventing that particular storied gossip making a return, it really would be best to make an appearance so they have no reason to talk."

I went still, fiddling my thumb over a chip in the end of one of the piano keys. No one knew the truth of what had happened between George Wickham and me, but the most vigilant had drawn their own conclusions. Rumours of the son of the former estate manager and the daughter of the house trying to elope caught like the driest kindling.

Time had quietened the whispers, but I knew they lay dormant rather than dead, ready to be reignited by the right spark. It would still be better than the truth being spread, the one that involved a pretty girl and an unlocked door and a blackmail threat, but only marginally.

"I shall think about attending," I promised Elizabeth.

It was the best I could do, stuck between two disagreeable notions. Evenings of stilted small talk and men stepping on my feet were far from my preferred way to pass the time. Still, the rumours Elizabeth spoke of had the potential to blacken not only my name specifically, but the Darcy name as a whole. My family had a reputation to uphold, and a wayward daughter had no part in it.

"Kitty will be able to accompany you next month," Elizabeth said. "Being the topic of gossip never much bothered her, as I'm sure you'll learn as soon as she gets here."

When my brother married Elizabeth, I inherited what seemed like endless family members.

For the longest time it had been just Darcy and me, with both our parents dead, but now I had a sister, and she in turn had four more, each more of a character than the last.

Jane visited often at Pemberley, her good nature making her a favourite houseguest of the household staff. Mary rarely left Longbourn but wrote often to Elizabeth, dreaming wistfully of Pemberley's library. Lydia was welcome to visit but didn't, on account of the invitation not extending so warmly to her husband, who himself was the reason I'd not met the younger three Bennet sisters. There had been a risk of him attending Darcy and Elizabeth's wedding, which made it certain that I did not. My brother would not risk me running into George Wickham, and it was a matter I would not argue with him.

Elizabeth had plenty of stories about most of her sisters, but Kitty seemed to inspire few of her own. She was often at Lydia's side in a tale, but never the focus. While her sisters planted roots, she spent much of her time with Elizabeth or Jane. Her visits to Pemberley had not yet overlapped with my own, but now that I had returned from London to stay indefinitely, I would undoubtedly be seeing much of her.

"What time is she expected?" I asked.

Elizabeth turned to the clock on the mantelpiece, comparing it to her pocket watch and sighing when they didn't match.

"Probably not long—maybe half an hour? Will you play me something before she arrives?"

I was happy to oblige, opting for a simple Scottish air I knew by rote. As I played, Elizabeth settled beside the window and tapped her fingers on her knee in time with the music. She recounted fond tales of the ball, perhaps a more subtle way to encourage my attendance next month. I found it hard to imagine my awkward elder brother dancing and making merry, but Elizabeth always did bring out a different side to him. She was midway through a story when she suddenly stopped abruptly, sitting up and squinting out the window.

"It's Kitty!" she said, grinning and jumping to her feet. "It must be. Are you coming, Georgiana?"

"I'll join you in a minute," I promised, seeking one last moment alone to rally myself for introductions.

Elizabeth disappeared out of the room, swiping another gingerbread round as she passed. I finished the song I'd started before leaving the piano for the window.

The light from the coach making its way down the path could only have been a dot in the distance when Elizabeth first saw it, for it was barely in view even now. It had been sent after dinner to collect Kitty for the final stretch of her journey, so it was one of Pemberley's own, but in the fading light it was unrecognisable from any other.

If I leant far enough forward, I could see Elizabeth already on the front steps. As the coach drew closer, my brother stepped out beside her and offered his arm, which she quickly took. I watched the two of them talking and smiling, imagining the jovial teasing to which Elizabeth was likely subjecting him. He bore it all with the same besotted look as always.

The coach pulled up at the bottom of the stairs, and Darcy stepped up beside it to offer Kitty a hand down the step. She barely took it, flying out of the door and pulling Elizabeth into a hug. There was a pang in my chest at the sight. Elizabeth felt most like my sister when her real sisters weren't there for comparison.

Kitty Bennet, like all the Bennet sisters, was

a variation on a similar theme. They all had the same bright eyes and blonde curls, yet no one could ever accuse them of looking alike. Even from a distance, I could see the differences. Her face was rounder, her features softer. She looked angelic, like the kind of person who could float one inch above the floor, ethereal and one step removed from the plane the rest of us called home, but chose not to. When Elizabeth took her arm and led her inside, Kitty's heavy steps would have made my former governesses wince. I couldn't help the smile that played at the corner of my lips.

As tempting as it was to stay upstairs and keep practising, I knew I had to show my face. My absence had already been mentioned by Elizabeth once, and I didn't want to give her further reason to be concerned. Besides, Kitty mattered to Elizabeth, and Elizabeth had come to matter dearly to me. Playing the part of the dutiful sister-in-law, I shut the piano lid.

I could hear the excited chatter between sisters from down the hallway. When I got to the door, I lingered just out of view for a moment, acclimatising myself to the vibrancy of an atmosphere so at odds with my day of practise and contemplation. I wasn't as quiet as I imagined, because I didn't even make it a full minute before Elizabeth caught my eye.

"Georgiana!" She grabbed my hand, dragging me into the room. "This is my sister Kitty."

Kitty's eyes were still shining with ripples of laughter as she dipped into a curtsey.

"Pleased to finally meet you, Miss Darcy," she said with all the hallmarks of a greeting right out of the pages of an etiquette guide.

I curtsied back automatically. "Likewise, Miss Bennet."

It was a well-rehearsed script, but neither of us was fully committed to the performance. Kitty was barely suppressing her excitement to be back with her sister, squeezing her lips together to dampen her grin.

I wish I could say my own good graces were genuine, but without years of deportment lessons ingraining the gestures into me, I would have been reduced to a wordless statue. Kitty Bennet was stunning. The light in her eyes and the life in her cheeks animated her every feature, her fingers fidgeting with a need to be in motion. It was enough to make someone wish to take her hand in theirs just to tether her down to one place, for that place would surely be better for having her there.

I was now well acquainted with Elizabeth, had been present for many of Mrs. Jane Bingley's numerous visits, and had heard enough stories of Mrs. Lydia Wickham that it felt as if I knew her, but Kitty Bennet was by far the most intriguing of the Bennet sisters. That she was one of the only two left unmarried seemed incomprehensible. From looks alone, she was exactly the kind of girl it would be all too easy to fall in love with.

"Georgiana, could you perhaps show Kitty to the kitchens? Ruth promised to set aside some supper for her after her journey," Elizabeth said, clearly trying to encourage a friendship.

Kitty had been to Pemberley before and no doubt knew exactly where the kitchens were, but I didn't protest.

"Of course," I said to Elizabeth, before turning to Kitty. "Miss Bennet, if you'd be so kind as to follow me."

"Certainly for the best," Kitty said with a note of teasing. "The house is palatial enough for me to get lost. Let us begin our voyage, Miss Darcy."

I was too out of sorts to laugh, even if her tone suggested I ought to. If I opened my mouth, there was every chance my laughter would be too loud and too wild, revealing the disruption Kitty had caused in my mind with only one smile.

As much as I wanted to abscond to my room and pretend I felt no attraction to the girl in front of me, I forced a smile and led her through the hallways of Pemberley. If Kitty noticed, she said nothing of it.

The marble stairs, oak panelling, and painted ceilings had never felt dark before, but Kitty seemed to shine light into rooms I had not even realised were lacking it. I'd walked the corridors for as long as I'd known how and crawled them before I was steady on my feet, but they had never been missing anything until Kitty walked them beside me, filling them with endless talk of her journey and her family. She stopped only to ask questions, steaming on once she had received my baffled answers. It was impossible to keep up with her in conversation as well as on foot, since she was very much the one leading me to the kitchens.

"What is this?" she asked, scuffing her shoe over a chip in the marble floor, one that had been there since before I was born.

"An accident with a dropped statue," I explained, holding back the full story. I would never get through the necessary number of words an explanation would require.

Darcy had told me of how he had accidentally gotten under the feet of a man moving in a new bust, doing permanent damage to both the floor and the statue itself, which still bore a noticeable crack if you knew where to look. Pemberley was full of tiny imperfections that most people never noticed. Many of the causes had been Darcy or me, for however well-behaved children were, a house could not be expected to raise two of them and come out entirely unscathed.

My brief answer seemed to satisfy Kitty, prompting her to dive into another story about Lydia knocking over a statue in their garden back home in Meryton. She was fascinating to watch, her eyes bright and her cheeks flushed from the exertion of her storytelling. She spoke equally with her hands as with her voice, illustrating each facet of her tale with enthusiastic gestures.

"Perhaps we need to get you to Meryton," Kitty said, as if it were a casual sort of invitation that would mean little to me. "Then you'd have some context for all the stories. I'm sure Lizzy tells them, too. My mother adores your brother enough that all Darcys will be in her good graces for the rest of time, so you'd no doubt be welcome."

She grinned up at me as we descended the stairs to the kitchens, and I knew in that moment that Eurydice had not resented Orpheus for looking back at her as they walked out of the Underworld. If his smile had been anything like Kitty's, she would have been thankful for a glimpse of it, regardless of her fate.

I felt something in my chest tighten, and I knew, for my own sake, I would have to limit myself to small doses of Kitty. After all, it had ended rather poorly for Eurydice.

The kitchens at Pemberley were Ruth's domain and had been for as long as I could remember. I always loved spending time there, sneaking gingerbread and hiding from houseguests, so the usual warmth of the stove and smell of dinner hanging in the air were comforting despite Kitty's unnerving presence.

"Ruth!" Kitty exclaimed, hurrying across the kitchen to greet the cook with a hug.

The familiarity surprised me, even though I knew Kitty had visited before. I had never assumed she'd spent much time in the kitchen.

"I'm glad to see you've arrived safely," Ruth

said, pulling back to survey Kitty the way she always did me when I'd been away. No member of her household was wasting away on her watch. "I've set out all your favourites."

She shepherded Kitty over to a table laid with a plate of bread and sliced meat. Beside it was a dish of small honey cakes and gingerbread rounds. Rather than start with the savoury portion of the meal, Kitty bit into a cake almost as soon as she sat down. Her hum of delight turned the tips of my ears red.

"It's as good as I remember," she told Ruth, who only beamed and thanked her.

It wasn't often we were in need of supper at Pemberley, so this was later than Ruth would usually work. Strands of her dark hair, streaked with wisps of grey, were starting to escape from under her cap, and her eyes were shadowed with the weight of the day. I hoped we would not keep her up much longer. Despite her tiredness, she picked up a plate from the side and handed it to me with a wink. On it was another gingerbread round. Even though I had eaten a plateful earlier, I always had room for one more, and I savoured the warmth of the spices as I bit through the outer shell.

It was almost enough to settle me, until I once again caught sight of Kitty so at home in the kitchen I had grown up in. She fit the picture too neatly somehow, making it warmer and more compelling as she pulled Ruth into conversation. Her boundless enthusiasm was captivating, but I knew all too well the dangers of being taken hostage by beguiling girls.

Noiselessly setting my empty plate down beside the sink, I slipped out of the kitchen. It was entirely rude and certainly not what Elizabeth had in mind when she asked me to escort Kitty, but I could not bear it in there any longer. I needed to put some distance between myself and Kitty, and calm the flutters starting to whip around my chest. Her presence seemed as if it would only feed the flames of attraction, and I was keen not to let them develop into anything more substantial.

Chapter Two

A night of sleep managed to put Kitty Bennet from my mind, but when I made it downstairs for breakfast, she proved herself to be very real and very present. It was a Darcy family trait to awake slowly and with a certain level of irritability, but the Bennets had a rather different approach to mornings. Elizabeth met each one with a startling vitality, and Kitty, too, was already beaming at her sister across the table as they gossiped between bites of honey cake.

"Good morning, Georgiana," my brother

greeted me from the head of the table with a tone of relief in his voice, likely thankful to no longer be the sole subdued figure at the table.

I returned the greeting, extending it to Elizabeth and Kitty, and was grateful for the cup of tea Elizabeth pushed my way. Darcy relied on coffee to chase away the lingering tendrils of sleep, but even when I heaped it full of cream and sugar, I couldn't stand the taste. The way he drank multiple pitch-dark cups was bordering on criminal.

Ordinarily I forced myself to make conversation with Elizabeth in the morning, since she wouldn't get much out of my brother until the coffee started to work, but I was relieved to find Kitty a far more willing conversation partner than I was. I was less pleased by her choice of conversation topic.

"I was so disappointed to have missed the ball," she said, turned to try to include both Darcy and me in the conversation. It was thoughtful, but somewhat wasted. "Mother so desperately wanted me to attend, but that streak of bad weather was rotten luck in delaying the trip. I had to put up with days of her complaining about the lost opportunity to find a match."

She pulled a face that chased a laugh from me,

surprising both of us. It only succeeded in pulling her attention my way.

"Did you meet any suitors we can expect to come calling?" she asked.

I was entirely grateful I had already swallowed my latest mouthful of tea, or it would have risked choking a coughing fit from me.

"No," I said, perhaps too quickly.

Elizabeth looked like she was about to provide context, but I caught her eye and quickly shook my head. I didn't wish to get into a discussion of my dislike for assembled crowds over breakfast, especially not when Kitty clearly had no concerns with shining brightly amongst veritable strangers.

Before I could summon a suitable explanation, a footman approached the table with a tray of papers, and my attention was lost to the best part of breakfast: the delivery of the newspaper and the day's incoming correspondence. The tray was set down beside Darcy as usual, but he passed over the newspaper without me having to ask, turning his attention to the small pile of envelopes.

It was yesterday evening's newspaper, the trip from London not a quick one, but I coveted it all the same. The rich scent of ink and paper made it worth the dark smudges it left on my fingers and the headache I got from squinting to read the tiny, blurred text. I skipped the advertisements and sales notices and the gossipy article about a high-society wedding, instead focusing first on the newly published book list. I was pleased to see a new novel by Mrs. Sarah Green and made sure to commit it to memory to request it be purchased, certain Elizabeth would want to read it. I had just moved on to the paper's recollection of the latest affairs in Parliament when Darcy's voice won my attention.

"Your aunt once again requests your presence at Rosings Park," he informed me, reading over a letter I could see in her foreboding, spiky script. "I am a poor influence on you, and she could have you married to a suitable match within the year to restore the good name of our family."

Anyone who did not know my brother might think he was genuinely contemplating the request, but I could see the hint of a smile at the corner of his mouth. He mocked the suggestion in his airing of it, rather than considering it.

"Lady Catherine's optimism is impressive," I said, choosing my words carefully. She may not have been present, but I had been raised better than to directly insult my relatives, even if my aunt had been rather insufferable to Darcy since his marriage to Elizabeth. She deemed her too far below him. "If it is all the same, I would like to remain here, with my poor influence of a brother."

His smile was overshadowed by Kitty's laugh, punctuated by a particularly unladylike snort. She covered her mouth with her hand, but her eyes still showed her amusement.

"You'll find that a full house at Pemberley is probably more similar to Meryton when we were all in residence than you might expect," Elizabeth said to Kitty, not quite hiding her smile behind her teacup.

"So I see," Kitty replied with a grin.

The weight of her attention on me, with that bright smile, squeezed my breath from my chest, and I raised the newspaper higher to sequester myself behind it. The report of a man hanged at Newgate wasn't usually something I would linger on, but I read each word intently just to focus on something other than the freckles across Kitty's nose.

"Charlotte writes from Hunsford," Elizabeth said.

When I peeked over the top of the paper, I found her reading a letter of her own. Charlotte was one of the people who wrote to Elizabeth the most, a friend from when she'd lived in Meryton who had married the Bennets' reportedly rather trying cousin.

"How is she?" Kitty asked, genuine interest in her voice and eyes.

As if she could sense me looking, she turned back to me. I ducked behind the paper again, my cheeks burning like I'd been caught doing something wrong.

"She's with child again," Elizabeth said. "I'm not sure staying at home is doing her much good. I ought to go and visit her."

From what I knew of Charlotte Collins, she lived far too near my aunt for me to voluntarily offer to accompany Elizabeth as I otherwise might. Journeying close to Rosings seemed too dangerous a trip if I wanted to return home unmarried.

"Is there anything of interest to report?" Darcy asked me, prompting me to lower the paper. This felt familiar, our usual breakfast routine of swapping opinions about the military's actions on the Continent or the latest law to be passed into effect.

"Debates over tax increases in Parliament," I summarised, knowing Darcy cared little for the gossip columns on the actions of the Prince Regent.

He sighed. "They might as well reprint the same article every day."

"Can I see the newspaper, when you've finished with it?" Kitty asked.

I blinked at her, surprised. She hadn't struck me as the kind of person who would be interested in politics. I handed over the paper, unable to stop myself from watching her as she turned to the ship logs and scanned down the reports of what vessels were arriving into and leaving from the ports. If she was looking for something in particular, she didn't seem to find it, but she lingered over each entry. Her fingertip picked up a dark smudge as she skimmed it over the text.

Once Elizabeth had refolded her letter from Charlotte and returned her attention to the table, Kitty passed the newspaper back to Darcy and started up another conversation with her sister. There appeared to be a lot of gossip to catch Kitty up on, with endless tales of betrothals or babies from within the walls of the estate and amongst the tenants of its lands. She surprised me by taking a genuine interest, recognising names from previous trips and making enquiries of her own after those she'd befriended.

She expressed joy at the good news and sorrow at the bad, her compassion evident. It was strange to think she had connections to Pemberley that I knew nothing about, and it unsettled me to see her fit so easily into the picture. This Kitty Bennet was not the one from Elizabeth's stories of her two youngest sisters, but I liked her all the better for it.

The deeper into the gossip the two Bennet sisters delved, the less respectable the subject matter became. It was impossible to be certain of the veracity of a tale so much retold that no one could remember the original teller, so I trusted the stories no more than I trusted the pages of my novels. That did not, however, mean they weren't just as enthralling, and I found myself leaning closer over the table to listen in.

Darcy tolerated local gossip more than he actively participated in it, and I never quite felt qualified to join in, with nothing to contribute myself, so it was usually an uncommon activity. But knowing her new audience well, Elizabeth spun a more lurid tale. So divorced from its source that it came without names, she launched into the story of a local family suffering from the scandal of their youngest son, who ought to have been courting respectable ladies, caught with a servant girl from the kitchens.

It was the kind of story that probably wasn't true. I suspected perhaps that the anonymity was why she chose it, with no one to actually be hurt by its telling. There were no details, no recognisable figures, no known consequences. It could have happened in any town from Land's End to Gretna Green. Yet I still felt my face burn.

The way Elizabeth told it, how the clandestine couple had been caught trying to steal some time alone, it was all too familiar. There were several key differences, of course, but the room they had thought locked and the bursting in of someone who was never meant to see... I tried not to make connections to what remained the most terrifying moment of my life. The squeak of a door hinge and the sadistic tutting of someone who knew the power of the information they'd just gained—it still haunted my nightmares. I'd sworn to forget the whole thing, even if it meant brushing the good aside with the bad, the two inextricable.

But did anyone ever truly forget their first love?

My brother professed he had married his, although I questioned what he'd been doing with his life to have gotten to the age of eight and twenty and not found himself drawn to a woman. Elizabeth had likewise confided in me Darcy was the first man she'd truly loved, but to say otherwise would be too improper to consider. I could not have been the only person to have felt the clench of my heart before I was even truly supposed to be seeking a partner.

It had happened so easily and so quickly that I'd wondered if I was mistaking one feeling for another, but it was not something I could speak to Elizabeth about, as much as I'd come to trust her. Not when the object of my heart's desires had been my best friend and a fellow student of my governess. Well-behaved young ladies did not fall in love with other girls. That particular rule wasn't in the etiquette guides, but I daresay only because it was such a scandalous thought to begin with that there was no need to even suggest otherwise.

My head found itself in such a spiral at Elizabeth's story that I didn't notice I'd stopped eating and was staring at my hands in my lap. My blush had spread across my cheeks and down my neck, burning a gentle heat at the memory of soft fingers that had once, and only once, traced the same path.

"Mrs. Darcy, I fear your sense of impropriety is scandalising my sister," Darcy said, giving Elizabeth a warning look as he misunderstood the source of my emotions.

Elizabeth just laughed. "Oh, Georgiana doesn't mind, do you?"

In truth, it gave me a thrill to be included, to be treated like another of Elizabeth's sisters rather than a child. There was simply no question of me admitting the reason for my blush, but I didn't want the present company to believe me so naive that one story of misplaced affection could unsettle me.

"Not at all," I promised, trying my best at a look that read unruffled.

Elizabeth's resulting smile was directed at my brother, self-satisfied and victorious. More a smirk than anything else. But Kitty's look was reserved for me, and she beamed. Her surprise was painfully evident, but I had given her little reason to think me anything other than an innocent little mouse of a thing who hid from company and never had anything to say. I could not be blamed that it was always far more interesting to listen.

Perhaps it was simply the way Kitty's grin lit up her face, unabashed and unrestrained, or maybe the intrigue in her eye as she looked at me—I couldn't be sure—but it pulled at something in my stomach. A tug that entreated me to follow after it, after Kitty, to see where it led.

It was a feeling I knew all too well, and one I swore I would not give in to again.

Darcy disappeared to his office and his financial ledgers to ensure the estate kept running as it should, but Elizabeth, Kitty, and I retired from breakfast to the front parlour to make the most of the morning's light. I had unearthed a book from the sofa cushions, settling in to continue the tale, when the footman appeared in the doorway.

"Ma'am," he said, addressing Elizabeth, "there is a caller here to see Miss Darcy."

The look of confusion on Elizabeth's face

was almost certainly also present on mine. I had never once received a caller at Pemberley by virtue of never going anywhere to meet someone who might want to come calling. No doubt plenty of visits were made to other houses in the days following a ball, but there was no reason for anyone to call on me.

"A male caller?" Elizabeth asked.

The footman nodded, handing over a calling card. "A Mr. Honeyfield, ma'am."

That only strengthened my confusion. The name rang a faint bell in the recesses of my memory, but I could not put it to a face. I wasn't convinced I had ever met this man personally before, which meant his call was entirely unconventional. I was within my rights to turn him away, but there was a chance it wasn't a call from a suitor. It could be news from someone I'd known in London, something too important to put in a letter.

"Have him shown in," I said to the footman. "Thank you."

As soon as he left, Kitty spoke up.

"Who is Mr. Honeyfield? A suitor?" she asked, fidgeting with her embroidery in her lap.

"I don't know," I admitted.

Sticking her needle into the fabric stretched across her embroidery hoop, she climbed to her feet and placed her project down on the side table.

"I think I'll go and ensure my things are unpacked" was the only explanation she gave before she hurried out of the room.

I couldn't blame her for leaving when it was what I most wanted to do, too. At least Elizabeth could be trusted upon to stay. Young ladies did not take callers, particularly male callers, without a chaperone.

"Georgiana—" she began, but before she could get anything meaningful out, the footman ushered in a man who, just as suspected, was entirely unfamiliar to me.

"Miss Darcy," he greeted me with lacquered enthusiasm. "How kind of you to take the time to receive my call. I had been hoping to see you at the recent Pemberley ball, but when you made no appearance, I felt I should call upon you to ensure you were in good health."

I rose to my feet and offered a curtsey, as was the polite thing to do. He was a tall, slender man, every limb an inch too long. When he bowed back to me it seemed perfectly measured as to not topple over his stretched frame.

"I do not believe we have been introduced," I said, making certain he could hear the insinuation that he was breaking social conventions. Men ought not to call upon ladies until a proper introduction was made.

Mr. Honeyfield's smile was wolfish, baring his teeth.

"I can only express my offence that you do not remember me. Why, we have known each other for over a decade now. Our fathers did business together. James Honeyfield." He introduced himself with smooth and polished words.

With the additional context, I could tease out a memory of running around the lawn of Pemberley with a gangly young boy, thrilled for the company while Darcy was away. We had met before. Technically he was within his right to visit, and he knew it, a self-satisfied smile betraying him at the corner of his lips. It was an unfortunate loophole.

"Of course." I forced a smile in return. "Thank you for the reminder. What brings you to my home?"

"As I said, I was most keen to ensure your good health. Shall we sit? Perhaps reminisce on happy childhood memories?" he asked. "If Mrs. Darcy does not mind?" He looked to Elizabeth.

I wished I could beg her to refuse him. If this was purely a social call, I had no interest in it. Mr. Honeyfield was wasting his time if he thought showing up unprompted would be endearing to me. Even with written notice a week in advance, I still had no desire to be courted.

When I looked at him, I felt fear. He had not personally done anything to frighten me, but he represented the kind of life that would stifle me. It would be unfeeling and shackled, and every second of it would be a lie. The intentions of his visit were clear: He wished to court me, propose to me, and make me his wife. All it did was remind me that I would never want that from any man. Instead, I could only compare how I felt about him to how Kitty had made me feel in the little time she'd been at Pemberley. It made that attraction all the harder to ignore.

Be that as it may, turning him away immediately after his arrival would be unthinkably rude. I had been backed into a corner, and I wasn't quite as good with loopholes as he appeared to be. Gritting my teeth, I was ready to resign myself to at least half an hour of talking about the weather, making polite enquiries after his family, and peppering him with suggestions that he should be thinking about leaving.

I had only just retaken my seat when Elizabeth spoke up.

"If only you had given us some notice, Mr. Honeyfield," she said. "I'm afraid we can spare only five minutes this morning before we must be on our way. We have promised to make calls of our own."

We had promised absolutely no such thing, but I was not about to disagree with her. I could endure this for five minutes, after which I would be spending another ten thanking Elizabeth profusely for having the mind-reading powers of a clairvoyant. If I was to be forced into social situations where men viewed me as a prize to be won, I wanted her there beside me to redirect them with undeniable politeness but irrefutable cunning.

Chapter Three

Despite how many years had passed, my mother's touch lingered on Pemberley. My father had preserved much of her influence after her death, and Darcy had been just as reticent to make any changes that diminished her memory, so many of the rooms rarely seen by visitors were almost two decades out of style. It was a welcome thought to know she'd picked the fabrics and the wallpapers, even if their comforting warmth could easily be mistaken as dark and cold by someone with no understanding of their significance.

My favourite place on the entire estate, however, was wholly of her creation, and it was to there that I absconded the moment Mr. Honeyfield took his leave. Between his unexpected visit and Kitty's enduring presence, I needed the solitude.

Manufactured out of the side of one of the hills in the grounds, the shell grotto was a place rarely visited by anyone but me. Its entrance was covered by a wall of shrubbery, concealing it from all those unaware it was there. My brother knew of its existence, of course, as did most of the staff, and I had shown Elizabeth a few months after she had married Darcy, but Kitty likely had no idea. Which made it the perfect place to hide from her.

Developing any kind of fondness for Kitty Bennet was out of the question. That kind of thing did not end happily. I had learnt plenty of lessons throughout my life, but I knew that one would stay with me the longest. Rather than linger in her presence and feel the threads that pulled me to her tighten, I picked the densest Latin text from the library and took it to the grotto in the hopes of staying out of sight and keeping my mind occupied.

The grotto was older than I was, so I hadn't been around for its construction, but I'd been told my mother had made it her project, dedicating years to the design and then the selection and placement of thousands of shells. They swirled from the floor up and across the ceiling, forming complicated patterns with unending intricacy.

The only light source was a circular hole in the roof, disguised from above as a well, that let in a column of sunlight. It bounced off abalone and mother-of-pearl, revealing the true beauty of the hidden cove, but it didn't provide quite enough light by which to read. With a candle, a book, and a bag full of Ruth's gingerbread, I was perfectly set for a long afternoon of seclusion. Anyone who truly needed to find me would know exactly where to look, but those new to Pemberley, including girls with angelic curls and permanent smiles, wouldn't have the slightest clue where I'd gone.

I was forty pages into my book when I realised I'd been interrupted. Quite how long Emma had been standing there, I wasn't sure, but when I looked up to reach for another biscuit, I instead found myself clutching my chest to calm my surprise at the sight of a figure in the doorway.

"My apologies," Emma said, her smile suggesting she wasn't particularly sorry.

After Darcy had married Elizabeth and I'd moved back to Pemberley for good, I had convinced him I was too old for governesses. There was nothing academic left they were willing to teach me, my education instead continuing in the pages of Pemberley's books. I had tired of being told I was wilful for requesting to be allowed to practise my Greek rather than my sewing. To my relief, Darcy had hired a lady's maid upon my return home, and it did not take long for relief to turn to delight as I got to know Emma. Sharp, skilled, and willing to collude in my feeble excuses to get me out of social engagements I couldn't bear to endure, she was one of my favourite people at Pemberley. Even if she did sneak up on me in silence.

"How did you find me?" I asked her, setting aside my book.

"You were not to be found anywhere else, which meant there was only one place you could be." She sat down beside me, lit by the flickering glow of the candle. "It has been a while since you have hidden yourself away here. Is everything all right?"

The last time I had spent a full day amongst the shells had been when Darcy brought me back to Pemberley after all but rescuing me from the clutches of a fortune-hunting, power-hungry man who knew enough about me to barter with my freedom. One could hardly consider that an unreasonable seclusion, but Emma had yet to be appointed then. If she had been there to speak to, I likely would have been less keen to hide alone. Telling her a part of what had happened, even a year after the fact, had eased the knot it still tied around my lungs.

"Who says I am hiding?" My visits to the grotto had always been frequent, if admittedly shorter.

"These are provisions for days"—Emma gestured to the bag of gingerbread between us—"and you told no one where you were going. Your brother was getting concerned. So what is it that brought you here?"

The problem with excellent lady's maids was the potential for their perceptive nature to see far more than you intended them to. I wished I hadn't put my book down, lamenting my lack of something to hide behind as I felt my cheeks go pink.

"I just needed some peace and quiet," I explained softly. "I can come back to the house, if my brother needs me for something."

Emma squeezed my arm. If I was spending extended periods of time in the grotto, it was usually because I wanted to feel closer to my mother. Guilt gnawed at me for allowing Emma to think that was what this was, but I couldn't explain the truth. I couldn't bear the thought of someone I cared about looking at me differently.

"Stay," Emma said. "I'll tell Mr. Darcy you're safe and sound. Perhaps make sure you talk to him after dinner? He worries about you. As do I."

"No, it's all right, I can—"

"It is fine to take some time to yourself," she insisted. "If you need it, no one in that house would begrudge you that. Just come back before you forget your way there. And call for me before you go to dinner, because you have been playing with your curls and they look terrible."

I hadn't realised I had done it until she pointed it out, but I'd been pulling on the locks of hair that framed my face, stretching out their coils until they hung limply. I tucked them behind my ears to hide the worst of it and assured Emma I would not go to dinner so dishevelled. She left me with a promise she would reassure my brother no harm had come to me and, unlike the governesses I'd had, did not say a word against me picking up my hefty Latin tome again. Her patience was endless, even though I knew she would enjoy working for a normal young lady who needed dressing up for balls and subsequent visits from suitors. I was rather boring in comparison.

I read my way through the wax of an entire candle, lighting a new one with the stub of the first. It was only when my supply of biscuits ran low and my back began to ache from sitting on the hard, shell-encrusted bench set into the wall that I finally ventured back to the house. Instead of heading straight for my own rooms, I took myself to Darcy's office and knocked on the half-open door.

"Georgiana," he said, surprise in his voice as he looked up to see me. "Emma said you wanted some time to yourself. Is everything all right?"

Like he always had, he set down his pen and pushed aside the letter he was writing, ready to listen to anything I had to say. Even when I'd been an endlessly curious child who always had one more question, I had never been denied his time. My multipage letters to him at school had been answered just as lengthily, and to my knowledge he had never once lied to me. If he didn't know, he said so. If he did know, he told me. He was the only person to truly take me seriously. So perhaps I was the worst sister imaginable for harbouring so significant a secret.

But I'd never read a single happy ending for someone like me. All the privilege and kindness in the world could not win me something that did not exist. I didn't want to put Darcy in the position of having to be the one to damn me, and it was almost certain he would. I would not be the first woman to be thrown out of Pemberley for this particular indiscretion.

The memory of Frances, one of our chambermaids, being dismissed only days after my father's death occupied a gaping, painful chasm in my chest. No one had told me why, of course, but the remaining staff could not help but submit to the allure of gossip. At first I heard her referred to as a fallen woman, her name spoken sharply like it cut tongues. I assumed she was pregnant, a conclusion that seemed confirmed when the whispers about her cavorting with a servant on a nearby estate were no longer held back. Until, one week after her dismissal, I heard something new: "The other girl has been sent away now, too."

It was the first I had ever heard of *other girls*, and at twelve years old, it sounded a note inside me that strung together a collection of moments like a melody. I had never connected them before, but suddenly I saw the thread between the way I could never imagine having a husband like other girls dreamt; the way I would sketch women over and over but draw men only if asked; and the way I'd developed what I now understood was a childish infatuation with one of the scullery maids, following her around and no doubt entirely getting in the way. It all made sense with those two words, but in the same moment I had been forced to confront the reality that my brother, who had always been my favourite person and was now in control of my life and my fate, had exiled a woman from Pemberley for the same sin now singing in my bones.

So I sat myself in the chair across from his desk, pulling up my legs to tuck them under me, and I pretended everything was fine. I tried to let him forget I'd been acting strange at all, but the conversation quickly turned to a topic I had not wanted to discuss.

"Elizabeth mentioned you had a caller," my brother said cautiously, well aware it was not a common occasion. "The son of one of our father's associates. Are you... interested in the gentleman?"

He was only marginally more comfortable than I was with the matter. I wondered if he was thinking of the last time I'd made a decision regarding romance and marriage, and quite how poorly it had gone. Perhaps he was trying to be particularly careful to avoid another attempted elopement.

"I do not really know him," I said, being sure my words were true, but diplomatic. "Until his call it had been many years since I had last spent time in his company."

"Are you planning to start seeking a suitor?" Darcy asked.

The idea seemed to make him wary, but any concerns he might have had would be dwarfed by my overwhelming hatred of the idea. Mr. Honeyfield's call had lasted barely five minutes, and it was still more than enough experience of courting to last me a lifetime.

"'It is an honour that I dream not of,'" I said,

quoting the words of Shakespeare's Juliet, which I knew my brother would recognise.

He narrowed his eyes.

"You and I are both aware of how that play ends," he said, and I had to laugh.

"My fate will not be the same," I assured him. "Presently, I do not feel any need to pursue marriage. There are too many books unread and languages unlearnt."

"When you change your mind, I would like to know the names of any men you plan to consider," he instructed me. "In the meantime, I will make enquiries regarding James Honeyfield."

I did not tell him that it was not a matter of "when," or that any enquiries into Mr. Honeyfield would be entirely pointless. For most young girls, the presence of an overly protective elder brother might be an annoyance, but I wasn't going to protest if Darcy deemed every man in England to be an unacceptable match. Whether for his reasons or for mine, no man would ever suit me.

Not trusting myself to continue to navigate such treacherous waters, I simply smiled and nodded and moved the conversation back towards topics that did not unsettle my stomach. I spoke of the books I'd been reading and the music I was writing. I asked for news of our cousins and suggested Ruth deserved some extra days off to visit her newest granddaughter. Even Darcy's tentative mention of next month's ball was met with a forced smile and a promise I'd consider attending.

It was a comfort to play the part of normal. When I left his office half an hour later, I felt almost as if I'd taken to the act well enough to truly adopt it. There was a lightness in my heart that I revelled in while Emma fixed my hair and helped me choose a dress for dinner. It carried me all the way down to the dining table, where Kitty's smile reminded me of the bitter truth of it all.

I continued in my solitary manner for days. If I was not practising the piano or the harp behind a firmly shut door, I hid myself away in the grotto. It was hardly the sort of isolation Elizabeth would want from me, but she had no idea of what was at stake. I could not allow myself to fall for Kitty, not if I wanted to avoid Frances's fate, and I knew all too well where my weaknesses lay. Prolonged exposure was all it would take.

Two weeks after Kitty's arrival at Pemberley, Elizabeth raised her concerns with my frequent absences, catching me after dinner before I could feign exhaustion and a need to turn in.

"Where is it you've been keeping yourself? We never have the pleasure of your company nowadays, so you must be getting up to mischief somewhere," she said, trying to joke. When I didn't laugh, her smile dropped into concern. "Is something wrong?"

"No, nothing," I promised. "I've only been trying to finish the sonata I've been working on."

Elizabeth's scepticism wasn't entirely alleviated, but my words, paired with my best attempt at a reassuring smile, placated her enough that she put up no further resistance when I excused myself from her company. I had no particular reason to hide from my sister-in-law, but she and Kitty could often be found together in the evening. Rather than risk being caught in that situation, I once again retired early. The walls of my bedroom had never been so familiar to me.

Despite having little else to do, I struggled to

find sleep. It eluded me even when a suitable hour for rest ticked by. Closing my eyes brought me visions of blonde curls and bold smiles I couldn't bear to see. After hours of staring at my ceiling, I admitted defeat.

Rolling over, I pulled open the drawer in the table beside my bed. Inside was a collection of items without a home—some candles, a pencil, a hair ribbon, and a button—but at the back was one thing I always kept close. It had followed me to London, to Ramsgate, and now back to Pemberley.

It was a small volume, so worn the spine was cracked and the leather cover was scuffed and peeling. The gilded title, *The Disposition of an English Lady*, had long gone dull, but I didn't need to read the words to be able to remember them. I had every sentence, from cover to cover, memorised. Newer etiquette guides were now favoured, but this one had belonged to my mother.

She had underlined passages, folded down corners, and studied it until the paper had gone soft. She had not lived long enough to teach me any of its lessons herself, so reading her book was as close as I would ever get to hearing her words of guidance. I was not a perfect daughter, but I tried my best to follow the rules set out in the book.

Leafing through the pages, I hoped to find an answer to my current predicament. How to be a good daughter and a polite host without falling victim to attraction to a kindhearted girl with a smile that could warm rooms. I already knew it was a fruitless task. I could quote every page in the book, the strict guidelines for social situations a lifeline when I would otherwise be at a loss of how to conduct myself, but it did not tackle this specific scenario.

With the book that usually settled my thoughts a lost cause, I replaced it in its drawer with a sigh. This evening required a distraction. Kicking off my blankets, I forwent shoes, a hairbrush, and respectable dress in favour of keeping on the worn shift I slept in. The companions I would find where I planned on going would not judge me for it.

Pemberley suffered from the same affliction of so many houses of its size—it was impossible to keep warm in its entirety, especially at night. Used to the chill that lingered in the hallways, I pulled on an old dark green tailcoat. It had been

Darcy's once, but when he'd deemed it too worn for his own use, I'd inherited it through incessant pleading. It was far too large for me, and the fabric was threatening to turn threadbare at the hem. The cuffs fell well past my palms, and several of the brass buttons were missing, but I still donned it whenever I felt cold within Pemberley's walls, out of sight of those who dealt in rumour-fuelled scandal.

There was a map of Pemberley catalogued perfectly in my mind, intimately detailing which floorboards creaked and which doors squeaked on their hinges. Now that I was no longer a child, there was no real reason for me to sneak, but the habit was too ingrained in me to walk freely. I let the light of the moon guide me where it peered through windowpanes, lighting my candle only when I was safely inside the library.

Nowhere felt more sacred to me than a room full of escapes. Floor-to-ceiling shelves held tome after tome, waiting to take me somewhere new or teach me one more answer to the complexities of the world. Elizabeth had added more modern works to it since her arrival, and I loved nothing more than to discuss them with her over hot tea, safely ensconced in one of the wing-back armchairs in front of the fireplace. But when it was just me in the library, I gravitated towards heavy Latin volumes or tested my still-struggling Greek. If I was translating as I read, I had no spare focus with which to worry.

Settling beside one of the shelves, I found a safe place for my candlestick and eased out the copy of Ovid's *Metamorphoses* I'd been working through. My place was marked with a hair ribbon that I slid out from the pages and wrapped around my wrist. The floor was far from the most comfortable place in the room, but there was something reassuring about being so close to the bookcases that I could smell the wood of the shelves and the richness of the leather bindings. It was all-encompassing.

I was several pages in when I heard footsteps in the corridor outside. Logically, there was no reason for me to panic. Yet I still shuffled back against the shelf and held my breath, hoping whoever was passing would ignore the room and go on their way.

In my hurry to delve into a book, I hadn't shut the door properly. My eyes widened as they fell on the candle still burning beside me. I blew it out, hoping the lack of light would conceal me better, but I was too late. The door creaked, and whoever it was padded into the room. I wasn't doing anything wrong, and no member of the household would punish me if they did find me—the staff would probably pretend they'd never seen me, and Darcy and Elizabeth would likely be more worried about my lack of sleep than anything else—but I was in no kind of mood to navigate a conversation.

The world made the decision to present me with the one person I was least prepared to see. For all my attempts to avoid her, now there was nowhere to hide.

"Oh!" Kitty's eyes were wide with surprise when she found me sitting on the floor. "My apologies. I saw the light and assumed someone had left a candle burning."

She looked at me intently, the light of her own candle flickering in her eyes, and I realised with horror what she was seeing. My hair was wild around my shoulders; my shift had long forgotten its days of being pristine, white, and crisp; and my toes curled against the wooden flooring, tucked under the edge of an ornate floral rug. My coat gave me some form of modesty, but it was as inelegant as the shift it hid. I was certainly not dressed for polite company and could only imagine what Kitty was thinking. *Such a mad girl, to be running around half dressed in the middle of the night.*

Kitty's own appearance was significantly more put together than mine. Her hair was tied up under a nightcap, a few curls escaping down the nape of her neck, and she'd had the good sense to put on a navy dressing gown.

"Do you mind if I join you?" she asked. "I assume you also had trouble chasing sleep?"

I was too startled by the request to deny it. There were ample choices of seating options in the library—from the armchairs to the sofas to the window seat—yet Kitty dropped down next to me and relit my candle with her own to extend the bubble of light around us. Trying to make the motion look as natural as possible, I shut my book. The movement left no space for me to replace the ribbon to mark the page, and I carefully tried to commit my place to memory for next time. Although for how long I could fence off a corner of my mind to think of anything other than Kitty was yet to be seen.

"Oh, don't let me interrupt you," she said as I pushed Ovid back into his space on the shelf.

"I was already finishing up for the evening," I lied.

Kitty reached out to trace the tip of her fingers across the spines of the books, her touch delicate and lingering. I resolutely tried not to imagine it against my skin.

"Should you not have finished up for the evening hours ago?" she asked. "What book was so engrossing that it kept you up this long?"

"It is not the book that kept me up," I said, although I'd never been able to explain my frequent inability to sleep. Sometimes it felt like there was far too much knowledge out there in the world to waste my time sleeping when I could be discovering it; other times I wanted nothing more than to close my eyes and rest, but my brain recycled inanities regardless.

Humming, Kitty seemed to listen to my answer but have nothing to say in response. She continued to dance her fingers across the shelves for a moment, before she shifted the topic of conversation entirely.

"Why are you avoiding me?"

If I'd been uncomfortable with her presence in the library already, now I actively wanted to expire rather than stay seated beside her. For a concerning moment I considered setting fire to the sleeve of my coat to form a distraction, but I rather liked the garment and I wasn't sure I wanted to endure the pain of burns unless it was an absolute necessity. Marking that as my backup plan, I made lying my first choice.

"I haven't been avoiding you."

"I have four sisters, all but one of whom are well practised in the art of holding grudges. I know perfectly well when I am being avoided," Kitty said with a laugh. "You likely have a very good reason for wanting to stay out of my company, but until I know what it is, I will not be able to apologise for it. And I would like to apologise."

Even in the dim, flickering candlelight, her smile was disarming. It made me want to tell her every word of the truth, but that was out of the question, so I opted instead for something not entirely a lie.

"It is nothing you've done."

"So you admit you are avoiding me?" she teased, nudging her shoulder against mine.

"Yes," I admitted. "Forgive me, I am…"

There was no good way to end that sentence. I ducked my head, fiddling with a button on the cuff of my coat. For a long few moments, Kitty didn't seem sure what to say, either. Until she shifted to face me, rather than sitting at my side, and straightened her back.

"Well, perhaps we need to start again. Pleased to meet you, Miss Darcy. My name is Catherine, but you are most encouraged to call me Kitty. I am here in your home because spending too long with my mother and only other unmarried sister is insufferable, and I am truly sorry if my presence is equally intolerable to you. If there's nothing I can do to fix it, I will make arrangements to return to Longbourn as soon as I can."

"No!" I said, far too quickly. I could tell she was being sincere, and I really didn't want her to leave. She seemed happy at Pemberley and, even if I had to hide from her for my own sanity, I wanted her to stay that way. "Please, there is no need for you to go."

"Then tell me," she said, leaning forwards and floating her hand just above my knee—not touching, but still close enough it made me shiver, "how can I make you comfortable in your own house again?"

Unless she was willing to stop smiling at me,

to stop looking so unfailingly beguiling whenever she laughed, there was little hope for me. I didn't even truly want her to stop.

"You...I...I will join you and Elizabeth tomorrow," I promised. "It is my problem and not yours, Miss Bennet, I assure you."

"I must insist you call me Kitty," she said, letting her hand fall on my knee properly this time.

My coat didn't cover my legs, so all that was between Kitty's fingers and my bare skin was the thin fabric of my shift. It felt like gossamer, not putting up any resistance at all to the weight and warmth of her hand.

I was getting myself into something dangerous. There was only one way this kind of thing ended, and it would not be happy. There were no blissfully wedded pairs of women in the pages of the novels that graced the library shelves. Even tales like Frances's were so unthinkable they were banished from literary tradition. But when I was faced with a pretty girl, I struggled to remember why that was.

"Kitty," I repeated back to her, hoping the flickering candlelight masked the worst of my blush.

"May I call you Georgiana?" she asked, her hand still on my knee. I needed her to move it. I never wanted her to move it.

There was nothing scandalous about her using my first name. It was common amongst friends of similar standing, and even more so amongst those with family connections. Now that her sister was married to my brother, we were entirely within our rights to refer to each other by our given names. It made sense, even, when there was still more than one unmarried Miss Bennet. No confusion could occur if I called her Kitty.

And it tasted so sweet on my tongue.

I nodded, unable to stop myself. I likely would have given her anything she asked for in that moment, but it was a lucky coincidence that this particular request was something I was not entirely opposed to. And not a single thing about it broke any written or unwritten rule of etiquette, except for the way her hand was still warm on my knee and my name on her lips sung in my ears. It was probably best to ignore those specific features of the moment.

Chapter Four

Keeping true to my word, I did not retreat to the shell grotto the next morning. Instead, I joined Elizabeth and Kitty on a walk around the gardens. Neither Kitty nor I made any mention of the library, but the conversation was continuous enough. I let the two sisters do the majority of the talking, content to simply listen as they shared tales of home and excitedly discussed the ball I still was not certain I could bring myself to attend. Both were subjects I could not have weighed in on even if I wanted to, my knowledge of Longbourn sorely lacking and my excitement for the ball nonexistent.

I was unsure exactly what my promise to Kitty entailed when it came to how much time I needed to spend in her company. Ordinarily, even when not actively avoiding guests, I spent much of my day alone. The solitude of the library or an empty drawing room with a freshly tuned piano was too enticing to pass up, but I did not want Kitty to think one morning in her company was all I could bear. When she, Elizabeth, and Darcy retired to the brightest and airiest sitting room downstairs, I decided to join them.

My brother read a letter from Mr. Bingley, while Elizabeth penned one to Jane. I pulled my book out from between the sofa cushions and tried to reacquaint myself with the world of *Gulliver's Travels*, but it had been so long since I'd last read any of it that it was more of a chore than a pleasure to reorient myself in the story.

Easily distracted, I watched Kitty instead. She'd taken up a pen and poised herself ready to write a letter of her own, but after barely one or two lines, she returned her writing box to the side table. Walking a circuit of the room, she inspected the paintings and ornaments that adorned it.

Kitty stopped in front of each one for minutes at a time, tilting her head as she took in the detail of the landscapes hung on the walls. She studied the stunning vistas, rolling hills, and endless countryside as if they might hold the answer to a question only she could hear.

Unable to stop myself, I set my book aside and crossed the room to join her. I rarely got the chance to share much of the knowledge I had amassed from Pemberley's library, and I hoped Kitty would welcome my intrusion. That, and the chance of making her smile. This was safe. This was allowed. Elizabeth and Darcy were looking on, and all I was doing was talking about art.

"It's a Vernet," I explained, gesturing to the painting of a ship leaving harbour at sunset that had currently captured her attention. "He was famous for marine paintings."

Kitty offered me a soft smile I could have lived on for days, before taking a step closer to scrutinise the ship in the centre of the image.

"Where is it of?" she asked.

I didn't have an answer, but I desperately

wanted to give her one. Hoping for help, I turned back to my brother and was surprised to find him watching us, with his attention drawn away from his letter. I took a step away from Kitty.

"That particular view is imaginary, I'm afraid," he said.

"Pity," Kitty said, "but I suppose that means it could be sailing anywhere."

Her words were wistful as she moved on to the next painting. My feet carried me after her, and soon we were on a stroll of the room's artwork, with me telling her as much as I knew about each pictured location. A few were from this isle, but most were from further afield, windows into the far-flung beauty of the Continent. I'd never seen any of the places in person, but I'd read enough of the travel books in the library to give some context.

Kitty's eyes sparkled as she asked endless questions, many of which I couldn't answer. Darcy occasionally interjected with the information Kitty seemed to crave, drawing on the knowledge he'd amassed on his Grand Tour several years earlier. Firsthand research always did exceed the anecdotal musings found in books.

Perhaps it was Kitty's enthusiasm for knowledge or the way she lit up with each scrap of information she gained, but I found myself utterly incapable of refusing her anything. After a full circle of the room, investigating every painting and several vases, she turned her attention to the chess set on the sideboard.

"Do you play?" she asked, picking up a knight and trotting it around the edge of the board.

My brother's snort of laughter was masked with a cough, but it earned him a glare from me all the same. Even Elizabeth had to hide a smile. Luckily neither seemed to win Kitty's attention away from the chess piece in her hand.

"I play a little," I said cautiously. Then, because this girl made me do foolish things, I added, "Would you care for a game?"

And because the scales in the universe had to be balanced, I was duly punished for my foolishness—she did indeed want to play.

I had played many a game of chess before in my life, but never one quite so absorbing as one played against Kitty Bennet. She focused intently, propping her chin up on her hands to stare at each piece like it held the secrets to victory. Each time she took her turn, the tip of her tongue would rest against the corner of her parted lips. Studying her was far more intriguing than watching the board, and I had never been more grateful that I could reliably play a game of chess five moves ahead of any opponent. It required very little effort to manufacture the outcome I wanted, leaving most of my faculties free to admire a far more appealing sight.

I did not play to win. Kitty knew the rules of chess perfectly well, but she was less versed in the strategy. Her moves were predictable and easily defended against, and even when she forced a more complicated order of moves from me, I could tell it was luck rather than skill that prompted it. The game would have been over in minutes if I'd wanted it to end, but I didn't. I wanted to keep staring.

People in general preferred to win the games they played, and sure enough, Kitty was keen to play again after I led her to a manufactured victory, making the most counterintuitive of moves to ensure she had no option but to instigate a checkmate. I could feel Darcy's eyes on me, and when I turned to look at him, I found confusion and amusement greeting me. He knew better than anyone that I was not playing properly.

It was the third game that revealed my deception. I had been too focused on handing Kitty another victory that I failed to notice she was calculating her moves just as much as I was. As soon as she had my king trapped, she challenged me.

"Why don't you want to win? I left openings for you at least four times. Lydia could have won that game, and she only looks at the board once every few moves."

Colour rushed to fill my cheeks.

"I must be distracted," I said, the words no shade of a lie. Even if I had intended to win, I wasn't certain I could depend on my ability to focus. "My apologies."

"I confess I haven't been much better. If you wish to keep playing, perhaps Mr. Darcy will take my place?" Kitty suggested.

My brother didn't even look up from his letter as he replied.

"That won't be happening." He turned over his sheet of paper, either oblivious to or unaffected by Kitty's confusion. "My sister has been going easy on you. I have never seen her lose a game she wanted to win, and while she may be kind to you, I would not get the same treatment."

Kitty turned to me, clearly expecting me to confirm my brother's words to be in jest, but everything he had said was true. It was all I could do to suppress a sheepish smile, and in return she grinned, surprised and perhaps a little impressed.

"You are a constant enigma, Miss Darcy," she declared. "I daresay we could sell you to a travelling curiosity fair. So you have not been playing me truly?"

I shook my head, rubbing my thumb along a familiar ridge down the edge of the chessboard.

"Do you want me to play fair?" I asked.

"Yes, of course."

"Are you sure?"

"Should I not be sure?" Kitty asked with a laugh, already resetting the pieces.

I won in six moves. She stared at the board, checking what I already knew was certain. When she confirmed for herself there was no way out, she grinned—and that was almost better than the endearing focus she'd shown in the first three games. She swiftly reset the board again, that single-minded concentration returning as she tried her best to defend against my attacks. I had never imagined one could be jealous of a chess piece, but I'd never seen Kitty Bennet devote all her attention to something before and I desperately wanted to take the place of the queen, to feel Kitty's gaze on me and her elegant fingers touching me so assertively. Distracted, it was ten moves before I took the game. It was almost disappointing, but Kitty still looked impressed.

"How do you do it?" she asked.

"Chess is an excellent equaliser. You cannot win with superior strength or physical fitness. I was determined to best my brother in something, and this seemed far more realistic than shooting or fencing," I explained, blushing at the memory of my childish competitive spirit.

"That may be the why of it, but it is not the how," Kitty said, leaning forwards as if there were a string pulling her in.

I had to disappoint her. There was no trick I'd learnt, no single key to unlock the skill. Chess had simply always made sense to me—I could see the path to a checkmate far more easily than I could read the tone of a conversation or judge a character. Once I had realised I might have a manner of skill, it had just been a matter of practise. It was a thoroughly boring answer to give, but instead of politely changing the subject, Kitty listened to every word, enthralled. Then she reached for the pieces to reset the board.

"Again," she demanded, before wincing. "If you want to keep playing, that is. I don't wish to force you to perform against your will like a circus animal."

If she thought she was going to learn to beat me genuinely after observing a few games, Darcy's ongoing refusal to play against me should have shown her otherwise. But she seemed keen to try again regardless, so I started setting up my line of pawns. It had been a long time since anyone had willingly sat through more than one game with me.

Sleep evaded me again that night, despite my lack of rest the day before. That alone wasn't a rare experience, but it was unusual for me to know exactly what was keeping me awake.

Kitty.

I wondered if she was in the library again, tracing soft leather spines with gentle fingers. If she was there, did she want my company? I lay there considering it for almost an hour before I climbed out of bed. Even if Kitty was not there, the books still would be, and they were perfectly adequate company on their own. *The Disposition of an English Lady* would not be enough to settle my thoughts.

Pausing to look in the mirror, I took in the old shift and my unkempt hair, loose around my shoulders. Usually, I had little chance of seeing anyone, but knowing I could stumble across Kitty, I felt more conscious than ever of my pitiful state. Short of waking Emma for help dressing, I'd likely only make myself look worse. I didn't even own a dressing gown, which had never felt like more of an oversight than as I pulled on my secondhand tailcoat. It would just have to do.

My first stop was down to the kitchens, where I carefully wrapped some leftover gingerbread rounds up in a cloth. If I added a few more of the biscuits than I usually would bring for myself alone, there was no one around to notice or pass judgement.

The library was empty when I crept inside, and I tried to suppress the disappointment in my chest. The room was a comfort regardless of the absence of blonde-haired girls within its walls. I pulled out one of the most familiar books and curled up on a sofa, not in the mood for the cold floorboards. My candle burned cheerfully beside me, and I'd left the door to the room open. For absolutely no reason at all.

I got more absorbed in the book than I'd intended to, losing track of the material world around me. My reminder of it came in the form of two hands clamping down heavily onto my shoulders and a voice loudly announcing "Boo!" right beside my ear.

It was impossible not to jump. I held back a scream but dropped my book as the muscles in my body pulled tight against one another. I knew there was likely no real threat—the now-familiar giggling behind me was my biggest clue—but my heart was far less logical than my head. It raced laps as I tried to persuade it to calm down.

Kitty dropped onto the sofa beside me, stealing a gingerbread biscuit. Her laughter trailed off when she noticed the heaving of my lungs.

"Forgive me," she said. "It was supposed to be in jest. I think sometimes I forget I am not at Longbourn anymore. Lydia and Lizzy were quite used to a few scares, but I imagine you are not. Are you all right?"

With the question, she reached out to touch my cheek. I wasn't sure entirely what possessed her to do it, but she traced the back of her fingers across my skin as I fought to regain control of my breathing. Her proximity was doing little to help the matter. For my lungs and my sanity, I shifted away just a little so her hand fell away. I missed the contact immediately.

Seemingly just as displaced as I was by the moment, Kitty nibbled on my gingerbread and scanned her eyes around the room in the search of something on which to fix her attention. When they landed on the book now resting in my lap, she reached out for it. I didn't stop her.

"This," she declared, as she tried to read the first line, "is not in English."

"No," I agreed, hiding my smile. "It is not. It's in Latin."

Kitty's look of surprise had my heart crashing into my ribs, and I had never been more grateful to have it so confined, or it would surely leap even closer towards her. Her eyes were wide, her lips drawn together in the slightest of gasps. It was a picture I wanted to paint.

"You cannot read this," she said, her disbelief evident in every word.

"I assure you I can. Whenever my brother came home from school in the holidays, I would endlessly mither him about what he had learnt. I think he taught me at first just to keep me quiet, but I liked to learn and he rather liked to play teacher. I had my own little exercise book and everything," I admitted, my cheeks warm with blush at the admission. It had angered my governess that I so desperately wanted to study Latin and Greek rather than needlepoint or dancing, but Darcy had indulged me and she never felt she could argue with him.

"Well then," Kitty said, shifting just a little closer and holding out the book to me. "Prove it."

I took a second to recover from her increased proximity, her knee brushing against mine, but managed to collect myself enough to take the book back. I was a few dozen pages into Virgil's *Aeneid*, a copy my brother had used at school. There were small doodles in the margins that signified every time he'd gotten bored and his mind wandered. Trees, more often than not. I wondered if he'd been thinking of home, where the forests went on for miles.

When I started to read aloud, I knew exactly what was coming, for it was the Latin I let spill from my tongue. Just as I anticipated, Kitty nudged me with her elbow, laughing as she rolled her eyes.

"In English!" she protested. "Or else I shall have no idea what it is you're saying."

I just smiled. Seeing her laugh had been my hope, and I would have liked nothing more than to make it my only goal in life from that moment on. It lit her up from inside like someone had touched flame to a candlewick, her eyes bright and animated. I simply could not look away, and it was several long moments before I could bring myself to return my gaze to the page in front of me.

My teasing over, I slipped into English. It took a little longer to read that way, translating as I went, but Kitty hung on my every word. She watched my lips, my finger tracing under each sentence, my hair as it slipped from behind my ear. It thrilled me to know it was not Virgil's story holding her attention.

I read my way through a few pages before I set the book down.

"This is probably not to your taste," I said. "Even translated."

"I cannot pretend to be following much of the story, but it is no hardship to hear you read it," Kitty admitted.

I could do better than *no hardship*. Pemberley's library was always open to visitors looking for an escape amongst pages, but it was usually Elizabeth and Darcy who played host. I never got the chance to make use of my encyclopaedic knowledge of the shelves, and I was keen to introduce Kitty to a section I thought she would much enjoy.

Basing my choice on little more than a suspicion, I dragged across the library ladder to climb up to one of the shelves above the door. I surveyed the selection of books concerning the world beyond our shores and picked some personal favourites. There were a few diaries of notable travellers and several large compendiums that came with exquisite colour plates depicting the most popular and picturesque locations. Passing my choices to Kitty, I climbed back down to find she had spread them out over the rug before my feet had even made contact with the floorboards.

"These are beautiful," she said, her voice almost reverent as she admired a depiction of Rome.

"You wish to travel to the Continent?" I guessed.

"I would like to go somewhere I could be certain no one had ever met any of my sisters first," she said, sighing wistfully. "These places are stunning, but my mother says the only chance I have of making it out of the country is if I marry a man with an occupation that gets him sent overseas."

My heart seized in my chest, losing its rhythm at the idea of Kitty marrying. Of course she was going to marry. It was what respectable women did, what they had to do. There was certainly no world in which I would be free to marry Kitty. The very idea was laughable, and I pushed it from my mind as quickly as it had flickered up, snuffing it out like a flame. Kitty did not want that. I was not allowed to want that. It would simply not be allowed.

I wanted to be the one to travel with her. If she lit up like this at illustrations and paintings, then I wanted to see her reaction to the sights themselves. I had read endlessly about so many of them that I could keep her entertained for hours, because by some miracle she seemed content to listen to me ramble. Perhaps she might reward my inexhaustible facts with a kiss, even if just to silence me for a moment.

I pushed the idea from my mind. It was ludicrous, and it would do neither of us any good for me to dwell on it.

"I'm sure there is a way for you to find yourself overseas," I said, hoping there was nothing in my voice that betrayed my thoughts.

"What about you?" Kitty asked. "Do you have aspirations to travel? Perhaps you could meet other people like you."

I resisted the urge to freeze, aware even the tension in my shoulders might give away too much. I was so sure I'd been careful. Surely she had no idea of the thoughts that pervaded my whole mind when I looked at her, chasing out anything sensible or sane.

"People like me?" I asked cautiously, needing to be certain of what she was implying.

Then there was the other intertwined implication. *Other people.* Sometimes I dreamt there were places with people like that. Others who lingered too long in front of portraits of beautiful women, who dreamt of kissing rouged lips and holding delicate hands. It seemed ludicrous to imagine a place where that was accepted, but the very idea was paradisiacal.

"Those who are obsessed with knowledge and prefer books to people," Kitty said, her words at once a relief and a disappointment.

"I do not prefer books to people," I protested. Kitty gave me a doubtful look, raising an eyebrow, and I conceded her point just a little. "Not to all people."

There were several notable exceptions. The most recent was sitting before me, polishing off the last of my gingerbread. Not even Darcy usually got away with that.

Chapter Five

Spending time with Kitty made my days undeniably more interesting but left me with little time for music practise. My sonata was going nowhere. After a week of late-night meetings in the library and endless attempts on Kitty's behalf to beat me at chess, I managed to talk myself into a day of dedication to the piano. Well aware of how easily I could be distracted by the right person, I chose a room on the far side of the house, with a piano I rarely played.

I thought perhaps it was the unfamiliar

instrument that rendered my playing useless, but when I didn't improve after several attempts at easy pieces, I realised it was I and not the piano that was causing the problem. Kitty Bennet had driven me to distraction.

This was not the first time thoughts of a pretty girl had affected my music. A piece I had written two years ago in London remained one of my favourites, despite how much time had passed. My more recent compositions were more technically developed, but there was something about Helena's piece that made it stand out. I could hear the truth in it.

Inspired, I turned back to the new sonata with which I was struggling. It didn't sound awful when I played it through, but something still wasn't quite right. Rather than try to put her out of my mind, I let myself dwell on thoughts of Kitty. It seemed only natural to lift the piece to match her vibrance, with a more joyful tone. I scribbled down the new notations, playing through each bar when I changed one of its notes.

It took me almost an hour to get to the end of the piece. Once I had changed the final note, I played it from the start. There was no doubt it was better, but I still wasn't ready to deem it finished. The final few notes trickled from my fingers regardless, lingering in the otherwise silent room until soft applause sounded from the doorway. I turned, expecting Elizabeth to be standing there. Instead, I found Kitty.

"That's beautiful," she said.

I mumbled a thank-you, ducking my head to hide my red cheeks. Logically, there was no way for her to have any idea she had inspired the latest iteration of the piece, but I still felt far too transparent. Unaware exactly what she had been listening to, Kitty crossed the room and settled beside me on the piano stool. The sudden proximity of her body pressed against my side had me jumping, and my hand clattered down onto the keys, creating a cacophony. My blush deepened. Kitty just laughed.

"An excellent approximation of my own musical abilities," she said, pressing down a few keys in no discernible sequence.

"Did you never learn?" I asked, surprised. Most ladies of any standing could be expected to be at least moderately proficient at the piano.

"My mother tried, but with five of us and one piano, there was never really the time for us all to practise. Jane was passable and Mary was determined, and Lizzy often bored enough to try. Lydia was too impatient, and her solution to boredom was shop windows rather than pianoforte keys. I often neglected my own practise alongside her."

"I could perhaps teach you, if you liked?" I offered, my mind certainly on helping her navigate polite society and not at all on having her sitting close beside me on a piano stool again.

"But why should I learn when I can so freely listen?" she teased.

Diligently, I played a few bars from the start of my sonata, unable to stop my smile. It was as I let them fade out that I realised exactly what was missing from the piece. A piano could not accurately capture its new essence. It was too mundane, too simple. Kitty either needed to be represented by some newfangled instrument not yet invented—which would certainly be an impossible task—or something that captured an increasingly bygone age.

Jumping to my feet, I almost knocked Kitty off the stool. I steadied her by grabbing her arm, sliding my hand down until I could link my fingers with hers. There were countless reasons why

I shouldn't, and she undoubtedly had plenty of questions, but I ignored them all, and she didn't protest as I pulled her out of the room and down the hallway.

When I'd had my own sitting room redecorated, I had opted for a more modern design. There was elaborately patterned cream paper on the walls and duck-egg-blue panelling around the skirting, with a matching rug softening most of the floorboards. Elegance had seemed key, but the one matter on which I'd refused to compromise had been the inclusion of my mother's old harpsichord.

Despite the fact that the instrument was rather out of fashion, I was too fond of it to hide it away. I didn't play it often, but I did sometimes find myself sitting at it, wondering what thoughts ran through my mother's head as she struck the keys. It was ornately decorated under the lid with scenes of the English countryside, and I heard Kitty's subtle gasp as I propped open the top. When I sat down, she retook her seat beside me.

"How many pianos do you have?!" she asked, baffled.

"Technically, this one is a harpsichord," I said with a laugh.

"Does your brother not realise you really don't need to do this?" Kitty asked, sitting beside me on the bench. My heart immediately leapt to my throat at how close she chose to be once again. The room was full of alternative seating choices. "You have an impressive dowry, you have connections, you—how many other languages do you speak?"

"Four," I admitted, ducking my head. The French and Italian were expected and had been carefully trained into me by a governess. The Spanish was not uncommon, but the Latin was less usual.

Kitty's response came in the form of several notes of a scale, dancing her fingers across the keys. It was unpractised and clumsy, but she knew it by heart so she must have found at least a little time for practise in her childhood.

"I know you're not including the Greek you don't think you are practised enough in, so you really speak *five* foreign languages," she said, playing another scale and tripping up on the final note. She tucked her hands into her lap.

"And you are beautiful enough to render anyone speechless. Not to mention there isn't a man or woman this side of London—or any side of London, for that matter—that you couldn't best at chess. I should imagine you'll have your choice of eligible suitors regardless of whether you can regale a party with a Scottish air or two."

I wanted to protest Kitty's words, but they bounced around inside me in a way I couldn't restrain. She thought me beautiful. The notion was almost sacrilegious coming from someone with such depths of fire in her eyes and grace in the angles and curves of her features. I shook the thoughts away, forcing myself to think practically and scrambling for any words that constituted a sensible response.

"My brother does not make me do anything. I like to play."

"Oh." Kitty appeared to be genuinely surprised, as if the thought had not occurred to her. "Go on, then. Why did you bring me all the way here when there was a perfectly good piano in the other room?" she asked, nudging at my side as if that would do anything other than make me forget my own name.

My fingers worked independently from my mind as they fell into a familiar pattern, finding the keys for the melody I'd been working on. Other than early attempts on the harp, my practise had thus far been on a piano, and the difference in plucking the strings with each press of a key rather than striking them unlocked a door I had been unable to open. It was the perfect marriage between the two other instruments, and it captured the newfound essence of the piece with a lighthearted frivolity the piano had been lacking. For the first time, I finished the final chord of the sonata with a grin on my lips.

When I turned to Kitty, I expected her attention to be on my hands, on the harpsichord keys. Or perhaps appreciating the music with some far-off gaze into the distance, like so many did when they were pretending to listen avidly. Instead, she was watching my face.

She was so close to me that I could feel the warm rush of her breath across my skin. I could count the freckles across her cheeks. There was a smudge of brown in the blue of one of her eyes, just below the pupil. When I collected myself enough to take in the entirety of her expression rather than a series of enticements, I found her lips parted infinitesimally, her eyes wide with surprise but soft with fondness. It was an expression that lodged itself firmly in the depths of my heart.

I had been told all my life that I had to learn to sing, to draw, to play piano so that I could one day impress a suitor, but I had never much seen the point. If I practised anything, it was because I wanted to. Now, however, I understood. The burst of pride in my chest, the shaky feeling I was left with after knowing I'd impressed Kitty—perhaps that was what my governesses had meant. To have her look at me like that made me feel impossible. I could not truly have the value I did in her eyes, yet she seemed to see it anyway.

I looked away, unable to bear it much longer. Everything I had ever known—Frances's fate, my past with Helena, a life of manoeuvring amongst polite society—had taught me I could not have the things I wanted.

"What song was that?" Kitty asked, her voice rougher than usual.

"I wrote it. I've never been particularly good at titling my compositions, so I'm afraid it doesn't have one," I admitted.

"You wrote it," she repeated, the words more a statement than a clarifying question.

I had no idea how to reply, so I danced my fingers across the two highest keys, just to have something else to focus on. Now that the piece had so much of her, or at least how I saw her, in it, I wanted to know her thoughts. If she hated it, I'd throw it out and never think of it again.

"I don't think it is possible for you to be real," she said. "No one can be so... You..." She sighed before trying again. "It is a remarkable composition. You should be very proud of it, George."

George.

It was the first time anyone had ever called me that. Usually I was *Miss Darcy* or, more increasingly, *Georgiana*, but the nickname was new and thrilling. Perhaps I should have hated it, given it was the Christian name of a man I hoped never to see again, but when dripped in Kitty's soft affection, it sounded like an entirely different name, and I wanted to hear it endlessly.

Afraid to draw attention to it in case she never used it again as a result, I instead mumbled my thanks, letting my fingers drift over the keys in an approximation of the beginning of a Bach sinfonia.

Kitty's leg was warm against mine through her peach-coloured morning dress. As damned as it might have made me, I wasn't going to be the one to move. If I could not have anything real, anything tangible, I could at least have this one moment.

Chapter Six

Pemberley's monthly ball was fast approaching, but Elizabeth had known better than to extend a direct invitation. She talked about it openly and made it clear my presence was welcome, but the thought of an evening of socialising and having to remember every rule of etiquette still sounded like torture. I considered the rumours I'd only encourage with my absence and tried to find a solution that involved me hiding away in my chambers with a pile of books and an equally tall tower of gingerbread, while still maintaining my family's reputation.

No answer presented itself, so I resolved to put it out of my mind every time it came up.

Kitty and I didn't speak about it. We covered every other conceivable topic as we walked the grounds or met at night in the library—from our childhoods to the books I read to the countries she wanted to visit. It hadn't occurred to me she thought I would be in attendance at the ball until she brought up the topic over breakfast on the day it was scheduled.

"Are there many suitors vying for a space on your dance card, Georgiana?" she asked, spreading butter on a thick slice of toast. "How many more balls until you are married?"

I almost spat out my tea at the very thought. Having just a little more decorum than that, I choked it down instead, hiding my mouth behind a napkin.

"No!" I protested between coughs. I vehemently hated the idea of Kitty believing I had any interest in Lambton's most eligible bachelors. As soon as my throat was clear, I leapt to clarify things. "No suitors. No dance cards. Charming as I am sure they are, I prefer to avoid such events as this evening."

Elizabeth met my eye and offered what

appeared to be a sympathetic smile, but thankfully she did not add her voice to Kitty's.

"You're not going?" Kitty asked, eyes wide with surprise and, I perhaps deluded myself, a little disappointment.

"You know you are more than welcome," Darcy said, stifling a yawn behind his hand, still half asleep. "Your company is encouraged, even."

"Thank you," I told him. "I...I still am not sure whether I'll go."

"Oh," Kitty said. For several moments, she was silent, until she burst out with something like she could no longer keep it inside. "I want you to be there."

We stared at each other, neither sure what to say. My heart felt too tight in my chest, like it had grown two sizes without my consent.

"It is not really something I am much good at," I whispered. "Forgive me."

The level of sincerity felt out of balance with the context, but I felt so regretful to have to deny Kitty something.

Neither of us said much more as we finished our breakfast, with Elizabeth and a slowly waking Darcy carrying the conversation. The moment her plate was clean, Kitty made herself scarce. Not one to be outdone when it came to matters of seclusion, I hid myself away in the one place I knew she wouldn't be. I had shared the library with her, but I'd never had the occasion to take her to the shell grotto.

I sat on the bench and traced the rough texture of the walls, considering whether I could stay there for the whole evening. It was a tempting thought, but the underground cove went from pleasantly cool to bitingly cold at night. Sitting alone, trying to find meaning in trailing patterns of scallop shells, I thought over my answer to Kitty.

She wanted to see me.

When our hands brushed together in the library, she didn't pull away. She watched me play piano like I was Mozart, rather than merely an amateur. She delighted in losing to me at chess. I had never excelled in mathematics, but even I could admit there was something encouraging about it all when it was added up. One evening. I would never get a lifetime of this feeling, but perhaps I could allow myself just one night. I had learnt from Frances and from the Georgiana of the past, so incautious with Helena. I would be careful.

Leaping to my feet, I fled the grotto and headed for the house. There wasn't much time left.

It was not often I visited Emma's room in the staff quarters since there was rarely an emergency I wanted to bother her with, but I didn't know whom else to go to. My brother was out of the question, and I wasn't sure I could look Elizabeth in the eye when I was experiencing such unspeakable feelings for her sister. Of everyone else at Pemberley, I trusted my lady's maid the most. I rushed into her room quickly enough to give her a start. It was only when she jumped, stabbing her needle into her thumb from the surprise, that I realised I should've knocked first.

"My apologies," I said, my cheeks flushed. "I can come back. I never meant to—"

"It's not a problem," Emma said, smiling like I was an overexcited child who'd just run into her knees. She sucked her thumb into her mouth to stop the blood welling up. "Even without you to startle me, I prick my fingers at least once an hour. Is something wrong?"

I chewed on my lip, unsure exactly what I wanted to ask for. Despite the best efforts of my governesses and those I knew in London, I didn't often like to show my face at large gatherings. A roomful of people was so readily intimidating. In truth, I wanted Emma to teach me how to walk into a ballroom and not immediately want to lower my gaze, but that wasn't her job. She wasn't there to hold my hand. Instead, I opted for vagueness.

"Can you help me?" I pleaded, sounding as pathetic as I was sure I looked.

Emma set aside the chemise she had been mending and cocked her head to look me over. I probably seemed awfully desperate for a person clearly in no mortal peril.

"Of course. What is it you need?" she said, getting to her feet and brushing out her apron. Ready for duty. I was going to have to insist that my brother increase her wages after this.

Not able to bear meeting Emma's eyes, I appraised her shoes as I mumbled my specific request.

"I want to look pretty. The ball tonight... I want to go, and I..."

"Have someone to impress?" she guessed, picking up my sentence where I left it.

My cheeks burned, more than answering the question. I did not dare to open my mouth, afraid I wouldn't be cautious enough and would accidentally reveal far too many of my secrets. If I confirmed Emma's suspicions, she would ask me who it was, and Kitty's name could not pass my lips.

"Sorry, it's not my place," Emma said, once it was clear her teasing hadn't been received as she'd hoped. She cleared her throat and offered a smile. "If there was ever an occasion to wear that new pink dress of yours, I would think trying to catch a man's eye would be it."

I knew exactly the one she meant. It had been a farewell gift when I left London, and I had yet to find a chance to wear it. A coral dress finished with a gauzy top layer embroidered with tiny cream flowers, it was more elegant than anything I would ever willingly choose myself, but I wanted Kitty to think of me as elegant. While I treasured our clandestine meetings by candlelight, there was something horribly appealing in the idea of taking her breath away when she saw me. A threadbare coat and an old chemise were not going to do that.

"Yes," I said decisively. "That one, please. And will you do my hair? And just a little rouge, perhaps?"

"What would Mr. Darcy say about that?" Emma said with a laugh.

I was far more worried about what he would say if he knew for whom I was wearing it. His affection for Elizabeth's sisters seemed unlikely to hold up if he knew anything of the thoughts running through my head. His affection for me was something I did not want to question, but all I could see was the thin line of his lips as we stood on the steps of Pemberley, watching the carriage that took Frances as far as Lambton before abandoning her to her fate.

"I will bear all responsibility," I insisted. "You needn't worry about getting in any kind of trouble with my brother. I will happily tell him I did it all alone, if that would make you more comfortable."

"I'm only teasing you. I'd be glad to help. Perhaps we will see you prosperously settled soon enough."

Kitty was certainly not the suitor she had in mind, but Emma's words still filled me with warmth. The thought of Kitty left me more content than the notion of any other match ever had.

Emma stepped back to appraise her handiwork, frowning for a second before adding another hairpin to the elaborate style she'd arranged from my curls. She still wasn't satisfied, considering me again before riffling around in one of the drawers at my dressing table. Triumphant, she pulled out a large feather, fluffy and soft pink.

"No," I said with a laugh, needing to draw a line somewhere. "I am walking down the stairs of my own house, not being presented at court."

"Don't you have a man to impress?" Emma asked, running the feather under my jaw to tickle my neck.

Suppressing giggles, I pushed it away. I wanted to impress Kitty, but I did not want to become someone else entirely. Piles of feathers and gems were too much. I shook my head, making my decision clear, and breathed a sigh of relief when Emma returned the feather to its drawer.

"All right, if you're against feathers, then I think you're ready," she declared grandly, reaching for the cloth she had hung over the mirror.

I had not been allowed to see my slow transformation from subdued hermit to semireluctant debutante. Emma insisted on the element of surprise, so I would see what "he" saw for the first time. When she whipped the covering away, I didn't recognise myself. My hair had been wrangled into ringlets and pulled into a complicated bun, tendrils of curls falling to frame my face. Emma's own recipe of rouge stained my cheeks and my lips with the subtlest flush, like I had been paid an unexpected compliment. The dress had been made for me by a master dressmaker in London, and the skill of the craftsmanship was solely responsible for how well it suited me. I scrambled out of my chair so I could shift the skirts beneath my hands, imagining how gracefully they would move if I danced. I felt beautiful and so far from Georgiana Darcy that I almost believed Kitty might think me beautiful, too.

"Thank you," I whispered to Emma. "I don't know how you did it."

"Made you shine?" she asked. "You do that all on your own. You just hide it well."

There was a smile at the corner of her lips that betrayed her teasing, and I feigned offence, clutching at my chest as if I was aghast at the suggestion.

"Are you ready to go down? Guests have started arriving, so you can make an entrance."

"I don't want to make an entrance," I protested.

Emma laughed. "Dressed like that, how could you not?"

I pulled a face at her but let her make final adjustments to my dress and hair before she deemed me acceptable to show my face in front of good company. She offered to fetch Darcy to escort me into the ball, but I requested Elizabeth instead, hoping my sister-in-law would be less likely to pass judgement on my change in appearance.

I don't know why I even had the thought. The second Elizabeth stepped into the room, she stopped, her eyes going wide as she took in the dress and the hair and the rouge. Her lips spread into a grin, and she took both my hands, squeezing.

"You are more handsome than anyone down in that ballroom," she said, deadly sincere. "Just how many hearts are you planning to break?"

I shook my head, not able to meet her eyes. It was a level of praise I'd never heard spoken so earnestly, not to me.

"Can we go down?" I asked, wanting to begin the evening so its ending could come quicker. I was starting to forget why I had ever even considered attending this ball.

I remembered exactly why the moment I walked into the ballroom on Elizabeth's arm. Kitty was impossible to miss. Even if not for the fact I was always aware of her exact position in every room, she shone amongst the assembled crowd. Her dress was cobalt blue, trimmed with golden embroidery around the hem. It was the kind of thing that fit in perfectly in London but still turned heads up in Derbyshire. Even without the bright garment, she would still have cast every other guest in shadow. There was a curve to her lips like she knew your every secret, a sparkle in her eyes betraying a laugh she held inside. If he'd been looking for perfection, my brother chose the wrong sister, but I'd never been more grateful his head had been turned by Elizabeth.

All the words I'd ever known eluded me. I wanted to rush over to Kitty, to tell her she looked more regal than royalty, to take her hand like she had taken mine in the library, but my feet had sewn themselves to the floor. It was only when Elizabeth tugged at my arm that I realised we hadn't moved from the doorway. I let her pull me farther into the room, my eyes still fixed on Kitty. She was talking to a woman I distantly recognised as one of Elizabeth's friends, laughing gloriously at whatever she'd said, and I yearned to be the one to bring that light to her eyes. Unaware of where my attention lay, Elizabeth led me over to my brother.

"My love," he greeted her, kissing the back of her gloved fingers like they had been separated for weeks, rather than mere minutes. Then he turned to me. "Georgiana, it is lovely to see you in attendance."

The sentiment was genuine, but then he took a moment to take in the atypical nature of my appearance and a frown settled across his features.

"Doesn't she look stunning?" Elizabeth said, noticing the same look and diving in to my rescue.

My brother always found it difficult to disagree with his wife. He forced a nod, far from happy about it, and made his excuses to step away from the conversation, suddenly spotting a friend across the room. As if it weren't a room filled solely with his friends.

"Don't pay him any mind," Elizabeth said with a laugh. "He's just not yet ready to believe you a woman ready to marry, especially after..."

She cut herself off, but it was easy to fill in the gap she left behind. Especially after Wickham. The version of the story Darcy knew rendered me a naive child in his eyes, but the truth would be far worse. I nodded, fighting back numbness, and cleared my throat.

"If you'll excuse me," I said with a nod, hurrying away before anyone could insist I needed to be chaperoned. I was hoping this ball being in my own house, half full of people I already knew, would negate any need for close supervision.

I didn't realise my feet were leading me to Kitty until I looked up and found her a foot away, staring at me. I couldn't blame her for being surprised to see me, not after how adamant I'd been that I wouldn't be coming. My cheeks darkened beneath the rouge.

"George..." Kitty said, trailing off like she'd forgotten the end of her sentence along with the rest of my name.

"Miss Bennet," I said, adding a shallow curtsey. How could I not, with her dressed like that? The king himself would've bowed.

"Don't." Kitty smiled. "I hate being a *Miss Bennet.*"

I took her hand quickly, hoping the motion was disguised by our skirts, and squeezed her fingers in apology. I wished there weren't gloves between us. Before I could commit to any silly ideas of walking around the room with her on my arm, I stepped a little away.

"You came," she said.

"You asked me to. That is a beautiful dress," I said, although it wasn't what I meant. It was Kitty who made the dress as breathtaking as it was. She was the one who deserved the direct compliments. I just wasn't brave enough to give them, not there in the middle of Pemberley's drawing room.

"I borrowed it from Lizzy," Kitty said, plucking at the fabric of her skirts to pull them away from herself. "It was stupid, really. I should never have—"

I couldn't let her keep talking.

"It looks like it was made for you," I insisted, and I clearly was not the only one who thought so. The entire room seemed to be sneaking glances her way, with ladies envious and gentlemen unable to direct their attention elsewhere. "They are all looking at you."

"Silly." Kitty laughed, shaking her head. "It's you they are looking at. And I cannot blame them for even a moment."

It thrilled me to hear her say such things. I dared to hope, just a little, that she returned even the smallest amount of my feelings.

"Would you like to dance?" she asked, without a hint of teasing in her voice. "Or is your dance card already full?"

"With you?" I blinked at her, certain I was misunderstanding. There was no shortage of men at the gathering; it would be unnecessary for her to have to dance with me. She could have her pick of any of the eligible bachelors in the room, and probably any of those already married. No gentleman would be unsympathetic to her request.

"Yes, with me," Kitty confirmed, her head held high.

"I…" I took a step back.

I wanted to. Kitty was radiant, and I wanted nothing more than to stand up with her in front of the whole room and know she had chosen me over everyone else. I wanted to slide off her gloves, lace her fingers with mine, and let our skirts sweep the floor together as we danced through the steps. But everyone would be watching, and even if we could have explained it with a lack of gentlemen, I would not be able to feign the disconnect of a lady dancing with a friend or family member. It was too much of a risk. Everyone would know.

"I am not much of a dancer," I mumbled, conjuring disappointment on her face. "But I'm sure you'll not be short of partners. You really do look beautiful."

I all but fled from Kitty's company, looking around the room desperately in an attempt to find someone I recognised who wouldn't protest me forcing my way into their conversation. What on earth had I been thinking, wanting to go to this ball because of Kitty? We could not dance together. Nothing could ever happen. She would never even want it to. Only bad repercussions came of this sort of thing.

Not wanting to be left to navigate the ballroom alone, I searched for Elizabeth amongst the crowd. Instead, I found the gazes of half a dozen men watching me and whispering to their companions. I withered under the attention. My dress and makeup felt all too overdone.

I wanted Kitty to think me refined and

elegant, but turning up dressed as if for my debut in society meant I had inadvertently presented myself as a potential wife. I had money and my family had influence—it would be foolish for me not to recognise how powerful a match I would make. I could have been the plainest woman in the country and I would still have had my pick of suitors, but I didn't want any of them.

Longing to be out of the spotlight, I elected to sit myself amongst the chaperones and over-danced ladies already nursing pinched toes. Only the most forward of men would dare to approach, and I was hoping the presence of my brother would dissuade even them. Dancing meant courting, and courting meant proposals, and I was not inclined to encourage any of it. The further down that path I got with anyone, the harder it would be to rescue myself, and I had already been at the mercy of one man manipulating me into marriage; I would not allow another to use etiquette and propriety to do the same.

When I settled down onto one of the overstuffed chairs arranged around the fire, the abrupt change of conversation made it clear they had been talking about me. Thin-lipped smiles adorned the faces of mothers hoping I wouldn't steal their daughters' first choice of husbands. If they knew the kind of thoughts that plagued me, I wondered if they would be relieved or disgusted. Perhaps both.

The topic of discussion settled on the new modiste setting up shop in town. My usual lack of need for new dresses for balls meant I could afford to focus on something far more intriguing. Kitty. A room full of blind men would still have been drawn to her, and with the addition of her looks, she had no shortage of suitors requesting space on her dance card. I wondered which dance she would have saved for me, and what people would have whispered when we stood up together. My skin prickled at the thought. It would take one word from Darcy to have me sent away if he suspected me for even a moment.

Kitty was born to step out onto a dance floor. Her steps weren't always perfect, but her enthusiasm and her joy were evident from across the room. She took such pleasure in the twist of her skirts around her legs and in matching her movements to the music. I couldn't look away. With the fire heating my cheeks and the beat of my heart in my throat, I realised I wanted to spend every evening for the rest of my life watching

Kitty Bennet smile. Even if I didn't get to be the one to cause it.

I did not recognise the man she was dancing with, but I could not admit to paying him much attention. Kitty's focus didn't seem to be on her partner, either. She smiled at him and made what appeared to be polite conversation as they waited to go down a line, but she seemed distracted. Her gaze wandered the ballroom in search of someone. Her sister, I presumed, or perhaps the man she'd promised the next dance to. Only then her eyes found me and she glowed, her smile even brighter before the next turn of the dance took her away.

The passing of time seemed of no consequence as I watched Kitty dance her night away. She honoured no man with more than one number, showing no particular favour for any of her partners. I found some comfort in the knowledge that, while she could not be mine, she did not seem particularly inclined to be anyone else's, either.

When Elizabeth dropped into the chair beside me, she startled me away from my staring. I hoped desperately that she had not noticed whom my gaze had been following.

"I should warn you, before you start to worry every man in the room is spurning you, that your brother has met every request to be introduced to you with a glare that could melt metal," she said, barely concealing her amusement. "If someone has caught your eye, you would be wise to mention it before he is sent running for the hills."

"No!" I insisted. It was an intervention I was glad of if it kept me off the dance floor and away from men who thought they were charming. The only person who had caught my eye had already made my acquaintance. It was not lack of an introduction that kept us apart. "If I cannot sequester myself away in the hills for the evening, then the next-best option is to have everyone else sent there while I stay here."

Elizabeth's smile dropped from her lips, and her forehead creased with worry. I had tried to make my words light, but the truth behind them was too deep to be so easily concealed.

"If you hate it that much, neither Darcy nor I would be offended if you retired for the evening," she assured me, her voice low as she took my hand and squeezed my fingers.

For a moment, I considered it. Only then I

caught sight of Kitty over her shoulder, grinning as she danced a particularly complicated step, and I didn't want to be out of sight of that smile for even a moment.

"Thank you, but I think I will stay at least a little while longer," I said, the unstoppable softness of my voice surely betraying my fondness for something beyond the dancing and fireside gossip. I resolved to say nothing more.

If Elizabeth noticed, she did not mention it. She sat with me awhile, sharing idle talk and pointing out various guests I should know of, but I could tell the Bennet-sister inclination to revel in the centre of the action did not stop with Kitty. Elizabeth was soon summoned away to walk the room, blessed with far more friends than I.

I watched as the current dance came to a close, the musicians settling to take a short break before striking up another tune. Kitty's cheeks were flushed as she curtsied her farewell to her partner, and I found myself on my feet, keen to fetch her a drink. I had taken barely three steps before I was intercepted by a painfully familiar figure. Mr. Honeyfield stepped into my path and bowed, giving me no choice but to stop.

"How lovely to see you again, Miss Darcy," he

said. "I trust you have nowhere else to rush off to tonight. May I beg your next dance?"

The question had sounded so much more appealing coming from Kitty. I knew I couldn't refuse Mr. Honeyfield without surrendering my participation in all further dances for the evening. It was considered rude to reject one man only to then partner with another, but I had no intentions of partnering with any man, so the opportunity was a welcome one. I wished only that turning down the offer of one dance allowed me to turn down all offers of dances, courtship, and marriage for the rest of my life.

"Thank you, but I think I ought to rest my feet," I said as demurely as I could manage.

Etiquette dictated Mr. Honeyfield should escort me to a chair, wish me well, and take his leave of my company. Wherever he had studied the finer points of social interactions, we had not been taught from the same book, because he barely held back a snort of laughter.

"You have spent most of the evening sitting down. And I cannot imagine the journey here was all that arduous—one flight of stairs? Two?" he teased. When my cheeks flushed from a mortifying blend of anger and embarrassment, he either did not notice or chose to deploy tact for the first time in the conversation. "One dance is all I ask, Miss Darcy," he insisted.

It was an impertinent response. While he was annoyingly astute when it came to how I had passed my time at the ball, he had no right to comment on it. I considered constructing a lie about injuring an ankle in the days prior, but I could never sustain any kind of ruse. If I myself did not let slip the truth, someone else would surely reveal my lie, and then I would be no better than Mr. Honeyfield when it came to following the rules of social etiquette. Cursing myself, I took his arm and allowed him to escort me to the dance floor.

If my brother was going to choose a moment to rush in and rescue me from the flirtatiousness of a young man, this would have been the ideal time, but I knew he would never make a scene unless I was in genuine danger. I caught a glimpse of him across the room, Elizabeth on his arm. He was watching me carefully, eyes narrowed, jaw clenched. Neither of us was happy about the situation.

James Honeyfield was a terrible dancer. He might have no longer resembled the gangly child with no proper grasp of where his limbs ended, but his movements were just as uncoordinated. He was never quite sure where he was supposed to be, each step either too slow or too fast, and his focus was entirely on his feet. All my energy was channelled into preventing him bumping into me—I had none left to worry about what Elizabeth or Darcy or Kitty thought of the whole affair.

If Mr. Honeyfield had thought asking me to dance was going to lead to any kind of affection for him in my eyes, he was sorely mistaken. Once the arduous experience came to an end, I curtsied as politely as I was able and begged my leave. Turning around to reacquaint myself with the rest of the room, I noticed at least three men making their way towards me. Now that a way around my brother's protective tendencies had been found, anyone with even the slightest prior interaction with me was going to extort it in exchange for a dance. One had been more than enough.

While they might have been willing to bend the rules of acceptable social cues, I felt certain they would not cross my brother himself. I scanned the room, hoping to find Darcy and plant myself at his side to deter further unwanted attention, but before I could locate him, a hand landed on my arm. My initial reaction was to shake it off and protest that laying a hand on me without my consent was unquestionably out of order, but after my arm had tensed up at the sudden contact, it relaxed again almost immediately. Someone was tracing a familiar circle with their thumb. I knew exactly who was touching me, and there was nothing unwelcome about it.

"Do you want to get some air?" Kitty asked, the earnest look in her eyes betraying the escape plan she was offering me. I nodded, probably far too quickly and too enthusiastically, and her smile lit up the whole room. "Come on, before they have you surrounded," she whispered.

I was all too keen to follow her. She looped her arm around mine and pretended to lead me in a stroll around the ballroom. When we passed close to the doors, open onto the garden, she nudged me out and followed quickly after, freeing a candle from a candlestick on a sideboard just inside. I felt laughter bubbling up inside me as I followed Kitty away from the house, not wanting to lose her amongst the hedges.

My shoes weren't intended for anything but

ballrooms, and I felt the grass through the thin soles. The moon hung full and high in the night sky, and between that and Kitty's candle, we didn't suffer from lack of light. We weren't the only ones to have sought the reprieve of cool air, but the voices of other couples soon faded until I could believe it was just the two of us in the world.

In the semidarkness, Kitty's cheeks lit by the flickering orange glow of candlelight, I couldn't help but feel the same comfort as I did in the library. There was a smile on her lips, mischievous and endearing, until something seemed to occur to her and it dropped into a frown.

"So who was he?" she asked, her indifference clearly feigned.

"No one," I insisted. I could not bear the idea of her thinking I held an ounce of affection for Mr. Honeyfield, not even for a second. "I knew him as a child, but truly, I barely remember him."

"I see," Kitty said, worrying her lower lip between her teeth. Her expression was hard to read in the dim light, and she quickly shook it away. "Come on. Show me the gardens."

She'd seen the gardens before, walked miles around them on plenty of occasions, but I didn't dare mention it, or the fact it was too dark to see much of anything. I was terrified to break the spell of the moment by letting too much of reality in. It would be dangerous to call attention to the way my arms prickled in the cold or how close candle wax was dripping to Kitty's gloves. Instead I led her farther into the gardens, keen to put more distance between us and the house.

If I had been walking with anyone else I knew as well, I would have taken their arm. Elizabeth and I had covered all of Pemberley's grounds in such a fashion multiple times over. With Kitty, it all felt too perilous. Rather than stroll at her side, I kept a cautious distance, walking just ahead. Out of the reach of the glow of Kitty's candle. The moon was bright enough to guide my feet but showed me only so much of the ground in front of me. When I turned back to steal a look at Kitty, the safe footing ran out before I could draw my attention away and I felt myself plummet.

Chapter Seven

For one moment of fear, I was in free fall, my front foot having nowhere to land. I tried to grab for the wall but succeeded only in driving my knee into the sharp edge of the bricks and scraping it against them as I fell.

"George!" Kitty screamed, scrambling to the edge of the wall. "How do I get down?"

The pain of the hip that had broken my fall and the knee staining my dress red made it difficult to think. I was worried if I stopped biting my tongue long enough to speak, all I would let forth would be sobs. Blinking through the haze of pain, I looked around to register where I'd landed. Noting the orderly rows of planted vegetables, I realised I'd tripped over the edge of the walled kitchen gardens, dug into the side of a slope to hide it from view of the house.

I gestured shakily farther down the wall where I knew there were steps. Kitty's frantic reassurances faded for a moment before she reappeared at my side, crouching beside me.

"How bad is it?" she asked, before taking one look at my knee and going pale. "Can you stand?"

I still couldn't talk, pressing my lips together as tightly as I could, but I tried to get to my feet. The second I put any weight on my wounded side, a bolt of agony ran up my leg and I collapsed against Kitty with a cry of pain.

"We need to get you back to the house. Send for a doctor," Kitty said, fussing over me. She pushed my hair back from my face, her gloved fingers ghosting over my cheeks.

I wasn't sure I could walk as far as the house, but Kitty's touch took away some of the pain, and coherent thought began to make its return. If we were in the kitchen gardens, then we weren't far from my mother's grotto. It had a bench and a roof and would be as safe a place as any to wait alone for Kitty to fetch help.

Leaning myself heavily against Kitty's side, I climbed to unsteady feet and gritted my teeth to stave off the pain. She supported my weight as I limped a little way down the wall and under an arch that took us close to the grotto's entrance.

"The house, George," Kitty tried to insist.

I shook my head, dragging aside the bushes that concealed the grotto. Kitty was close enough that I heard her tiny inhale of surprise, but she didn't hesitate to help me inside.

The moon shone down through the well in the ceiling, glinting off the glass tiles embedded in the floor and the shiniest chips of mother-of-pearl. I rarely saw the space at night, and it looked almost ethereal, impossibly beautiful in its intricacy. Kitty must have thought so, too, but her focus was solely on me as she settled me onto the bench and knelt in front of me.

"Hold this," she said gently, handing me the candle and pulling off her gloves. She tugged at the hem of my gown. "Is this all right?"

I would have said yes to anything she asked, nodding almost embarrassingly quickly. With the candle flame so close, I looked down to survey the worst of the damage. The outer layer of my gown was shredded from my thigh down to the hem, with the pink silk underneath torn at my knee. The petticoat had fared no better, baring my ripped stocking. Every layer was stained with blood, sticking to the gash in my flesh.

Kitty carefully peeled away the layers of my dress, tucking them up above my knees. I couldn't focus on the pain anymore, not when I felt my heartbeat pounding just under my skin. Under any other circumstance, the intimacy of the situation would have overwhelmed me. I wanted Kitty so close there was barely any room between us to breathe, but her touch was almost clinical. She reached for my petticoat, and I expected her to similarly push it out of the way, but instead she gripped the hem ruffle between her hands and pulled until the stitches ripped and the strip of fabric came free. I startled, but Kitty seemed to know exactly what she was doing as she separated the ruffle and smoothed it out.

"I have four sisters," she reminded me, guiding me to move my leg up so it lay flat along the bench. "One of us invariably ended up in a scrape at least once a week. Not so often Jane or Mary, but Lizzy, Lydia, or I could be relied on to make up the shortfall."

She wrapped the fabric tightly around my knee, stemming the bleeding. It didn't seem to bother her that her hands were stained crimson or her dress was newly embellished with smudges of blood and dirt. I felt myself, against my better judgement, fall even further. Fresh tears sprung up in my eyes, following the tracks of their predecessors. Seconds later, soft thumbs brushed them gently away.

"Does it hurt that badly?" Kitty asked, concern heavy in her eyes as she took the candle from my shaking hand and propped it up in an upturned shell set into the wall beside us.

I considered lying, but I didn't have the energy left in me. My knee was throbbing, and there was blood soaking through the ripped ruffle of my petticoat. I wanted to sink into Kitty, to hide away. To erase the terrible turn the evening had taken.

"My pride is more wounded than anything. I went to all this trouble with the hair and the rouge and a dress I am not even sure I really like and all because…" There was no going back if I said it. But if I didn't say it, it was going to kill me, taking up all the space in my chest until there was none left for my lungs. "I wanted you to look at me. It was a childish folly," I admitted, unable to meet her eye if I wanted my cheeks to remain unflushed. Instead, I focused on poking my fingers through the holes in my skirts, but when Kitty's hand rested on mine to still my fidgeting, I had no choice but to pay her my full attention.

"All I have done all night is look at you," she said. "You cannot take my breath away anymore, George, because you took it the first time I saw you, and you have never given it back." She tugged my hand to her lips and kissed the back of my gloved fingers with a tenderness I felt through the fabric and down to my bones. "I am in a constant state of breathless awe around you."

The pain in my knee was a forgotten inconvenience, my mind too focused on the overwhelming joy flooding in. I had never hated my gloves more for getting in the way, and I shook off Kitty's grip to strip them off, tugging at each fingertip before letting them fall to the floor. I wanted to lace my fingers with hers, but I caught myself the second before I did, unsure exactly what she wanted from this.

As if she could sense my hesitation, Kitty reached out and took my hand, her skin soft and cool as it ghosted over mine. It was a featherlight touch, until I met her eyes and she tightened her grip. Emboldened, I traced circles over her knuckles with my thumb.

Neither of us said anything as we sat there, bathed in moonlight, clinging to each other. I could not entirely believe my luck, that I got to look at her so freely. Her hair was escaping its confines, and I could see the traces of exhaustion collecting in her eyes, but she was still the most beautiful person I'd ever seen.

I was reaching for her before I knew what I was doing. An escaped lock of hair had curled just in front of her ear, and I tucked it away, but I could not bear to stop touching her once I had started. Her skin was too warm, too real, and I lost my fingertips in her hair, my palm hot against her neck.

She kissed me first, and I would be forever grateful for it. If it had been left to me, we might have stayed in that moment of heavy gazes and brief touches eternally. But Kitty shifted forwards, her fingertips cautiously lingering at my jaw to steady me as she brushed her lips against the very corner of my mouth. I couldn't help my contented sigh, or the way it spun into a whine as she settled back. It wasn't enough. With Kitty, I wasn't sure it ever would be.

When she sat back, there was fear in her eyes, as if she couldn't believe what she'd done, and I couldn't allow her to think she'd made a mistake. I reached out to pull her close, my fingers sliding over the silken fabric of her dress at her shoulder, and thankfully she responded with no resistance, pressing her lips to mine with unpractised enthusiasm that I returned almost as inelegantly. My practise with Helena, no matter how brief, served me well enough, and the security of the grotto calmed my fears of discovery. It was just Kitty and me left in the world.

With her advances returned, Kitty seemed to shake off any remaining hesitations. Her hands found my hair, playing aimlessly with some loose tendril, before her fingers started sliding out my hairpins and dropping them to the floor with gentle clicks against the glass tiles.

"That took forever," I mumbled between her kisses, but I had to fight to keep my laughter at bay. I was too giddy to be anything but happy.

"Sorry," Kitty replied, shifting to kiss my

cheek. "Only I've been wanting to do this since the first night I saw you in the library."

I thought perhaps *this* meant kissing me, but once Kitty had finished her quest to unpin Emma's elaborate styling and my hair was tumbling down my back, she ran her fingers through the curls, brushing them out before losing her hands in them. I felt dizzy, like the hairpins had been the only thing holding me together.

We kissed for long enough that the impromptu bandage around my knee bled through with sticky crimson. Physicians had been wrong all this time. It wasn't opium that best eased pain; it was Kitty Bennet. I couldn't think of anything but her lips against mine and her skin under my fingertips, my injuries quite forgotten. They ought to sell her by the bottle, but I selfishly wanted her all for myself.

I had no plan for what was going to happen once we walked out of the grotto. What we were doing would be viewed as reprehensible to anyone who saw, but I still didn't want to stop. The only other time I'd done this, the choice had been taken away from me, Wickham's interruption controlling my fate.

It seemed history was keen to repeat itself.

Elizabeth gave us as little warning as Wickham had given Helena and me, rushing into the grotto with a frantic chaos about her. Kitty wrenched herself away from me, scrambling to her feet before I could even organise my thoughts.

It was all going to happen again. The blackmailing and the fear and the consequences. I cursed myself for being so stupid, for making the same mistake twice, but I hadn't been able to help but fall for Kitty.

Maybe Elizabeth hadn't seen. It was dark in the grotto—perhaps we'd been in shadow, or Kitty had been quick enough to put some distance between us. I tried to gauge whether there was disgust in her eyes, but she was wholly focused on Kitty.

"You need to come with me," she said, grabbing her sister's arm and hauling her towards the door like she was a child.

"But—" Kitty tried to protest as she stumbled over her feet. She didn't look at me.

"Now."

With that, Elizabeth pulled her away. She spared me an apologetic glance, barely even properly seeing me as she left me in silence, my only companion the flickering candle.

I sat there, numb, as I regained my breath. With Kitty gone, there was nothing to distract me from the pain of my knee. My leg thrummed with pulses of agony, and my heart beat a similar rhythm of anguish. Every time I let myself get attached and allowed myself to give in to my wayward feelings, it ended badly. I tried to reassure myself that this was different, that Elizabeth was nothing like Wickham, but it still felt like I'd lost Kitty, just like I'd lost Helena. If Elizabeth told Darcy, I might lose Pemberley, too.

I hoped she'd come back. Even if Elizabeth was admonishing Kitty, I thought at least she would send help for me once she'd been told of my fall. There was no way for me to accurately measure the time that passed, but I was shivering in my ridiculous, destroyed dress and the candle was starting to burn low. If I didn't get myself back soon, I would have no light by which to do so and no movement left in my frozen limbs.

Without Kitty to support my weight, standing was difficult. Walking was even harder but, candle in hand to guide the way, I made the walk back to the house step by painful step. I could still hear the noise of the ball spilling out from Pemberley's windows. If I had been the talk of the town in my prior absences, returning midevening with tearstained cheeks, ripped skirts, and a blood-soaked bandage tied around my knee would truly cause a scandal. For a moment, I considered it. Mr. Honeyfield would lose all interest, as would any other viable suitor. From my perspective, it sounded ideal, but it would bring shame to Pemberley's door that my family name should not have to bear on my behalf.

Changing my course to head through the kitchens, I prayed to find them empty but instead stumbled across Ruth peeling potatoes.

"My days!" she said, horrified at the sight of me. "Miss Darcy, what happened?"

She dropped the knife and potato she was holding into the bucket of scraps, cleaning off her hands on a towel before hurrying over to fuss.

"No, I'm fine," I insisted. I needed to find Kitty, to make sure she wasn't in trouble. "Mrs. Darcy and Miss Bennet? Where are they?"

I was convinced there was a psychic connection amongst Pemberley's staff. Information spread quicker than the plague through London, jumping between rooms and across floors in minutes. If there was something to know, Ruth would know it.

"Their carriage just departed for Longbourn, miss. You should sit down."

She tried to usher me towards a chair, but I stood firm. I couldn't bear the idea of Kitty being taken away because of what we had done, not before I had a chance to talk to her and try to reason with Elizabeth. It was all my fault.

If they had only just left, perhaps there was still a chance I could catch them. I ducked past Ruth and headed for the main entrance. The pain in my knee was of no consequence. I just needed to get to the front steps as quickly as possible. Ruth called after me, but I left her voice behind as I limped through the halls. I could hear the vibrancy of the ball bleeding through the house, but I didn't care who saw me.

I heaved open the front door and hoped frantically that the carriage would still be at the bottom of the steps. Stumbling out into the cold, I found the drive empty. If I squinted, I was almost convinced I could make out moving lights far in the distance, but they were much beyond the space I could cover with my feet or my voice.

There was nothing I could do. I sank to the floor, my shaking legs no longer able to hold me up, and clutched my knees as I let tears fall from my eyes. I'd ruined my own life when I'd kissed Helena, but now I'd ruined Kitty's, too. She didn't have a prosperous marriage lined up to save her from scandal. I let everything hit me—the pain in my knee, the breathlessness Kitty had left me with, the fear bubbling in my stomach. It was too much to bear.

I wasn't sure how long I sat there, the cold seeping through my dress and the music from the ball carrying through the open door behind me. My tears cooled on my cheeks, chased by fresh tracks when I considered the potential of never seeing Kitty again. She had turned my life upside down in a matter of weeks, but when she was beside me I'd never felt off-balance from the change in orientation. With her gone, my blood was pooling in my head, leaving me sick and dizzy.

It was a voice that eventually disrupted my downward spiral.

"Georgiana?" I heard my brother calling, but it felt like the words were passing through water before they reached me. He had to be right beside me, though, as I felt his hand rest on my shoulder. "Ruth told me you were hurt. Do you need a doctor? What on earth happened?" When

I couldn't find the words to answer, he got more and more frantic. "Talk to me, Georgiana!"

Telling him truthfully what had left me in such a state was unthinkable. Unless Elizabeth had already told him as she ushered Kitty away, but there was no bite to my brother's words, no malice behind his concern. His temperament suggested he had no idea what I had been doing.

Feeling years younger than my age, despite the rouge and the dress, I turned my face into Darcy's shoulder. Like he always had for a skinned knee or a bruised elbow, he stroked my hair and mumbled something reassuring, but too low to hear in its entirety. Usually it was a promise that everything would be okay, but he could not guarantee me that anymore.

"Can you walk?" he asked.

I shook my head, certain I had drained the last of the fear-induced strength left in my bones. Darcy picked me up like I was a wounded child, one arm behind my back and one below my knees. The motion jostled the cut Kitty had wrapped what felt like a lifetime ago, and I had to bite back a cry of pain.

Darcy carried me up to my room, kicking open the doors in his way. Ordinarily, I would protest at being made to feel so juvenile, but I didn't have it in me. Darcy didn't speak, either, his teeth gritted. His arms weren't shaking under my weight, so it didn't seem like exertion making him tense.

My bedsheets were the first soft thing I'd felt since Kitty's skin, and I wilted into them, rubbing my cheek against the fabric in search of comfort.

"Sit up," Darcy said abruptly. When I flinched, he softened his tone. "I'm sorry. Your knee needs attending to. Does it hurt badly?"

We both looked down at the bloodstained bandages visible through the tears in my gown. I was too numb to feel anything, but Darcy blanched, immediately retreating to ring the bellpull that would summon Emma. Rather than return to my side, he paced the floor.

"What happened?" he asked, concern lacing the words.

"I fell," I mumbled, sharing the only part of the truth safe to tell.

"No." Darcy turned sharply on the ball of his foot to start another line. "This did not happen from tripping on a step. Why were you outside alone in the dark? What happened to your hair?"

Kitty happened. Kitty's fingers combing through my hair, getting caught in my curls. The memory, so recent but already feeling like it was fading, brought with it a fresh wave of tears.

Darcy's frustration turned to panic, and he flew across the room, hovering awkwardly.

"Please don't cry," he implored. "I am not angry with you. I just need to know who did this. I want to fix this, Georgiana. Please let me."

He wasn't going to relent without an explanation, but my brain was swimming with too much to fashion one. I thought through the least damaging version of events, clumsily erasing Kitty from the narrative in the desperate hope I could still save her reputation somehow. Before I got further than how I could have possibly wrapped my knee alone, Emma burst through the door.

Probably expecting to help me dress for bed, excited at the prospect of an evening's gossip, she froze when she saw Darcy. Confusion clouded her eyes, only for them to widen in horror when she processed the state of me.

"Mr. Darcy," she said, bobbing into the slightest notion of a curtsey before hurrying over to me. "What can I do?"

I grabbed Emma's hand, keen for the comfort

of a familiar figure who wasn't in control of the fate of the rest of my life. The urge to tell her everything had never been stronger.

"It is nothing," I managed, but I was fooling no one.

Emma clucked her tongue and dragged over a chair so I could prop my leg up. I winced to force it straight, clutching at the bedsheets. She knelt beside me, tucking one side of my skirts up around my thigh.

"Forgive me," I said, "for ruining the petticoat," because I knew she'd been the one to make it and now it was beyond mending.

"That's not what I'm worried about," Emma said. "Tell me if you can't bear the pain."

She picked at the knot Kitty had tied in the fabric until she could loosen it, unwinding it one loop at a time. She had to peel away the sections saturated with sticky blood while I fought to keep my face neutral.

Darcy had resumed his pacing, resolutely keeping his eyes averted from either my bare legs, the sight of blood, or both.

"I need a name, Georgiana," he said, almost an order. "If it was someone at this ball, they are someone Elizabeth and I considered trustworthy.

I need to know who betrayed that trust." He paused, cocking his head to the side. "James Honeyfield. I saw him dance with you. Did he…"

"No!" I insisted.

As much as I preferred not to be in Mr. Honeyfield's company, he had done nothing to deserve being thrown to the wolves. I didn't doubt my brother would fight a duel over my honour if he believed a man responsible for its destruction. I had seen him move heaven and earth to protect me before. When he thought my decision to run away and marry Wickham had been simply the actions of a misled child, he had still done everything in his power to ensure I would not be tainted by my poor judgement.

What I'd done with Kitty would leave my reputation in tatters even if she'd been a man. I wondered what Darcy would do if he knew. I had no idea what had become of Frances, thrown out the way she was without a reference or anywhere to go. If I was turned away from Pemberley in the same way, I had no one to turn to.

"Truly," I said, begging him to believe me, "no one hurt me. I fell off the wall around the kitchen gardens." My words tumbled into a hiss of pain as Emma prodded at the skin around my knee to test the stability of the bone.

"What were you doing out there in the dark?" Darcy pushed, finally looking at me again, but keeping his eyes firmly fixed on mine.

"I needed a moment away from the ball," I explained, avoiding a lie as best I could.

Darcy scrutinised my gaze, searching for something. I hoped he couldn't read me that well—I was keeping too many secrets.

"Mr. Darcy, sir, could you ask the kitchens to send up some boiled water and clean bandages? And some vinegar?" Emma asked.

I had never heard her request something of him so boldly. My brother was not a frightening man, but he could certainly be intimidating.

Darcy blinked in surprise, as if Emma's presence had slipped his mind.

"Should I not call for a doctor?" he asked.

"It needs to be cleaned and wrapped, but she is not on death's door. Perhaps request a full examination in the morning, but for now she'll make it through the night and will probably benefit from the rest," Emma said, before her eyes went wide. "Sir," she added, with a bob of the head.

Ordinarily I wouldn't be sure how Darcy would take being given orders by a lady's maid, but he nodded like her words were the tether he had been looking for and left us with a terse bow.

The moment we were alone, Emma took both my hands.

"If there's something you're keeping from him, can you tell me?" she asked, desperate. "Did a man...? Your skirts are ripped."

I shook my head, squeezing her fingers.

"I fell," I promised.

"And your hair?" Emma pressed, not so easy to misdirect as Darcy. "That did not happen from a fall. Forgive me if it's not my place, but it would not be the first time a man tried something with a vulnerable young lady."

It would not be the first time a man tried something with me. I could hear the insinuation under her words, aware of Wickham's manipulation in the same way Darcy was—the more palatable version that erased Helena from the story. Physically, Wickham had never hurt me. He had not even tried, valuing my money above anything else. Still, I could not bear the idea of

Kitty's hands in my hair being misconstrued as something taken rather than freely given.

"She's gone," I said, unable to keep it inside. I couldn't tell Darcy, but maybe Emma was a safer option. Maybe she would understand.

"Who's gone?" she asked, her brow furrowed.

"Kitty."

Her name fell from my lips without my permission. I ached to say it. What if she hated me now? What if she never wanted to see me again, or if she told everyone I'd kissed her? In the moment it had seemed as if my feelings were reciprocated, but a little time and perspective might bring Kitty some sense. If not, stern threats from her sister certainly would.

"Miss Bennet?" Emma asked, confused.

I dragged a pillow into my lap and hugged it tight, staring intently at my own toes rather than meeting her eyes.

"She left with Mrs. Darcy," she said, trying to be helpful. "That was the word downstairs."

I bit back a sob, but not quickly enough. The bed dipped beside me as Emma took a seat.

"I see," she whispered.

I whipped my head up to look at her, finding surprise, confusion, and a little pity, but not a hint of disgust. There was no way she had understood, not truly. Still, I watched her carefully for a long moment to be sure. If she told Darcy, she could ruin my entire life in one action. Kitty's, too. The notion that Elizabeth might have seen too much was bad enough, but she would at least want to protect her sister. Emma was employed by Darcy, owed her allegiance to him, even if she was kind to me.

We sat in silence, Emma still holding my hand, for several minutes. Before I could find the words to break it, Darcy was pushing his way back into the room. Rather than send a maid with what Emma had requested, he bore the load himself, juggling the supplies in his arms.

Emma worked quickly to clean and rewrap my knee, dousing it with vinegar and all the while assuring my brother the scrapes were not as deep as they looked. I was too exhausted to do more than wince at each twinge of pain. Darcy tried to question me more about how I'd gotten hurt, but when I had no answers for him, he eventually bid me good night with a worried frown and left me. There was still a ball going on, after all, and they'd already lost their hostess.

Emma stayed until I was on the cusp of sleep,

gathering up my ruined clothing and promising she'd mend what she could. I was too tired to tell her not to bother. Even if it was fixable, I never wanted to wear that pink dress again. This was not an evening I wanted to remember.

Chapter Eight

Whether or not I had a tangible memento of the previous evening, the throbbing pain in my knee reminded me at my first moment of consciousness.

I considered my options. There was every chance news of my indiscretions had now made it to my brother, and I doubted that conversation would go well. The urge to lock myself in my bedroom and sequester myself away until I expired from lack of sustenance was appealing.

Seclusion also meant never seeing the library

again, or the shell grotto, and never even getting a chance of finding out what happened to Kitty.

Rising on shaky legs, I pulled on my second-hand coat, sinking into the familiarity of its embrace. I got as far as the door before it opened in front of me, Emma in the doorway.

"You should not be out of bed," she said sternly. "I have only just talked Mr. Darcy down from summoning every doctor within thirty miles. Do not make me regret it."

She gave me little choice in the matter, blocking my escape with the tray in her hands. Perching on the edge of the mattress was about as obliging as I could bring myself to be. Emma set the tray down beside me, passing over a cup of tea.

"I need to change that bandage again," she said. "And a letter came for you this morning, sent back from Lambton with the carriage."

My heart leapt into my throat, leaving no space for the tea I was trying to drink. Spluttering and coughing, I spilt a wave of liquid over the tray as I set down the cup and snatched up the letter just in time to rescue it from soaking.

My name was scrawled across the front in looping script I'd seen spill from Kitty's pen. I tried to talk myself to calm as I ripped open a hastily formed seal and unfolded the paper, keeping it close to my chest as I read.

> *My Dearest George,*
>
> *I am writing this in the carriage as we travel, so please do excuse the occasional wandering line. Pemberley is still in view, and I hate that I am leaving you behind, particularly in such a haste. Despite my most ardent pleading, Lizzy was adamant there was no time. I think she was still a little in shock after how she found us. But rest assured she has spoken not of it, and I do not believe she seeks to punish us. Perhaps she does not fully understand what she interrupted. She has not said a word to your brother. Even if she had wanted to, there was simply no time.*
>
> *Tonight a messenger brought word that Father is ill and Mother wants us back at Longbourn at once. She fears he will not recover and that we must say our last goodbyes, but she would fear that if he had but caught a chill. Still, it would be a terrible thing if he were truly unwell and we did not go to him, as I am sure you can understand.*
>
> *I will return to Pemberley as soon as I can, if you wish me to. In truth, I think the only thing that could keep me from seeing you again is a request from*

you that I stay away. I do not pretend to understand these feelings, or flatter myself to think you might share them, but you stun me, Miss Darcy, and leave me quite at odds with sanity. I rather think I like it.

Yours humbly and reverently,
Kitty

I traced over Kitty's name, allowing myself to smile for the first time since she left me in the grotto. It seemed like the best news I could've hoped for. Elizabeth had to at least have her suspicions regarding what she'd seen, but it wasn't her chief concern.

"Good news?" Emma's smile was knowing but kind.

I nodded, carefully refolding the letter and slipping it between the pages of *The Disposition of an English Lady*. It felt too dangerous to keep it out in the light. As terrible as it was to think news of the Bennets' ailing father to be a positive thing, I couldn't help my relief.

"Do you know where my brother is?" I asked Emma.

"That is a question I will only answer once I've seen to your knee."

I huffed but sat obediently while Emma cleaned and rewrapped my wounds. The cuts looked almost pitiful in the light of day, raw and pink but unbloodied. It seemed inconceivable that they could've caused me so much pain. The skin around them, however, had darkened to an ominous purple, mottled right across my knee-cap. Even after a night of healing, it continued to twinge whenever I flexed my leg. As soon as Emma tied off the new bandages, I cautiously got to my feet and waited expectantly, balancing my weight on my good leg.

"He was in his study ten minutes ago," Emma obliged. "Would you not like to dress for the day?"

"No, thank you." I rushed through the words, not wanting to miss Darcy. If I had my way, I was going to need something more substantial than morning dress.

I found Darcy in his study as Emma had said, standing beside his desk with Pemberley's steward and going over a book of accounts. When he saw me lingering in the doorway, he broke off midsentence to usher me to a chair.

"You should be resting," he scolded me,

before turning his attention back to the steward. "Thank you, Mr. Adams. I trust the estate will be in capable hands until I return, as always."

Mr. Adams bowed his head, ignoring the presence of his employer's woefully undignified younger sister. My hair had not seen a comb since the ball, and I certainly was not dressed for polite company. As soon as Mr. Adams had left, I started talking before Darcy could send me back to bed or call a doctor.

"Where are you going? Did you hear from Elizabeth?"

"I did," he said, pulling a letter from his jacket pocket. "Her father—"

"I know."

I had interrupted before I had time to think, my teeth clacking together as I closed my mouth a moment too late. Darcy raised an eyebrow.

"You know? How do you know?"

I considered my options. No obvious lie came to mind, and I tried to make a habit of lying to my brother only when there was no other choice. I preferred it when he had no reason to doubt me when I absolutely needed to hide something. I had secrets too dangerous to swear any vow of total honesty. But Kitty writing to me was not, on its own, any kind of crime. If Elizabeth had not alerted him to what she had seen, Darcy had no reason to think a single letter suspicious. As long as he didn't ask to read it.

"Miss Bennet wrote to me," I said, resisting the urge to cross my fingers behind my back. "She said their father was unwell."

Darcy showed no sign of mistrust as he nodded, absentmindedly unfolding and refolding his letter from Elizabeth. He had no need to conceal its contents. I suppressed a bitter wave of jealousy.

"Elizabeth has asked me to join her. I have spoken to the staff here and will be on my way before noon. In all official capacity, Pemberley is under your care, but—"

"I want to go."

For a moment, Darcy only blinked at me in confusion, trying to interpret my words.

"To Meryton?" he checked.

"Yes."

I fought against my cheeks' desire to turn red, hoping they didn't betray me. If I stayed at Pemberley, there was no telling how long it would be before I saw Kitty again. Even if her father recovered, I could hardly expect her to return immediately, and if not, the selfishness of me desiring her presence would pale in comparison with her duties as a bereaved daughter. Even if I got to see her for only a moment, I needed to know every word of her letter was true. I wanted to take her hand and kiss her fingers and ask if she had felt these kinds of feelings before.

I still remembered the confusion and self-hatred I'd fought through, alone, in London, and I didn't want her to endure the same. To have someone beside me, reassuring me that my feelings were not a curse or a punishment or some kind of twisted abnormality would have meant the world, and if Kitty needed that, too, then I wanted to be that person for her.

Darcy took a seat behind his desk, looking me over.

"Are you sure you would be well enough to travel?" he asked, gesturing to my knee.

"Absolutely," I promised. "I can walk, and it doesn't hurt."

What was one more little lie?

"And if you find yourself in the way at Longbourn House, you will return here or go on to your aunt's without complaint?"

I barely restrained myself from pulling a face at the mention of my aunt. Any notion that I was a human being in her eyes rather than a pawn in a game of matrimony had vanished the day Darcy had defied her wishes that he marry her daughter. Rosings Park, the de Bourghs' home, was the last place I wanted to go, but I would have agreed to anything for the chance to see Kitty.

"Yes, fine."

Darcy considered it longer than I'd hoped, but eventually he relented.

"Elizabeth would no doubt like to see you. And I think I would feel better if I was able to keep an eye on you. If you remain attached to this story of an accidental fall," he said, fixing me with a sceptical stare.

I stared back, unwilling to recant an explanation that at least mostly embraced the truth.

"Have Emma pack your things," Darcy said. "I would prefer to get to the Bennets' as soon as possible."

I suppressed my grin, fleeing before he could change his mind. My heart beat wildly as I traced my steps back to my room. Now that the potential of seeing Kitty had become a certainty, my emotions were harder to keep in check. I desperately wanted to see her, but I couldn't even imagine what I'd say.

What I wanted was entirely incompatible with what I could have. If I were a gentleman, I'd have offered Kitty my hand in marriage after our first meeting in the library. Only a fool would wait to convince a lady so intriguing of their attachment. But I would never have that option. The most I could offer Kitty was stolen moments carved out in shadows of privacy. She deserved so much more, but however long we could claim together was preferable to no time at all. And I would have no idea of Kitty's thoughts on the matter until we could finally talk.

When I made it back to my own room, I rescued the letter from my mother's book.

You stun me, Miss Darcy.
I rather think I like it.

I dared to let myself hope.

Elizabeth often spoke of Longbourn House as if it were a person, so it existed in my imagination in vivid brushstrokes. Despite not having seen it myself, I felt as if I knew the building like an old friend. I couldn't help myself from staring wide-eyed and childlike when it came into view through the carriage window—the redbrick walls and creeping ivy were just as I'd always pictured.

As the carriage pulled to a stop, the gravel of the driveway crunching beneath the wheels, the door flung open. Elizabeth's smile was too bright for the condition of her father to have worsened since the letter that summoned her and Kitty home, and I felt one worry in my chest subside. Kitty's security relied on his health until she married, and I didn't want her forced into a match or left to depend on the good nature of relatives—even if I was sure Elizabeth and Darcy would not see her homeless and suffering. Besides, Mr. Bennet, from what I knew of him, was a kind man much loved by people I cared about.

Elizabeth embraced Darcy the second he stepped down from the carriage, the moment too intimate to directly observe. He brushed hair out of her eyes and cradled her cheeks, speaking in low murmurs so earnestly it was as if they had been separated for months. Turning to give me a hand to get down from the carriage was certainly an afterthought, but I appreciated my brother being aware of me at all while he had his beloved so near.

Once Elizabeth had reminded herself thoroughly of my brother's existence, she turned her attention to me. Darcy had sent word ahead, so she greeted me with less surprise than if I'd shown up unannounced.

"Welcome to Longbourn," she said with a smile. "These might not be the most cheerful circumstances for a visit, but I hope, regardless, you enjoy your time here."

The words themselves were perfectly civil, but they felt stilted. Rehearsed. I could see beyond her smile, and it was guarding something.

She knew what she'd seen.

I trusted Kitty hadn't said anything, for her own safety even if not for mine, but Elizabeth had been there in the shell grotto. Kitty and I had been too close to explain any other way. My journey to Longbourn had been spent largely occupied by thoughts of Kitty, but I hadn't considered facing Elizabeth.

If she chose to tell Darcy, I wasn't sure what would happen. I loved my brother, but I was also painfully aware of how much I relied on him. If he disowned me, I would have no access to my own money and no legitimate defence to claim it through the courts. There was no one I could go to. Elizabeth held my future in the palm of her hand.

Impulsively, I stepped back, stumbling a little when my knee threatened to give way. Elizabeth's careful mask of neutrality gave way to concern as she reached out to steady me, supporting my elbow.

"Is your knee that bad?" she asked.

So Kitty had told her something.

"It is fine," I said. "Just a scratch."

I wanted to ask after Kitty. Impatience was gnawing at the edges of my consciousness. When I'd envisioned this moment, she'd been there on the doorstep waiting for me. I'd imagined her embrace, finally calming the stress I'd been unable to escape since our kiss. Perhaps she was out on a walk. Darcy had sent word I was travelling with him, but Kitty wouldn't have known the exact time of our arrival.

"You should sit," Elizabeth said, taking my arm and guiding me inside, leaving Darcy to liaise with the staff regarding the luggage.

Longbourn House was far cosier and more intimate than Pemberley. There was no grand entranceway with soaring ceiling, but there was dark-wood panelling and a sense of homeliness. It reminded me of my favourite parts of my home, the parts untouched since my mother had passed.

Elizabeth settled me in the sitting room, in an armchair that had long forgotten what it was like to be properly stuffed.

"Jane will be arriving later today," she explained as she pulled over a footstool for me to prop my leg up on. "Although, even without her, the house is still plenty full. Father is resting upstairs, but I'm sure I can scare up the others."

Before I could protest that I didn't need a welcoming party, Elizabeth was already gone. When she came back, she had three figures in tow.

"My mother," she said, introducing a middle-aged woman with the standard Bennet curls peeking out from under a white cap.

I tried to get to my feet to greet her properly, but Mrs. Bennet fussed over me the moment I tried. "Sit, my dear. Once everyone is settled, I'll have to join you. You can tell me of Pemberley. I do always want to hear more of the place my daughter calls home, and she is never forthcoming enough in her letters. How does Lambton fare for eligible young men? I suspect you've got a sweetheart, handsome as you are?"

Mrs. Bennet was exactly as Elizabeth had always described, speaking a mile a minute and immediately turning her attention to matchmaking. I would have laughed, had I not been too conscious of the fact that the only person within a hundred miles of Pemberley that I had ever considered anything close to a sweetheart was her second-youngest daughter.

"Okay, Mother!" Elizabeth thankfully interrupted, forcing a smile. "It's been a long journey; let's allow our guests to rest." She ushered forwards someone else in order to shift Mrs. Bennet out of the way.

"Georgiana, this is my younger sister Mary."

The middle Bennet sister carried herself like a woman twice her age. Her face was set in a serious expression, appraising me silently, and she offered a curtsey almost as an afterthought. After Mrs. Bennet's enthusiasm, her reserved composure was rather a relief.

"How do you do?" I greeted her.

When it became clear she was going to offer

up no more than a mumble in return, Elizabeth moved on. She hesitated for a moment, but continued before anyone else could catch her reluctance.

"And you already know Kitty."

Chapter Nine

It had been a matter of days since I'd last seen Kitty, but the sight of her still took away my breath. I'd been avoiding looking directly at her, delaying the moment until I knew I'd be able to focus solely on her. She was hovering in the doorway, shuffling her weight awkwardly. Even as Elizabeth said her name, she did not raise her eyes from the floor.

"Miss Darcy," Kitty said, curtseying painfully formally.

Her tone was so void of affection, nothing like the Kitty from the shell grotto, not even like the Kitty I had first met in Pemberley's drawing room. All the hope that had been building in my chest came crashing down at once. My throat was bubbling with things I wanted to say, questions I wanted to ask, but none of it could be voiced in the presence of our families.

I could not trust myself to say her name without my voice betraying me, so I greeted her with a nod. She still wasn't truly looking at me.

If anyone noticed the strange way we were acting, they didn't mention it. Mary disappeared the second she was no longer being directly addressed, and Mrs. Bennet clearly found my brother of more interest than me. She insisted on showing him to his and Elizabeth's room herself, despite the house being one with which Elizabeth was rather familiar.

Left alone in the sitting room, Kitty and I sat in silence. She'd raised her gaze from the floor but now focused it on the door as if she was longing to leave through it. With my knee still injured, I wouldn't have been able to stop her.

This was nothing like the way I'd envisioned it. The second we were alone, I thought perhaps she might want to kiss me again. Her letter had been so fond, but there was nothing in her demeanour that echoed the warmth of those words. I had no idea what I could have done to upset her while not even in her presence.

I could only assume she'd had time to think things over. Overt affection between women in that way wasn't acceptable. Anyone who dwelled on the idea would come to the same conclusion. It was something I had come to terms with and elected to ignore, but if Kitty had decided otherwise, it wouldn't be fair to judge her.

Trying to find the words to explain that I understood her decision, I fiddled with the cuff of my spencer. It was Kitty who broke the silence, speaking only after she had taken a deep breath and turned towards me. Her gaze still landed somewhere near my shoulder.

"How's your leg?" she asked, gesturing to where it was stretched out in front of me.

I didn't think about her pushing up my skirts, or touching my skin. I didn't think about her kissing me, pulling the pins from my hair, leaving me breathless. The only person I was torturing was myself.

"Fine," I said, but I couldn't bear the silence

that followed, so I added more words but no further information. "Better. It doesn't hurt so much."

"I'll leave you to rest," she said, fleeing the same way Mary had gone earlier.

I resisted the urge to cry, pulling a cushion into my lap to trace the inelegant needlework. Perhaps it was Kitty who was responsible for the clumsy depiction of roses. I certainly could not imagine Elizabeth sitting still long enough to get through more than one petal.

As much as I wanted to ask Darcy to allow me to return home, I'd need to explain why my visit had been such a short one when I'd been so determined to accompany him. There was no way I could spin a story that avoided the truth but stayed in the realm of believability. Things were getting so hopelessly tangled. I was stranded at Longbourn House until my brother returned to Pemberley.

When I heard footsteps on the stairs, I couldn't help the speed with which I looked up, hoping Kitty would come through the doorway. Instead it was Mrs. Bennet who bustled into the room, evidently done with settling in Elizabeth and Darcy.

"Right, my dear," she said. "Jane and Mr. Bingley will be arriving this evening, so I'm afraid we're running a little short on rooms."

This was my chance to go home. I could insist to Darcy that my presence was the imposition he'd feared, beg him to let me return to Pemberley so the Bennet family wouldn't have me under their feet at a time of great unhappiness and anxiety. I was about to express my deep apologies to Mrs. Bennet and offer my solution, when she delivered the worst resolution I could have imagined in that moment.

"Kitty's letters home mentioned how marvellously the two of you were getting on, so I'm sure you'll have no problem sharing her room. Lydia's old bed is still in there, and it's all made up for you."

I had to force myself to remember to express my gratitude for her hospitality, all the while my lungs were threatening to choke me in their hurry to circulate air. An hour ago, I would have been unspeakably thrilled at the idea of sharing a room with Kitty. There was little chance of sneaking away to the library together for late-night conversation in a house so bursting with people, but we wouldn't need to sneak anywhere if we were already in the same room. Except something had clearly changed. Kitty didn't want me there.

If I couldn't flee to Pemberley and we were going to be in such close quarters, I could not simply ignore Kitty, even if she sought to ignore me. Perhaps I had misread the tone of her letter, but I was certain I had not imagined her kiss. I would not pursue something she didn't desire herself, but we both needed confirmation of secrecy from the other. When Mrs. Bennet offered to have me shown to my room, to Kitty's room, I accepted.

If the last person I wanted to see turned up at my house, I would hide myself in the room in which I felt safest. Kitty had never spoken of having a particular affinity for any potential parlours or libraries that Longbourn House might have so, particularly considering the absence of her younger sister, I imagined Kitty's more desperate escapes would be made to her bedroom. Sure enough, when the Bennets' maid knocked on the door before calling out and pushing it open, Kitty was scrambling off her bed. She shook out her skirts in an attempt to calm the wrinkles one got in their clothes from curling up into a ball.

"Miss Darcy, miss," the maid announced me, before curtseying and taking her leave.

I'd meant to ask her to check on how Emma was settling in amongst the Longbourn staff, but she was gone before I got the chance. Kitty seemed minded to race after her, inching towards the door.

"I will not tell anyone," I assured her quickly. "If that is what's concerning you. I have just as much to lose."

If not more.

I didn't verbalise the addendum, but we both understood it even so. I wasn't entirely sure it mattered. I had a fortune and a higher social standing, but we would both end up in the same place if we fell. We risked ostracization from our families, with no friends to take us in. Without money or shelter, it was a bleak reality at best and a short one at worst. I could hardly blame Kitty for fearing it.

I assumed the floorboards had been the same for the entirety of Kitty's residence in the room, but she still seemed to find them greatly more fascinating than she found me.

"Are you going to ignore me forever?" I asked, tears prickling at the corners of my eyes. "I'm sorry. I never meant to...I...*Please*, Kitty. If I made you uncomfortable, please forgive me. I won't...I won't talk to you, won't even be alone with you if you'd rather it that way."

It wasn't a promise I was entirely sure I'd be able to keep, given the proximity of the bed I'd been allocated, but I would have said anything to get her to look at me. Yet she still didn't. Instead she clenched her fingers around the fabric of her skirts, her knuckles turning white from the force.

I thought perhaps she meant to ignore me until I left, but then she reached out and took my hand. A far cry from the strength with which she'd gripped her dress, her touch on my skin was featherlight and almost reverent. Her fingers ghosted over mine as she coaxed my hand to her mouth, gentle lips brushing against my knuckles. I felt a crackle of something warm and exciting at the contact, and I was unable to stop the smile that tugged at the corner of my mouth. Until I realised her touch wasn't doting affection.

The shift of the angle of her neck allowed me to get a glimpse of her face. Tears streamed down her cheeks, dripping to the floor when they reached her chin. If she was scared, confused, or overwhelmed, I understood entirely—it had all felt the same when I was coming to my own conclusions about myself. I brushed away the droplets with my spare hand, cupping the curve of her face.

"It's all right," I reassured her, although of what I wasn't entirely sure. "If you need to cry, you can cry, but I promise nothing is wrong we cannot fix."

When I received no reply, I began to wonder if she'd taken a vow of silence. She let go of my hand, letting it fall to my side. As she stepped away, my other hand slipped from her jaw.

"Are you in trouble?" she asked, finally letting me hear her voice. I would have been thrilled, if she didn't sound so concerned. "Is that why you came? Because your brother wanted to keep an eye on you?"

"I asked to come. I wanted to see you, and I thought you wanted to see me, too. I received your letter."

A fire of panic ignited in Kitty's eyes.

"Did you show it to anyone?" she asked, desperation colouring the words.

I shook my head. It was carefully tucked into the lining of my valise, as it felt safer to bring it with me than leave it unattended at Pemberley, but no one else's gaze had fallen across it.

"No, of course not." I tried to take a step towards her, but she took one away. "I have said nothing to no one, about any of it. My brother only knows I fell and hurt my knee." But I thought over that evening in my mind and realised I was not entirely being truthful.

"What?" Kitty asked, picking up on the way I flinched and the guilty bite of my lip.

"I said nothing exact, but I...I was not entirely in my right mind when I returned to the house and found you had left. I was afraid and in pain and it was not possible to contain all of it and—"

"What did you say?" Kitty pushed, her voice acidic. "Who did you tell?"

"Emma, my lady's maid, connected my state to your absence. But she's as trustworthy as the most loyal steward, I swear it. I confirmed nothing specific, and she would never tell my brother, or your sister."

Kitty's legs appeared to collapse from under her, and she settled onto the edge of her bed, chewing at the side of her cheek. Tentatively, I sat on Lydia's bed. It was barely five feet away, all too close to be to someone who wasn't happy with your presence. But my knee was starting to protest, and at least Kitty and I would be at eye level if I sat, too.

"Your maid has kept this kind of secret for you before?" she asked.

I wondered what answer she was truly after. Was she solely concerned with Emma's trustworthiness, or did she instead seek to enquire after my history of kissing girls under the cover of darkness? From the intensity of her fears, I imagined my total in that arena to be greater than hers only because her experience was evidently limited to me. I had already experienced some of the worst repercussions of that particular sin.

"No," I said, honestly. Since Emma had become my maid, I'd had no active secrets she would need to have kept. She'd been hired precisely due to the extended consequences of my first foray into kissing another girl.

"Then what makes you sure she will keep your secret now?" Kitty asked, clearly frustrated. She got to her feet and started to pace the room. "We should never have done it."

That hurt more than I anticipated. I'd never gotten to dissect a kiss after it happened before, but I imagined both parties were supposed to be feeling far happier with the situation. Like Kitty had seemed in her letter. Like how I'd imagined she felt, for a moment, as she kissed my hand not minutes earlier. It was enough to make my head spin.

"Well, we needn't do it again," I said, softly.

Kitty's resulting look was far from the relief I expected. She seemed anguished at the resolution, lacing her fingers together and pulling tight. If things had been different, I would have taken her hands and teased out the tension until I could separate her fingers and wind them with my own. Nothing about the situation suggested she wanted that.

Except she had kissed me, in the grotto. She had written me a letter so full of fondness it alone had summoned me to Meryton. Some part of her must have wanted to do those things, as I was certain I'd never forced her. The connection I'd felt in the library at Pemberley was not one-sided. But this entire thing was too fragile to be encouraged in someone hesitant.

When Kitty left the room without another word, I gave in to the urge to lie back on the bed, shifting so I could prop up my leg. It hurt less if I could elevate it, and although I felt guilty for taking Kitty's own room hostage, I needed to close my eyes for a few moments and process everything that had happened.

 I couldn't stop the tears that fell or the sobs I muffled with the back of my hand. Kitty's presence in Pemberley had felt like a dream. Each smile I'd earned from her was a gift, and every time she'd touched me, my skin felt hot in her wake. I had sworn I would never again give in to the tug I felt to pretty girls like that, but I'd been unable to refuse myself the chance to follow what felt like signs of affection from her. But nothing had changed. Pretty girls with soft smiles and soft curls and soft hands were still a bad idea.

Chapter Ten

I could avoid the other members of the household for only so long. It would not do to invite yourself to someone else's home and proceed to hide upstairs for the entire duration of your stay. No one disturbed me until there was a call for dinner, my injured leg likely earning me my solitude, but eventually there was a soft knock at the door. For a wild moment, I hoped it was Kitty, but the hope building in my chest turned to dust when instead Emma offered to help me dress for polite company.

As she helped me—a task made a little trickier

by my newfound inability to rest all my weight on one of my legs—I considered whether or not to warn Emma against spreading rumours, if she knew anything of what had happened that night. But it seemed likely to only make things worse. If she had only her suspicions, this would confirm them. Besides, she could know only that I had feelings for Kitty. Dwelling on the matter in any way might make her aware Kitty had feelings for me.

If Kitty even did have, or had ever had, feelings for me. It was a fact I was now painfully doubtful of.

All the etiquette guides one could possibly read on the subject laid out the clear rules for conversing with potential suitors over refreshments. Since there was no one around the table that any such guide would consider a possible suitor for me, I took that as an invitation not to converse at all.

Even with their father ill upstairs, the Bennet sisters and their mother were a lively group. Jane and Mr. Bingley's arrival had swollen the ranks of the party even further and made it possible to overlook my silence and Kitty's absence. I pushed a potato around my plate, trying to rearrange the food so it looked like I'd managed more than a mouthful. My appetite had lost itself amid the grief in my heart.

It felt inconceivably selfish to be nursing a wounded ego and broken heart while Mr. Bennet wrestled genuine illness, but if inconvenient feelings could so easily be tamed, I would not have found myself suffering these latest developments in the first place. With no confidante trusted enough to discuss them with, I was doomed to the bickering of the voices in my head as they fought amongst themselves to decide whether I wanted to scream at Kitty for being so frustrating, or wrap her in my arms for being so confused.

When I returned to the room to find several sprigs of wildflowers tied hastily together with a lilac hair ribbon and set on my pillow, the voices advocating for screaming got a little louder. It was Kitty's ribbon—I recognised it from one of the many times I'd found myself staring at her curls, fascinated by the way each one had its own opinions about where it was going and how it meant to get there. Any logical person had to therefore deduce that Kitty had left the flowers. Except she was nowhere to be seen, and she seemed to want little to do with me, and I was rather losing track of what I was supposed to be feeling.

I relied on Darcy to provide me with any level of entertainment. Elizabeth's opinion of me was still unclear, so a ridiculous chain of conversation was set up, where I asked Darcy to ask Elizabeth if I might borrow a book, and she in turn lent it to him, and he passed it on to me. If Darcy had any thoughts on the matter, he kept them to himself. My leg was still healing, and he seemed inclined to coddle me at least until I could walk without a limp.

The situation continued for two days. I barely saw Kitty—even at night, she curled up away from me and faced the wall, always gone by the time I woke up. I didn't make eye contact with Elizabeth, too afraid of what I might find. I simply tucked myself into a corner, longing for my own books and my own instruments, and tried not to draw attention to myself. It seemed to be working, until midafternoon on the second day, when Elizabeth came to find me.

"Will you take a walk with me?" she asked,

before her eyes fell to my knee, propped up on a cushion. "A short walk. To the end of the garden."

I half worried I would never make it back, but Elizabeth didn't seem the sort to solve her problems with homicide. Besides, I was hopeful she loved Darcy too much to do something that would likely make him so unhappy.

I had largely kept to the house at Longbourn, so under any other circumstances I would have been glad for the opportunity to take the air, even walking as slow as I now had to. This walk was clearly not one of simple exercise or pleasure.

Tension hung thick between us as Elizabeth led me through the gardens until we reached a stone bench sheltered from the house by a row of trees. She gestured for me to sit. As much as I wanted to face her eye to eye for this conversation, I needed to be able to focus without the risk of my knee buckling under me, so I dutifully took a seat on the bench.

When Elizabeth spoke, her words were measured and calm, clearly rehearsed.

"Georgiana, I...I owe you an apology. I should not have taken my sister away so hastily. My father *is* unwell, as you know, but after what

I saw, I should have given her time to say her goodbyes."

I dropped my gaze, running my fingers over the rough surface of the bench. I'd promised Kitty I would not speak of it. When it became clear my chosen response was silence, Elizabeth tried again.

"What did I see?" she pushed.

"I don't know," I admitted, my voice barely loud enough to be heard over the wind.

"I think we both know that isn't the truth."

"I really don't know," I protested. "We got carried away. I...I did not...We just..."

Was it truly breaking my promise to Kitty if Elizabeth already knew what had happened? If she'd seen it with her own eyes, there was no denying it. I had to tell her something, and I was in no mind to craft falsehoods. The confusion had been building up inside me in layer after layer of conflicting signs and messages, and I was finally being offered a way to lighten the load. So I took it, the words pouring out of me.

"She went away so suddenly, but she sent this letter that made it seem like...I have read it so often over the last few days I have already torn holes in the folds. Now she barely even looks at me, but there were flowers on my pillow, and it is killing me not to know what she's thinking or whether she... Whether she truly feels the way I do."

I was almost out of breath as I finished. When I risked a glance up at Elizabeth, I found none of the horror I'd anticipated, but instead sympathy in her eyes.

"What way is that?" she asked gently.

"I am afraid to say it," I whispered, worried I was going to tear a hole in my skirts from how tightly I was twisting the fabric between my fingers.

Even if fear wasn't silencing me, the language to accurately describe my feelings would likely still elude me. People so often spoke of love, but how was one supposed to tell if that was truly what something was if they'd never knowingly felt it before? I had never loved Helena. I had been fond of her, certainly, and intrigued by how it felt to kiss her and confirm my suspicions about where my interests lay, but I now knew for certain I had not been in love, because what I had felt for Helena was nothing like the all-consuming ocean of *something* I felt for Kitty.

"I have never seen my sister so out of sorts," Elizabeth admitted. "Being apart from Lydia has done her good, and she has grown into a much more sensible young woman, but she doesn't seem to know herself right now."

"I'm sorry," I mumbled. "It is all my fault."

"No, that's not what I meant. You can be sure she has feelings for you, Georgiana. She would not be so affected if she did not. The precise nature of those feelings is not for me to pretend to know, but I watched her write you that letter from the carriage. She ended up covered in ink and sealing wax for her efforts, but the whole time she was torn between elation and concern. For you. It is only since we arrived in Meryton that she has come to withdraw. If I had any part in that, I apologise."

It was all I could do to remember how to blink at her, wondering with each pass of my eyelids across my vision if the image before me would be erased and replaced with one of anger, disgust, and blame. But the image stayed true—Elizabeth was far more understanding than I had ever imagined.

She took a seat beside me, reaching for my

hand and squeezing my fingers. "I do not judge you. Either of you. It is...a surprise to me, but heaven knows men are frequently more trouble than they are worth."

For a second, I just stared at her. It took a moment for her words to fully process, but once they had, I could not stop the wave of laughter that rolled through me. Elizabeth caught it, too, and soon we were both giggling uncontrollably. It felt good to laugh properly for the first time since the night of the ball.

When the laughter wore off, we were still smiling, and Elizabeth pulled me in for a hug.

"Do you want me to talk to Kitty?" she asked.

I considered it, but I wasn't sure if the confirmation of the depth of Elizabeth's knowledge would help anything or just make things worse. More than that, I was afraid she'd realise that, even without the fear of her sister's condemnation, I still wasn't worth it. Or, worse still, she had no real feelings for me at all.

"Perhaps not yet," I suggested. "I think she might still be...processing. It can be a lot to accept." I knew that all too well from experience. Time and space would help. It had helped me, and sometimes I still needed it. "My brother has no idea. If I could persuade you not to discuss it with him?"

Even with Elizabeth's support, if Darcy took issue with anything I did, I had nowhere else to turn. His word alone would see me turned away at the door of every family member we had left.

Elizabeth forced a sad smile, tucking an errant strand of hair behind my ear.

"He loves you," she said. "You must know he'd do anything for you. If you'd not approved of me, I daresay he wouldn't have married me. Truly, I owe you a great debt."

"He may be fond of me now," I conceded, because all evidence from the past seventeen years supported the statement, "but I cannot delude myself into believing that love to be unconditional. He... he once sent away a chambermaid for the same indiscretion, and I have nowhere else to go."

"He would not dare," Elizabeth said, squeezing my hand in hers.

Her reassurance was all very well, but we both knew she couldn't guarantee a positive reaction from my brother. While he was of no mind to imminently marry me off to a well-spoken member of the landed gentry, it was certainly an expectation he had for me in years to come. As much as I knew he cared for me, I had no true idea what the terms of that affection were.

Still, there was one person in the world who knew the whole truth and was still speaking to me. I had not anticipated how freeing such a notion would be. When Elizabeth put her arm around me, I leant against her and tried to hold back my tears.

Longbourn House felt far less lonely knowing Elizabeth did not resent me. I still retired to Kitty's room each night to find a new posy of wildflowers gracing my pillow, tied up in a different colour of hair ribbon. I collected the flowers in a vase I'd begged from Emma, displaying them on the dresser at the end of my bed. I braided the ribbons together, tying them around my wrist in a rope of light blue, lilac, and peach. If Kitty noticed either gesture, she said nothing to encourage or dissuade me.

It was on my fifth day in Meryton that I met Mr. Bennet. He was confined to bed for the most part, and while his wife and daughters dutifully made trips upstairs to sit at his bedside, I doubted the presence of a stranger would do much to improve his health.

With Elizabeth's permission, I'd begun to explore more of the house. I opened each door in fear I'd be encroaching on the space Kitty needed, but instead of finding her behind the latest intriguing oak door, I found a slender, almost gaunt man sitting behind a wide desk, surrounded by bookshelves. He was swallowed up by his chair, a blanket tucked over his lap and glasses sliding down to the tip of his nose as he consulted a large book open in front of him.

When he looked up, his face was already settled into a smile, but it quickly turned to confusion.

"I may be unwell, but unless I've taken to hallucinations, you are not one of my daughters," he said.

"No, sir," I said with a curtsey. "Forgive me, sir. I did not mean to intrude."

I turned to leave, my hand already on the doorknob when he called after me.

"Wait. If you are not one of mine, pray tell me who you are. Or I shall have to report an intruder in my home."

The threat was empty and, although Mr. Bennet's face was rather too pale for anyone healthy, his smile was still warm.

"My name is Georgiana Darcy, sir." I added another curtsey, because he looked exhausted and I was an uninvited guest.

"Ah, of course, Miss Darcy. How apt of you to have found your way to my library. My daughter tells me you like to read."

"Elizabeth spoke of me?" I was surprised to hear I made for an interesting topic of conversation with a man who'd never met me.

He corrected me so casually, it was as if there were no reason for the name he gave to cause any shift in my heart at all.

"Catherine. She told me all about her time at Pemberley."

I very much doubted he had been told *all* about what Kitty had done at Pemberley, or I was certain Mr. Bennet would have far fewer fatherly smiles to offer me.

I still had no understanding of what it was Kitty wanted from me. She avoided me at every possible moment, yet she spoke of me to her father. She left me flowers but wouldn't meet my eyes over dinner. With Mr. Bennet still looking at me, patiently waiting for a response, I pushed all thoughts of Kitty aside in favour of a smile.

"I do like to read," I confirmed. "You have a wonderful collection of books."

The room was but a fraction of the size of Pemberley's library and held, at a glance, a much narrower selection of volumes. But I would still take a boring book over no book at all, and there was something comforting in rows and rows of texts full of unlearnt knowledge, no matter how limited the number of offerings.

"You are welcome to read from the shelves here," Mr. Bennet offered. "My daughters make for a loud house when all assembled, and you seem to me the kind of person who prefers quiet solitude. Readers are often those people—Lizzy being an exception." He smiled wryly, no doubt imagining just how much chaos Elizabeth could cause. "Should you need a place to think, as I often do, please consider yourself welcome here. I am rarely well enough to sit here myself at the moment, and libraries exist to be used. When this room is empty, you may treat it as open for your respectful use."

"Yes, sir. Thank you, sir," I said.

Then I took a step towards the door, because it

had not escaped my attention that the room was currently not empty. He valued his solitude, too, and I was preventing him from enjoying it. With another curtsey and a final apology for intruding in the first place, I took my leave and ventured downstairs. Ruth wasn't here to indulge me with gingerbread, but perhaps the Bennets' cook could be persuaded to donate a sweet treat to a girl with a leg not yet fully healed and a heart that got more broken each day.

Chapter Eleven

I was halfway down the stairs when I heard the giggling and laughter from below. It wasn't Elizabeth. She and Jane could talk endlessly until almost breathless with excitement, but they at least kept up a pretence of refinement. Mary had not giggled once in the time I'd been at Longbourn. I could believe one of the voices was Kitty, but that left her with no one to be interacting with. And, as enthusiastic as I knew she could get, she was not causing all of that shrieking alone.

Curiosity piqued, I crept down the stairs so I didn't disturb the scene, like I was a child again and Darcy was waking me up early to show me the baby rabbits hopping around Pemberley's lawn.

It was indeed Kitty's excitement that had caught my attention. She was talking animatedly, waving her hands around as she tried to relay a tale to a young woman who hadn't even taken off her travelling cloak yet.

The new figure could only be the final Bennet sister. She had the same blonde curls peeking out from under a bonnet, but her features seemed more severe than those of the others. Angular cheeks and a sharp chin gave her an air of superiority when her face was at rest. In my surprise, I'd kicked my foot against the base of the door, and the childish gleam in her eyes faded to suspicion as she shifted her gaze from Kitty to me.

"Who are you?" she asked.

Of course Lydia would be here. I had never thought over the matter, but it made just as much sense as Elizabeth, Jane, and Kitty coming home to see their father. And Elizabeth and Jane had both been escorted by their husbands.

The thought of seeing Wickham forced every

rule from every etiquette book straight out of my head. Rather than answering Lydia's question or enquiring about her journey, I turned and ran.

I ignored both the confused voice—Kitty's voice—calling my name behind me and the twinge in my knee as I fled from the house. If that was where Lydia was, I had to assume that was where Wickham was, too. So I needed to be as far away from it as possible. Even the Bennets' grounds were too close. I was more than willing to get lost in the woods to avoid the monsters of my past, so I turned into the forest that bordered the property and weaved between the trees until my chest was heaving and my knee was protesting with enough conviction that I had no choice but to listen.

Stopping myself in my tracks with my hands against a tree trunk, I felt the bark scrape my skin. My blood was rushing in my ears from the shock and the exertion, and I turned to rest my back against the trunk and slide down until I was sitting amid the roots and fallen leaves. I felt the texture of them crunching under my weight but couldn't focus on sounds enough to hear them. I didn't hear Kitty, either, not until she was dropping to her knees beside me. It was only when her hands were on my face that I startled, realising she had followed me all the way out here.

"George, please," she begged. "Talk to me."

Despite everything, the nickname settled me just a little. I hadn't heard it in what felt like so long, and it proved Kitty still harboured some degree of fondness for me, even if she tried to convince herself otherwise. She was so earnest, her panic so reminiscent of the night of the ball at Pemberley. It was endearing that her concern for my well-being could overpower her concern of the dangers of getting too close. I dropped my head against her shoulder, my face turned into her neck while I breathed her in.

As I calmed down, Kitty calmed down a little with me. She wrapped an arm around me, keeping me close as she shifted to sit properly beside me.

"Please, tell me what's going on," she said, resting her chin on the top of my head.

"I had forgotten..." I tried, but I didn't know how to put it properly into words.

Understandably, it was not enough to lead Kitty to the intended conclusion. I could hear the confusion in her voice, feel it in the way her fingers tracing circles on my arm stumbled across my skin.

"Forgotten about Lydia?" she asked.

"That she is married to..."

I couldn't say it. I hadn't even thought about him so directly in as long as I could manage. Kitty shared no such reluctance.

"Wickham?"

I flinched away from the name, as if it could hurt me, pulling out of Kitty's arms and hugging my unwounded knee to my chest. Peering at her over my skirts, I watched her raise an eyebrow sceptically. She asked no question out loud, but I could see it in her eyes.

"I never stopped to think that perhaps he might be here," I tried to explain, assuming she would soon make the necessary connections.

"He never visits. Lydia came alone," Kitty promised. She reached out and squeezed my fingers at my resulting sigh of relief. "George, I still don't understand."

She sounded genuine in her confusion, but I could only presume it was an act of deception to attempt to reassure me not everyone knew the sordid details of my prior associations with Wickham.

"You cannot tell me you didn't hear," I said, bitterness seeping into the words.

Darcy had admitted to me that he'd laid the story out for Elizabeth, to explain away Wickham's lies, and apologised for telling her without any forewarning for me. I understood his reasons so I'd not even stayed upset, but it was clear Elizabeth had told at least her eldest sister. When I'd first met Jane Bingley, then still a Bennet, there had been so much pity in her smile that she couldn't possibly not have known. I assumed it was common knowledge to the entire Bennet family.

Only Kitty's confusion continued, too entrenched not to be genuine.

"I assure you," she said, as cautious as she might be with a wounded animal, "I have heard nothing that would give me any insight into why you ran. Are you hurt? Is it your knee?"

There were two versions of the story. I considered for a moment which version to tell her—the version I'd stuck to from the beginning, the one my brother and Elizabeth knew. Or what had really happened.

The false truth that had been shared amongst my kin made me look foolish. An easily led child, swept up in the affections of a charming older man and cajoled with compliments and flattery into risking her reputation to escape to be married at once. It was not an entirely impossible story—some girls did fall prey to such figures. Lydia Wickham had been one of them. Darcy had not doubted the tale for a moment. He had no reason to, for why would someone construct a fiction that made them appear so tragically misguided? Only when the truth made them appear even worse, of course.

Naive and misled was infinitely preferable to a corrupted temptress, living a life of sin and determined to take others with her in her fall. That was how Wickham had threatened to paint me if I did not do as he instructed. When he found me kissing Helena in a room we thought we'd have privacy in, I'd been given a choice. He would denounce us both as the immoral sinners we were, ruining our reputations and that of our families, or I could marry him.

It was my money he wanted, not me. I was worth both a fortune to him and nothing at all. The idea of marrying him, especially with how he'd looked at me like I was filth, was enough to turn my stomach, but there was no other viable alternative. I would never allow Darcy's reputation to suffer because of my decisions, something Wickham likely presumed would be the case, but I also couldn't let Helena's life end so tragically, either. She was all but promised to a viscount who would be able to provide a comfortable living for her. Wickham's threats would have seen her likely cast out by her family before that wedding could take place.

Just as he'd known I would, I'd agreed to marry him. Not out of misplaced girlish infatuation, but to protect the people I cared about. My hope had been that he'd drink himself to death before too long, leaving me free to navigate society as a widow. Unmarried but unbound by the rules that governed debutantes.

Darcy tracking us down and putting a stop to things could have proved disastrous. Wickham still had his blackmail material and hadn't won his prize. I could assume only that he was so relieved to have escaped my brother's wrath with his life that he knew better than to test it again so soon. Helena had married her viscount, and Wickham's place in society left him unable to touch her, but he could still destroy my life if he chose to. Refusing to think of him was the only way I kept calm about it.

That was the version I told Kitty. After the first time her face morphed into a mask of horror, I delivered the rest of the story to the sleeve of her dress. It was too overwhelming to take in her reactions visually, but I felt them through her fingers with each squeeze of my hand. She didn't let go for the whole time I spoke.

Once I was done, silence lingered for several moments until she finally whispered a question, like it pained her to even consider it.

"Did he...? I mean, were you hurt?"

The words themselves were vague, but the meaning was perfectly clear. Exactly how much had Wickham tried to take, or succeeded in taking, from me?

"No," I assured her honestly. "I think he thought he was being a perfectly upstanding gentleman."

"He was extorting you!" Kitty protested.

"I did do something wrong," I said with a shrug.

"No." Her tone was resolute. "No, you didn't do anything wrong."

I could not help the burst of hope in my chest. If kissing Helena had not been wrong, kissing Kitty couldn't be wrong, either. It seemed unwise to push the idea if Kitty had yet to land upon it herself, so I just watched her, waiting. She chewed on her lip, clearly debating something, but when she finally spoke, it was not what I expected.

"Did you love Helena? *Do* you love her?" she asked.

She was jealous. I had to fight to suppress my smile as I took in the hard set of her jaw and the clench of her fingers. Everything with Helena had happened so long ago that I thought of her only in the past. Even after the business with Wickham had settled and I no longer felt the need to keep away from her for her own good, our lives had gone down entirely different paths. Other than the secret of that one stolen, interrupted moment, we would likely have little to talk about over tea.

"I have not seen her in almost two years. She is married, and I think is now a mother," I explained gently. Boldly, I traced my thumb down Kitty's jaw.

"But do you love her?" Kitty insisted, seemingly desperate for confirmation.

"No."

I thought perhaps that would be the end of things. She had her answer, explicitly stated, and I assumed that was enough to settle the line of inquisition. Until she asked something else, something I had not expected.

"Do you love me?"

My breath caught in my throat, and a few seconds of hindered breathing made me feel lightheaded.

"You have ignored me," I reminded her. "The whole time I have been here. We…" I looked out into the forest, unsure how sensible it was to speak so freely in a place where we could so easily be overheard by someone hiding amongst the trees. I'd been candid about my history with Helena, but that did not incriminate Kitty in the potential earshot of her family. "After what happened in the grotto, and that letter, you have barely looked at me."

"I know," she said, her voice quiet and cracked. "It is no excuse, but I was… frightened. I have never done anything like that before."

I was not entirely void of sympathy for the notion, but I still vividly recalled the agony of the past few days. If she'd voiced her worries sooner, having this conversation days prior could have alleviated so much of that pain for both of us.

"You were the one who chose to do it," I reminded her, taking the gamble that our actions in the shell grotto were as emblazoned onto her brain as they were onto mine.

"I know." She was even quieter, forcing me to strain my ears to hear her words. "I told you, in that letter, that I didn't understand these feelings, and I don't. But I don't regret it, George. What we did that night. I regret how I've acted since you've been here, but nothing else. Being around my family unsettled some of the things I thought I was sure of, I have to admit to that, but now you're here and I can look at you and touch you…" She tugged my fingers to her lips and pressed a kiss to my knuckles. "I am so sure of them."

"Do you love me?" I asked, boldly.

She did not skip a beat.

"Yes."

The intensity behind the word surprised us both. It was impossible not to trace Kitty's bashful smile with the tip of my index finger, trying to memorise the shape.

"Even when I was trying to keep my distance,

I couldn't help but leave you flowers," she said, her fingers skimming over the hair ribbons laced around my wrist. "I had to express my affections for you somehow, or else they were going to overwhelm me. But now, if you have no objections, I'd prefer to express them like this."

She moved slowly, giving me plenty of time to move away or ask her to stop, but all I wanted to do was haul her closer as quickly as I could. I forced myself to stay put, letting her come to me. That seemed important. When she finally kissed me, it was worth the wait.

Her lips tasted faintly of the strawberry jam served with breakfast. She must have been in the kitchens, sneaking more of it on leftover bread, for it to have lingered this long. The image had me smiling, which did little to help the accuracy of the kiss but made it no less perfect. Her fingers were in my hair, and those that weren't were tangled with mine.

It was just as risky as kissing Helena. At least then we'd had a door between us and the rest of the world, and I had learnt the lesson to always keep that door locked. Yet here Kitty and I were, surrounded by a spectrum of leaves, every colour of brown and orange and yellow, out in the middle of the woods for anyone in search of some fresh air to trip across. It was foolish and dangerous, but Kitty was enough of a distraction that I could focus on little but her proximity. When she eventually sat back, I let her go only because we both needed time to refill our lungs.

"Does this mean I no longer get flowers?" I teased, the words buoyant with breathlessness.

The taste of her laughter was sweeter than strawberry jam against my lips as she kissed me quickly again.

"You can have all the flowers you want," she promised. "I'd give you the world if I could."

We sat like that, undeniably too close and too caught up in each other, for as long as we dared. The longer we were gone, the greater the chance of someone venturing out to look for us, and there were few worse situations we could be found in. Elizabeth might not have taken umbrage, but I didn't know how many of the other members of the Bennet family would share her acceptance. I could not trust Lydia, not with knowing who her husband was. Mrs. Bennet would hate me for distracting one of her still-unmarried daughters, if nothing else. Jane's and Mr. Bingley's demeanours were bright and cheerful, but that didn't mean they would be tolerant of something denounced as a sin.

And then there was my brother, whose love for me I had never doubted. Still, it was possible to love and hate someone in the same breath, and I couldn't bear to test the strength of the former in light of the latter. Kitty and I were both safest if we kept secrets.

Aware we were running out of borrowed time, eventually we pulled away from the moment. Kitty helped me to my feet, gently berating me for exerting my healing leg, and offered her arm. It was a gesture I had never thought twice about before. Women so often walked arm in arm with close friends, but now it seemed like so much was written beneath the surface of the action. At least I was still unsteady on my feet, in need of support. If anyone questioned it, we had the perfect alibi. My real reasons for wanting to be close to her could stay buried deep beneath the more convenient truth.

Chapter Twelve

Lydia Wickham, even with the absence of her husband, was a thoroughly confusing person to be around. Well aware of her status as a married woman, she carried herself with an air of superiority, but on the occasion she was denied something, her pettiness showed her youth.

She wasn't a fan of sitting to read. Even her needlework suffered from her lack of focus, with loose stitches and hanging threads, as she barely looked down at her hands, preferring instead to swap gossip. She was at her happiest when discussing others, or in town to observe people to gather gossip fodder for herself.

Lydia spent a token amount of time with her father but disappeared into Meryton at least once a day, often with Kitty in tow. Any invitation offered to me felt disingenuous, so I opted to decline on account of my leg. It certainly could have withstood a leisurely walk, but I was grateful for the easy excuse. As much as I liked spending time with Kitty, I preferred to do so alone. She felt less like my Kitty and more like the Kitty from Elizabeth's childhood stories when Lydia was around to encourage her in frivolity and idle gossip.

Making the most of my invitation to borrow from Mr. Bennet's library, I dug through his collection to unearth a book or two that would hold my attention and took them out to the garden. The next few days were spent like that, feeling the breeze tease my hair as I turned pages.

The nights were spent in Kitty's arms.

We made sure to be in our own beds by the time we fell asleep, to be safe, but the time between taking our leave from the household and taking our leave from the realm of the waking was not wasted.

It felt wrong to be deliriously happy on a visit to a dying man, but I was. The mood in the house was rarely one of melancholy. Occasionally Mrs. Bennet would have to excuse herself, owing to a sudden burst of tears, and at least one of Mr. Bennet's daughters would spend the evening sitting and talking with him, but his condition, though poor, seemed stable.

Longbourn House was full of people, and a house full of people would find it difficult not to be equally full of spirit. I had never enjoyed company more—from games of whist to being persuaded to play the piano of an evening, which Kitty encouraged at every given opportunity.

"Please," she begged, "one song."

The Bennets' drawing room was not well suited to as many people as it currently held. Extra seating had been dragged in from other rooms, but that still left too many people squashed together on one sofa, meaning no one could say anything about how close Kitty was sitting to me. It was enjoyable but also left me susceptible to her best cajoling tactics as she grabbed my hand and whispered so close I could feel her breath against my cheek.

"Just one," I warned her.

Elizabeth had sat at the piano stool in the absence of any other spare seat, but she quickly got up to swap with me, squeezing my shoulder as we passed.

"Play the one you wrote," she encouraged me.

My cheeks went faintly pink at the very thought. I knew it off by heart, of course, but it felt too private. Besides, I had already decided it sounded better on the harpsichord than the pianoforte. I instead opted for an easy, light tune, the kind of thing no one ever took issue with. It was soft enough to melt into the background if everyone else wanted to continue a conversation, but they listened politely as I played the gentle melody. The Bennets' piano was ever so slightly out of tune, but not so much that anyone else would notice.

When the last note faded, there was a swell of polite applause I would usually have hated, but Kitty clapped the loudest, beaming with pride, and I let myself smile back. She got to her feet and for a fleeting moment I imagined her coming over to reward me with a kiss, as if the very idea in front of her entire family wasn't absurd.

Instead she brought her smile closer, where its power over me only increased, and leant against the wall beside the piano.

"Play the one you played at Pemberley, in your drawing room," she insisted, asking for the same thing as Elizabeth.

"It isn't good enough," I said, although that was far from what I meant. It just felt too much like baring my soul.

"Please." Kitty batted her eyes in a way that was probably supposed to be comic but was simply effective. "For me?"

She didn't know that every time I played that song, it was for her. It existed only because it was for her. I had never found the time to tell her, and this definitely was not the best moment, but the least I could do was indulge her request to hear it.

It still did not sound quite right on a piano, especially one not wholly in tune, but Kitty lit up the second I played the first note, and that smile did not leave her face for the entire time I played. I barely looked at the keys, relying on years of practise to guide me to them as I focused on her. Everyone else in the room faded away until their applause at the end of the melody jolted me back to reality, reminding me that this moment was far from private.

I quickly evacuated the piano stool with a small curtsey to my audience, before stealing Kitty's old space, now beside Elizabeth. It left Kitty to take the piano stool as a seat, but I wanted to put some distance between me and the instrument, and between me and her.

Elizabeth squeezed my arm as I sat down.

"That was beautiful. Even better than last I heard it. You've changed it a little?" she asked.

"Yes," I admitted, but I added nothing further. From the knowing set to her smile and the way her eyes flicked over to Kitty, I didn't need to.

I hoped that someone else would be persuaded to play, taking the burden of attention away, but Lydia managed to do that without the help of an instrument.

"There's a town ball in Meryton at the end of the week," she announced to the room at large from the armchair she had claimed for herself. "And I thought we all might go."

There was a moment of silence where I was almost certain everyone else in the room was thinking the same thing—this was not a visit that ought to be celebrated. Mr. Bennet was still bedbound, and there was no clear answer to how his illness would end.

"Lydia," Jane began gently, "I think that might be a little improper, given the circumstances."

"But it might be our last chance!" Lydia protested. "Don't we deserve a little fun?"

It was a callous way of looking at things, but she was right that they would all have to endure a lengthy period of mourning if Mr. Bennet passed. There would be nothing near the realm of fun for a while, and Lydia gave the impression of one who thrived off attention and merriment.

"I doubt Father would mind, if we asked," Kitty added, not surprising anyone in her support of her sister's idea. "And it would be nice to be able to dance."

Her interest in turn piqued Mrs. Bennet's.

"I think it's a wonderful idea. It would be good to get you girls out of the house for a while," she said, looking pointedly between her two unmarried daughters. "I imagine it would be a great comfort to your father if you were to find husbands."

The implication of *before he passes* was unspoken but still clear in her thinly veiled attempt to guilt Kitty and Mary. I bit back my grimace. An evening of watching Kitty dance with eligible bachelors was not the delight to me that it was to her mother. I liked to watch her dance, but the constant threat of matrimony lingered in the back of my mind in a dark and ugly cloud, and I was keen to avoid reminders of it.

"I'm going to ask Father!" Lydia declared, jumping to her feet and rushing out of the room.

Elizabeth sighed. "I suppose it is good to see marriage has not changed her," she said, sharing a look with Jane that suggested they had both hoped it would change her just a little.

"Are we really going to go dancing with Father so ill?" Jane frowned.

"If he allows it, then I suppose there's no harm," Elizabeth said. "I can see the appeal for him in some peace and quiet."

"It's perfectly peaceful here," Mrs. Bennet protested, waving away her daughter's words and either missing or ignoring the smothered smiles of everyone else in the room. She was responsible for a large proportion of the lack of peace, and she encouraged much of the rest.

It was not long later that Lydia thundered down the stairs, almost tripping as she burst into the room to announce that we *had* to attend the ball in Meryton, as it was their father's fondest wish. Elizabeth included me in the amused look she shared with Jane—Mr. Bennet was definitely seeking a little peace.

I considered trying to avoid the ball. My last attempt to act like a respectable young lady enjoying a night of dancing had ended with me bloodied and crying myself to sleep, and I was in no hurry to repeat the experience. Only when I told Kitty I did not plan to go, her resulting pout was enough to pull at my heart.

"Please," she begged, pressing a row of three fleeting kisses up my wrist. "I want you to come."

"I have nothing to wear," I tried to argue. When I'd packed for Meryton, dancing and merriment had not been amongst the likely activities. There was no evening gown in my luggage.

But Kitty was having none of the excuse.

"You are in a house that has, until recently, housed five young women. Do you honestly believe there will not be a dress for you to borrow?"

"Perhaps, but—"

"George, please," she insisted. Her eyes were wide with deliberate intent to persuade. I both loved and hated that it was effective enough to work. "I will not be able to have a moment of fun without you."

"Oh, really?" I said with a laugh. "All balls have been an utter bore until now, have they?"

She took my innocent attempt to tease and twisted it into playful flirtation.

"Until now I have had no point of comparison. But yes, in retrospect, I do believe they have been."

Her lips were on my skin again, grazing my knuckles. No one could be expected to protest under such circumstances and, all too easily, I found myself giving in. If Kitty wanted me there, I would go to the ball.

There seemed to be no time to waste in the Bennet household when it came to preparations. Dresses were pressed and bonnets trimmed with new lace; lists were written of hair ribbons and other trinkets that needed to be collected from town. It was a finely tuned operation that I had no part in, so I kept a careful distance. Even after so long away, Jane, Elizabeth, and Lydia fell back into parts they clearly still knew how to play. Largely that meant Elizabeth and Jane were attempting to reel their youngest sister in just a little, but sometimes it was easiest to send her into town so they could breathe. Kitty was keen to go with her, leaving me to quiet contemplation in our room as Emma finished fixing my hair for the day.

The knock that came at the door was too soft to be Kitty, so I expected perhaps Elizabeth. Instead it was Jane who entered, holding a pale cream dress draped over her arm.

"I hope I'm not intruding," she said politely. "Only Kitty said you were in need of a dress for the ball, and I thought this might suit you."

She held the gown up by the shoulders, revealing a delicate creation that fully embraced its clear Grecian inspiration. It was a few years out of style, not yet caught up to the new fashions of deeper colours and more lavish decorations, but it was still a beautiful dress. There was a hint of pattern to the fabric, a subtle line of the palest green running down the length of the gown every inch.

"This was mine, before I married, and I had passed it on to Mary, but she has never worn it. It ought to fit you, if you would like to wear it. Nothing fancy, I know, but it is perfectly serviceable," Jane said.

"It's beautiful, ma'am," Emma said, taking it from her to lay it out carefully on my bed. She immediately started rummaging through my hair ribbons, looking for a matching shade.

As much as I'd liked the way Kitty had looked at me in my pink dress at Pemberley, I couldn't help but feel that this borrowed ensemble would feel rather more like me, especially when Emma triumphantly unearthed a soft green ribbon from the box that Kitty once said perfectly complemented my dark eyes.

"Thank you," I said to Jane. "I would love to wear it, if it is no bother."

"None at all," Jane insisted. "I would lend you something more lavish if I could, but I did not travel with many evening gowns, as I assume neither did you. Although I should have known it would lead to this, with Lydia around." She smiled, welcoming me into her teasing, before leaving me to finish getting ready for the day.

"This will suit you perfectly," Emma decreed,

looking over the spread of the dress and hair ribbon on the bed. "I assume it's still a no to a feather?"

I laughed. "Now more than ever, yes."

When Kitty returned from town, she appraised the dress carefully, told me I would look better in it than Jane ever had, and kissed me until my toes curled in my slippers. That was enough to give me total confidence to wear it to the ball.

A borrowed dress and a simple hair ribbon may have been all it took for me to prepare for the ball, but Kitty and Lydia both treated it like it was the event of the season. The day before it was due to take place, the two of them headed into town again for a final procurement of new ribbons and hair adornments from their carefully cultivated list.

Rather than entertain any notion of joining them in their walk, I retired to the library in search of a book small enough to fit into a reticule so I might take it to the ball. I had no high hopes of locating one amongst Mr. Bennet's collection, but there were several at Pemberley, so it was not out of the question. I was not even particularly concerned with the content on the pages, so long as there were words I could read to distract me as Kitty danced with eligible young men.

Mrs. Bennet, despite her husband's ill health or perhaps because of it, seemed determined to use the opportunity to matchmake for her two remaining unwed daughters. After Mary had made it clear she had no intentions of attending the ball, all their mother's energy had been refocused on Kitty instead. She had excitedly informed me the new hair ribbons were being funded by her mother for the occasion, rather than coming out of her pin money.

I wondered how likely Mrs. Bennet would be to provide the money if she knew Kitty was in need of new ribbons because she'd used several of them to tie together bouquets of flowers for me. I had returned them to Kitty to reuse, but the first three were dear to me and I still wore them, plaited together, around my wrist.

An extensive search of every bookshelf revealed nothing small enough to discreetly read in the corner of a ballroom, but I did discover a polished wooden chessboard high up on one of the shelves. A thin layer of dust coated the mahogany and pine pieces, collecting in a dark line across my thumb when I dragged it across the squares. Pulling over a chair, I climbed up to retrieve it and, balancing it as carefully as I could, set it down in the centre of the desk.

I reset the pieces that had slid out of place and spun the board around so I had white on my left and black on my right. Playing alone was useful when it came to testing out strategy and identifying the holes in your own defence, but it was dreadfully boring. At least the games lasted longer than those played against most other people, but I still ended up slouched over, resting my cheek against my arm where it lay on the desk. I moved each piece with a half-hearted push of my little finger as I tried to find a way to attack a well-defended king.

The window was propped open to allow an autumn breeze to whistle through, and when it carried with it the laughter and chatter of women's voices, I was quick to abandon the chess pieces, knocking over the white king to surrender to myself before peering anxiously down onto the road below.

Kitty and Lydia were back, strolling down the driveway arm in arm. I felt a flood of warmth in my chest at the sight of Kitty, admiring her unrestrained smile. Despite her absence lasting only a few hours, I still found myself missing her, so I abandoned the study in the hopes of coaxing her into kissing in her bedroom.

I was partway down the stairs when I heard my name.

"I just need to look for Georgiana," Kitty said, because it was unmistakably her voice.

"Fine," Lydia replied, with an audible pout. "If you must. She's just so dreadfully dull—always with her nose in a book. I can't see why you feel the need to spend any time with her at all. Just leave her with Mary. They can be tedious together."

My ears burned. My first governess always had warned me against eavesdropping, assuring me I would overhear something I would rather not know, and she had certainly been right.

I waited for Kitty to say something in my defence, to refute Lydia's words. Instead, she laughed.

"Yes, but she is Lizzy's sister-in-law and a guest here, so we cannot ignore her without it looking like a slight, no matter how much of a bore she might be."

My eyes pricked with tears. I could not

comprehend what I could possibly have done to turn Kitty's opinion of me. She'd kissed me that morning before leaving for town, promising to return with gingerbread from the cake shop, which was not quite as good as Ruth's but reminded me of home nonetheless. Doing my best to stop my lower lip from trembling, I descended a few more stairs until Kitty and Lydia could both see me. I said nothing, but my face alone must have told them what I'd heard. Kitty looked horrified, but Lydia was barely suppressing her laughter.

"Oh," she said, covering her smile with her hand. "Oh dear."

She offered no apology, and neither did Kitty. Wordlessly, I fled the staircase upwards and ensconced myself in the familiar comfort of the library. Sitting back in the desk chair, I pulled my knees up to hug them close to my chest and methodically set up the chess pieces again. Playing alone might be boring, but at least wooden pieces wouldn't insult me. My tears mixed with the dust on the board as they dripped off my chin.

Chapter Thirteen

I was two games in when the door to the study opened, but I didn't care to look up and greet Kitty, so I stared determinedly at the board.

"What are you doing in here?"

The unexpected voice startled me into decorum, and I uncurled my spine, pressing it against the back of the chair as I rubbed at my cheek. There was probably a red mark from where I'd been slumped, but that couldn't be helped.

It was Mary Bennet at the door. She had a book in her hand and kept her eyes fixed on me as she took several steps into the room and slid it onto a shelf, swapping it for the next volume in the set without even looking.

"I saw the chessboard and I—" I began, ready to launch into an apology.

"This is Father's study."

My mortification was instant and overwhelming. Mr. Bennet lay ill in bed, and I'd been curled up in his chair like it was my own. Even with his permission to borrow from the shelves, I was taking far too many liberties.

"My apologies," I mumbled, my entire face crimson. "Forgive me, I will—"

I climbed clumsily to my feet, knocking over half the chess pieces in my attempt to clear the board away and return it to its home. Mary rushed forwards to the other side of the desk, carefully helping me gather them up. She checked each one for any sign of damage, glaring at me even when she seemed to find them all unharmed.

"You ought not to treat them like toys," she chastised me. "It is a game of skill, if you know how to play."

"I know. I play a little," I admitted, stopping shy of the truth that I played so little because there were few people left I had not so frequently bested they'd lost their patience to play against me.

Mary's disapproval gave way almost instantly to intrigue.

"Can I interest you in a game?" she asked, feigning far more casualness than I could see in her eyes.

I answered with a nod, quickly helping her to reset the pieces. She dragged another chair over from the corner so she could sit on the far side of the desk from me, leaning forwards to rest on her elbows and get a better view of the board. It was a more relaxed demeanour than I'd seen from her so far.

I didn't take every opportunity she left me to attack, nor did I play so purposefully poorly as I had when I'd first played Kitty. There was something fun about the challenge of engineering the perfect game. A white lie of a conclusion was harder to manipulate than an immediate win, but eventually Mary called a checkmate and I conceded the victory. When I looked up from the board, she was smiling. It was a look of genuine contentment I wasn't sure I'd seen from her before.

"Where did you learn?" she asked.

"My brother taught me when I was six. Anything he knew how to do, I wanted to copy."

Mary nodded, listening but distant. "Father tried to teach all of us a few years ago, but Kitty and Lydia couldn't be persuaded to take interest. Lizzy was tolerable, but has always preferred books. Jane liked it best, besides me, but after she married, it was only Father who would sit and play with me, and then only on the rare occasion."

"I similarly lack opponents." I smiled, automatically moving to set up the pieces again. Mary didn't stop me. "Your sister still prefers her books, and my brother lives in fear of being bested by the one to whom he taught the tricks."

We began another game without formal declaration. Mary simply reached out and moved the first piece, and the rematch was afoot.

This time, I orchestrated a victory for myself, but a hard-fought one. A game that could have lasted less than two minutes stretched out to ten, but Mary didn't grow bored. She studied each move carefully, with such intent that I could practically see the pieces shifting on the board as she plotted several moves ahead. Her strategy was not unpractised, and I could see how her sisters might tire of playing with her—they would likely often lose, if they treated the game casually.

"You play well," Mary observed as she considered how to rescue her king from the check I'd backed him into. It could be done. She could even end the game with a win if she was clever about it, but probably not against me.

There was a knock at the door before Mary could make her next move, and we looked up at each other in surprise. No one else but Mr. Bennet seemed to use the room, and he would not knock to enter his own study. Likely presuming, as I did, that it was the maid hoping to dust the shelves, Mary called out for them to enter.

Kitty pushed the door open tentatively before stepping into the room and standing with her hands tucked behind her back, her head bowed slightly in at least mock contrition.

"May I speak with you?" Kitty asked. Her eyes fell briefly on Mary, before returning to me, heavy with intention. "Somewhere quiet?"

"I'm afraid you've found me busy," I said, still not making eye contact.

Mary moved a knight, and I quickly countered her attempted escape with my queen.

Before Mary could move again, Kitty cleared her throat. When Mary turned to glare, they had the kind of conversation only two siblings could engineer. It was entirely silent and deployed the language of a number of fierce glares, pointed looks, and exasperated sighs. Eventually Mary climbed to her feet with a huff.

"We will need to have a rematch, Miss Darcy," she said with a nod to me, before leaving without paying Kitty any mind.

I ignored Kitty for a few moments further while I reset the chessboard, watching out of the corner of my eye as she perched on the edge of the chair Mary had vacated. Once the final pawn was back in position, I looked up and made sure she saw my scowl.

"That was rude," I chastised her. "We were in the middle of a game."

"The chess pieces aren't going to go anywhere without you," she tried to joke, but my raised eyebrow made it clear I wasn't in the mood to entertain her comedy. "George, please, let me apologise."

"I don't believe I am stopping you."

"You know I don't think you dull because you

read. I love all the things you have packed inside your head," she insisted.

"Yet you mock me with your closest confidant," I challenged.

I did not care if she kept the true nature of our relationship a secret. Indeed it was the only way for both of us to be safe. But I doubted the notion that she couldn't hide from Lydia the fact she kissed me each night without cruelly mocking me behind my back.

Kitty reached across the desk to take my hand. I put up a pitiful show of pulling away, but surrendered the pretence as soon as she started tracing her fingertips over the inside of my wrist.

"*You* are my closest confidant. You cannot believe I tell Lydia anything of the way you make me feel?" she said, her voice low to prevent eavesdropping, but with the side effect of making me shiver. "I trust but one person in this world with the true depths of my heart, and she is standing before me, understandably grumpy but on the brink of forgiveness," she said, pushing hopefully.

"She sits before you. Disappointed, tired, and a little hungry."

Kitty retrieved a small parcel from behind her on the chair and set it on the desk in front of me. It was wrapped in wax paper and tied with string, but I knew it contained gingerbread. It was an admirable attempt at a peace offering, and I was putting an embarrassing amount of restraint into not opening it immediately, but I was still angry with her and to take it felt like conceding.

"Or would it make her feel better to trounce me at several rounds of chess?" she suggested.

"Kitty, stop," I said with a sigh, not in the mood to play games of any kind, linguistic or with thirty-two carved pieces.

"I truly am sorry," Kitty said. Her eyes were watery and fearful, like she was on the brink of losing something precious. It hurt to see her so upset. "I was overcompensating. Sometimes I get so scared that what we're doing is obvious, and I panic. I forget we can be—we are—friends. It doesn't help that when I am around Lydia, I am..."

"Not your best?" I suggested.

"Demonstrably my worst," she said with a laugh. "But it is good to know they teach tact so efficiently in London." She kissed my hand, the only part of me she could reach from across the desk. "There is nothing dull or tedious about you, Miss Darcy. You are an endless enigma I wish to dedicate my life to solving, and I don't anticipate I'll be bored for even one moment."

Her words stunned me. I couldn't even tell if she'd realised what she was insinuating. We were both taking risks each day, but we'd never sworn any part of the future to each other. It seemed entirely too impossible, but she'd laid the concept out with such casualness it almost seemed a foregone conclusion.

"You are lucky I love you," I managed, only just keeping my breathlessness out of my voice.

"Yes," she agreed. "I rather think I am."

She reached out and moved a chess piece, challenging me with one raised eyebrow. Laughing, I took the bait. We played three games in quick succession, holding hands beside the board. Kitty didn't complain for even a moment when I beat her in all of them, the entire process taking less than five minutes.

We left the library only because I was keen to unwrap my gingerbread and I knew better than to risk getting crumbs all over someone else's books. I did not much feel like joining the rest of the household downstairs while I was still hurt by Lydia's words, so I persuaded Kitty to walk with me in the garden. She had not changed out of the spencer she'd worn into town, so I sent her downstairs to wait while I collected something warmer from our room.

On my walk back past the library to meet Kitty, I noticed the door was ajar. Mr. Bennet had given me no rules regarding keeping it shut after I used the space, but I knew it was usually always closed and had to assume that was how he preferred it. Before I could pull the door flush against the frame, I heard the soft rustling of skirts inside and wondered perhaps if Kitty had not yet headed downstairs.

It wasn't Kitty inside. Instead, I found Mary curled up on the floor, her back against the side of the desk. She rubbed her eyes furiously when she saw me, hiding her face against her knees.

"Go away," she ordered.

I almost obeyed, knowing I was a guest in her house, but I didn't want to leave her while she was upset. Besides, her words had a touch of petulance to them, akin to how one sibling might try to get rid of another. The familiarity encouraged me to take a seat on the floor beside her.

"Are you all right?" I asked, tentatively hoping it was nothing I'd done that had left her like this.

Mary sniffled for a moment, contemplating, before she gave me an answer.

"This house used to be quiet," she whispered. "It was noisy all my life, and then Lydia left, then Lizzy and Jane. Kitty started to spend most of her time visiting anyone else. It was just me left, and there was no one to play chess with, but it was quiet." She spoke wistfully, like the memories were fond ones, before her smile fell. "Now everyone is back and Lydia's sharing a room that was always just mine because you're here and… and Father might die."

I was starting to understand. It was easy to see how the descending of family, and uninvited sisters-in-law, could be overwhelming.

"I'm sorry," I said, feeling guilty. "I never meant to impose. Truly, Mary, if you would prefer it, I can leave."

"No." Mary sighed. "Elizabeth wants you here. So does Kitty. And with Father bedridden, you're the only person who can put up any kind of defence in chess."

It was a weak attempt at humour, but I made

sure to grin widely enough that she'd know I found it amusing. Mary turned to look at me, weighing something up before she spoke. I assumed there was something she wanted to add to her soul-bearing monologue, so I tried my best to look open and willing to listen. No part of Mary's demeanour made me think I had to be guarded with my own, so I was entirely unprepared to mask my reaction when she challenged me.

"What are you doing with Kitty?"

The correct response would have been one of immediate confusion, with no frame of reference or context. Surprise had me instead show my true fear. I recoiled, any verbal response sticking in my throat. There was no clue to Mary's judgement on the matter in her voice, only simple interest, but I imagined the worst regardless.

If she told her parents, told anyone, our lives would fall apart. It had the potential to hurt Mary, too, of course. As an unmarried woman, she had to know the opinions suitors had of her family name mattered. A lady having an immoral, disturbed sister would be a consideration weighed up before a proposal was offered, and that was how people would see Kitty, see us both. Only Mary had shown no interest in marriage the entire time I'd been at Longbourn, so perhaps the risk to her own reputation was a moot point to her.

Far too late to be natural, I slipped on a mask of confusion.

"What do you mean?" I asked.

"You know exactly what I mean."

Mary's own casual demeanour wasn't an act, and I knew it could stand far longer than mine could. Dropping the pretence, I instead chose to bargain.

"You cannot tell a soul," I pleaded. "For Kitty's sake, please. It is all my fault. I was the one who... It was me."

I couldn't bring myself to say I'd seduced Kitty against her will, but the sentiment was still, I hoped, evident. It was the only way to keep at least one of us safe, and I would always save Kitty before I saved myself.

"It looked mutual," Mary said, sceptical.

I wanted to ask her what she'd seen and when, but I didn't dare. I didn't want to hear how she would describe it.

"Please, Mary."

I didn't know what else to do. If there was no convincing her she'd misunderstood, we were at the mercy of her next action. She could ruin our lives. I felt the weight of my ribs on my lungs, slowly compressing them.

"It doesn't matter to me what you do," Mary said eventually. "As long as you are not truly doing something Kitty doesn't want. You cannot be worse for her than Wickham is for Lydia."

I blinked at her, my words lost to shock. Perhaps she had indeed misunderstood, or I was misunderstanding her. It seemed impossible that she could be so accepting despite knowing the truth. But Elizabeth had been the same way, and had said nothing against Kitty and me since.

"Lizzy is happy. Jane is happy. Lydia thinks she is happy," Mary said. "Should Kitty not get that chance, too, even if it is this she wants?"

I managed a nod.

"You will say nothing?" I whispered.

Mary shrugged. "Who would I tell?"

Still too stunned to say more, I seized on to some rogue scrap of courage and reached out to squeeze Mary's hand.

When I left the library at speed, it was half

to flee Mary and half in pursuit of Kitty, whom I'd left waiting for far too long. At some point I needed to tell her just how many of her sisters knew exactly what was going on between us, but for now I wanted to walk a circuit of the garden in blissful ignorance of the rest of the world.

Chapter Fourteen

Such a party we were, we needed two carriages to take us to the assembly rooms in Meryton, and those two carriages wouldn't have fit one body more. I found myself packed in beside Kitty, opposite Lydia and Mrs. Bennet.

Lydia and I had not spoken since the day before. She didn't seem inclined to apologise, and I wasn't keen on sharing my time with her until she did. It was easy to see why Mary detested the presence of all her sisters at once when they could be so cruel.

Mrs. Bennet seemed oblivious to the frosty atmosphere that hung over us, chatting to Kitty at speed about the men she expected to be at the ball. She recited endless lists of names of suitors and how many dances she thought Kitty should offer them—one was simple courtesy, two indicated interest. She conveniently ignored the fact it was not Kitty who would get to do the asking. Ladies were allowed only to accept or decline, and even the latter came with caveats and rules.

Through the entirety of her mother's speech, Kitty kept her foot pressed against mine under our skirts. I wanted to take her hand and hold it tight, to distract her from thoughts of an endless parade of men. She had been the one to offer up the notion of a future together, but we still had yet to discuss the idea properly. I tried to ignore the inevitability of our position.

The town ball at Meryton was far louder than the intimate affairs thrown at Pemberley. Anyone could attend, so there was an air of competition that was absent from groupings of friends. This was about matchmaking and networking and displays of power. I hated it.

Far more familiar with Meryton than I was, the rest of the party quickly melted into the congregation. Jane, Lizzy, and Lydia no doubt had friends to catch up with, sharing gossip and updates of their lives. Mrs. Bennet headed directly for the chaperones and spinsters gathered on chairs in the corner. Usually that would be my first and only destination, too, but a gentle hand caught around my wrist and pleading eyes begged for my company.

Had Kitty not been at my side, I would have turned around and immediately returned to wait in the carriage. But when she linked her arm with mine, pulling me into the fray, I was powerless to protest. The music was lively, a dance already in motion as couples paired up opposite one another, waiting to go down the line.

Rather than throw herself into the prescribed list of activities her mother had detailed, Kitty stayed with me. She fetched drinks and kept up a constant, animated monologue in my ear as we traversed the edges of the ballroom. She was so in her element that I forgot I was not in mine, happy to be swept up in her enthusiasm. I could ignore everything I hated with her to distract me from it—I did not even lament my lack of reading material.

It was only after two laps of the room that I

realised Kitty's tactic was to keep moving so no man could stop either of us to ask to dance. It would have been rude to interrupt us while we were not seeking the attention of anyone else. If we kept walking and avoided any interference from her mother, I would not have to lose Kitty to the hand of a suitor, nor endure one myself. So I was surprised when, as the current dance came to an end, she pulled me to a stop.

"Dance with me," she requested simply.

The intensity with which I wanted to was overwhelming, but it was still out of the question. It had been tempting enough in Pemberley, when all that had passed between us were brief brushes of fingers and hands. I had not then let myself imagine a future. Now that I had, I very much wanted to treat her like every other young woman got to treat her suitor. Her beloved.

"We shouldn't," I said.

Kitty was not so easily dissuaded. She squared her chin and took a step back, holding out her hand like a man formally asking a lady to dance.

"In Meryton we have a custom that, should a woman not be asked to dance by a man, she is free to pair up with a friend. We've been here ten minutes, and if no man is sensible enough to see how astounding you are in that time, none of them deserve you," she declared.

I could not help but laugh. "We've been practically running away from anyone who might ask."

"Please," Kitty insisted.

I had no idea what I was thinking, or if I was even thinking at all, when I took her hand. This was a place where no one knew me. They could gossip all they wished, but eventually I was going to leave Meryton, and no rumours we started were likely to follow me. Kitty had plenty more to lose than I did. If she was willing to risk it, I ought to be, too.

We took our places for the dance alongside the other couples. There was no shortage of curious or confused looks, but none of anger. It made sense, I supposed, that no one would see us stood up together and automatically assume we were abnormal. If Kitty had been right about Meryton's customs, then onlookers were more likely to pity us as spurned debutantes than abhor us as heathens. I minded not what they thought, so long as they left us be.

The one smile we were granted came from right beside us, where Elizabeth had paired herself with Darcy. That alone was uncouth—married couples rarely took to the dance floor, in what was deemed an activity for the courted and courting. If you weren't dancing with a potential suitor, you were at least expected to be displaying your vitality and grace. But no one would deny a young married couple, clearly very much in love, a place in a dance.

"You look lovely, Georgiana," Elizabeth said. "It's good to see you at another ball. I was afraid your experiences at Pemberley might have put you off them forever."

I looked almost plain, my dress unadorned and my hair so simple Emma had begged me to allow her to add more curls. If there was anything noticeable about me at all, it was the girl standing opposite me. I risked a fond smile in Kitty's direction.

"It turns out I can be convinced to attend under the right circumstances."

Elizabeth laughed, a mischievous glint in her eye. "So I see."

"Is your leg strong enough to dance on?" Darcy asked, thankfully more preoccupied with my health than my choice of partner.

"I will be fine," I assured him. "It is hardly the most strenuous of activities."

Before he had time to argue, the musicians once again struck up their instruments and the dance began.

I already knew Kitty loved to dance, but I had never seen her smile quite so widely as when our hands met midway through a step. It felt everything and nothing like when I held her hand behind closed doors. It was just as intimate, even through gloves, but seemed almost monumental. Daring. As if we were challenging the whole room to find fault and brushing any potential protests aside. The rest of the guests might not have understood the significance of what we were doing, but we both felt it.

I was no stranger to the dance's steps, having been taught them all in precise detail, but they were buried further down in my memory than in Kitty's. I found myself relying on her knowledge of the steps to stop me making a fool of myself.

Kitty shone when she danced, beaming wildly and moving with a kind of ethereal grace that lifted her skirts as she turned. It was a privilege to dance opposite her. Despite likely bringing her shame with my lack of coordination and thoroughly mundane motions, Kitty directed every smile at me.

When the dance drew to a close, Kitty squeezed my fingers quickly.

"Another?" she asked, eyes hopeful.

"People will talk," I warned her, but it was teasing more than genuinely cautionary.

Kitty grinned. "Let them."

We were both being reckless, and that should have been what persuaded me to stop, but instead it was a twinge in my knee that forced me to take a break.

"I think I better rest my leg, at least for one dance," I said.

"I can sit with you?" Kitty offered, but I knew the dance floor was where she truly wanted to be, and I was in no hurry to begrudge her that.

Before I could insist she not let me get in the way of her fun, my brother stepped forwards with a rare and unexpected suggestion.

"If you are in need of a dance partner, Miss Bennet, it would be my honour."

Darcy rarely danced with anyone but Elizabeth. Even with only one of their balls at Pemberley for reference, it was clear to me that he preferred not to dance with people he did not know. I knew he was offering largely for Elizabeth's sake, familiarising himself with a family he had once judged. He did not need to know how much of a favour it was for me to see Kitty paired with my older brother rather than with a potential suitor.

Kitty gave me a panicked look, but I shook my head with a soft smile. She didn't need saving from this. Darcy could be intimidating, but she had no reason to fear him. I liked the idea of him warming to her, accepting her. It allowed me to entertain the fantasy of one day telling him where my heart lay.

"He would kill me if he knew," Kitty whispered in my ear.

"Best to find other topics of conversation, then," I replied, giggling.

I had no idea what was coming over me.

Kitty's fondness for dancing outweighed her apprehensions regarding my brother, and she took his proffered hand and let him lead her to join the assembling couples.

"Let's find you somewhere to rest your leg," Elizabeth said, holding out her arm.

She escorted me towards a row of chairs lined up along the wall, awaiting anyone who had worn ill-fitting shoes or danced one too many Scotch reels. This early in the night, most of them were empty.

With Darcy preoccupied, there was no clear obstacle between me and any man wishing to ask me to dance. I saw one or two heads turn my way, working out who I was and how much money I represented to them. I thought back to Mr. Honeyfield and knew these men would similarly not be above the finding of loopholes and bending of rules.

If they asked me to dance, I could always refuse on the grounds of my injured leg, but I'd be expected to sit out for the rest of the night and I had hoped to dance with Kitty once more. She had offered, after all. As much as I wanted to sit and watch her dance, I'd rather be able to stand up with her again myself, after a little rest.

"Can we go outside?" I asked Elizabeth. "I'd like some air."

Whether she saw my true intentions or not, she happily changed course, and we found our way outside the assembly hall, tucked around the side of the building.

"You make an attractive couple," Elizabeth said, the context absent but still clear.

I couldn't help my blush. "Thank you."

"Is it something you feel ready to tell your brother about?"

"No!" I yelped, my immediate reaction one of panic. "He would never understand. And unless I marry, he is in charge of my life."

"*You* are in charge of your life," Elizabeth insisted. "He would not punish you. He'd be mad to think I'd ever let him."

She was unspecific, but I heard the potential scenarios all the same. Sent to a hospital for the insane, kept locked up at Pemberley, denied access to my own money. Denied access to Kitty. I didn't want to believe my brother capable of any of it, but I'd seen him send Frances away.

"Please, you cannot tell him," I begged.

"Of course not," she assured me, squeezing my arm. "Not without your consent. Now you wait here. I'll liberate us some wine."

She returned back inside with a wink, leaving me to my own spiralling thoughts. No matter how I imagined telling Darcy anything of how I felt for Kitty, I could not envisage a happy ending without feeling like I was lying to myself. The risk was too great.

Sighing, I leant back against the side of the

building to take some weight off my knee. When I took in the figure walking towards me, I thought it a hallucination at first. Some kind of twisted mirage born from the speculation of a wandering mind.

George Wickham, in a scarlet jacket and freshly shined boots, was here in Meryton.

Chapter Fifteen

I'd never felt more betrayed than by the sudden inclination of my soles to root themselves to the ground. They left me standing there, as helpless as a startled hare on a hunt, and just as doomed.

"It has been too long, Miss Darcy," he said, sweeping into an almost comically low bow.

It hadn't been long enough. I could happily have gone the rest of my life without ever seeing him again. Despite my loathing, I found myself dipping into a curtsey. The courtesy was so well taught it had inscribed itself deeply under my skin.

"I thought Mrs. Wickham had come alone," I said, fear bleeding into my voice.

Wickham smirked as my voice wavered. Silently, I prayed for Elizabeth to return quickly.

"She travelled ahead, but I could hardly leave her alone in such a situation. It seemed wrong to impose myself on the Bennets at such a time, so I thought it best to stay at an inn."

He was avoiding my brother. While Darcy would not cause a scene in public, there was no guarantee of such restraint in private. But with Mr. Bennet's will potentially soon in need of proving, I presumed Wickham was hoping he might benefit from the death of his father-in-law.

"I must admit, I am surprised to find you here," Wickham mused, taking a step closer. "Or I was surprised, until I saw you sharing a dance with Miss Catherine Bennet. You just cannot help yourself, can you?"

I hated his smirk. I hated that he thought he was allowed to say Kitty's name. I hated that I kept standing there as he spoke.

"She makes a fine dancer, doesn't she?" he

said, every inch of his grin mocking. "I myself have had the pleasure on a few occasions."

My skin prickled at the knowledge he'd touched her, even with gloves between them.

"Don't" was all I managed, the rough texture of bricks digging through the back of my dress with how deeply I tried to hide myself in the wall.

"You seem determined to damn others alongside you. Poor Miss Bennet," Wickham said, mock sympathy dripping from his words like honey. "It would be most terrible for her if news of this particular indiscretion was to get out."

My heart stopped in my chest. Surely there was no reason left to blackmail me. He was married; Darcy had paid off his debts to encourage him to marry Lydia and save her reputation after they'd run away together. Neither I nor my money could be of any use to him.

"She has done nothing wrong," I managed, though my voice was far weaker than I was proud of. "Leave her alone."

Wickham only laughed.

"I think we've found ourselves in this situation before," he said. "You are the one with the power to determine what happens here. If you want me to do what you ask, I need something from you in return."

He got closer still, bracing one arm against the wall beside my shoulder so there was no way for me to escape. With his other hand, he tugged on the loose end of my hair ribbon.

"So what will it be?" he asked me, as casually as someone enquiring after someone's preferred breakfast choices.

The realisation of what he wanted sent a wave of icy cold fear through my body. He was talking about something far less innocent than marriage, something I would never give. Something he had no reason to even be requesting.

"You married Lydia Bennet," I reminded him, although I was sure he had not forgotten.

"Indeed I did," he said with a laugh. "But you are not a fool. No doubt you are aware that married men, particularly those less than fulfilled by their match, often stray?"

My pity for Lydia was not insignificant. I knew he had toyed with her from the beginning, worse than he had me. Every choice I'd made was just that, a choice. I'd known exactly what I was getting into and I'd chosen it anyway, even if I had to do so under duress. He'd made Lydia believe he loved her, but if he was willing to extort intimacy from me, I didn't doubt he was seeking it from others. It could be easily bought even when he didn't have the benefit of information as leverage.

As much as I felt sorry for Wickham's wife, I pushed the sentiment aside in favour of surveying the situation I had found myself in. I would not let him threaten Kitty, but I wouldn't let him hurt me, either. This was a chess game and I was a cornered king, one move away from a checkmate. There were two ways out of check. I either needed to move the king or have another piece come to the king's aid.

Both of Wickham's hands were pressed against the wall, caging me in. He was far too close, and I could smell the alcohol on his breath. When Kitty was that close to me, it took every bit of self-control I had not to kiss her, but all I wanted to do to Wickham was strike out at him. So I let go of my self-control.

I didn't have a good angle to put much power behind the punch, but I didn't need it. My brother had taught me how to make a fist and drive it forward, the lesson coming after he'd exhausted chess and Latin in knowledge he could bring me back from school. I'd never actually used this particular teaching before, so I had to drag it out of a hazy memory. My form was probably off and my power lacklustre, but it was enough.

My fist connected with the side of Wickham's jaw in a satisfying crack. I doubted I had broken his bone or even really done that much to hurt him, but the shock of my action was enough to have him reaching for his chin, rubbing at where I'd made impact. With his arm lifted, I dodged around him, freeing myself from the wall. The king was out of check.

"You little whore," Wickham growled, reaching out to grab me.

I stumbled out of reach, turning and running back in the direction of the assembly hall's entrance. Wickham wouldn't do anything in public, especially not with Darcy there.

Turning the corner, I ran directly into Elizabeth. The impact upset the wine in both glasses she was carrying, sending it sloshing over the rim and soaking into her gloves.

"Wickham," I explained before she could say anything.

Elizabeth's eyes darkened at the name. The king now had a rook at its defence. If I could negotiate the presence of a knight in the form of my brother, a checkmate would be almost inevitable—at least in my hands. Then I would have to worry only about the ongoing safety of my queen.

Even not knowing the truth of what had transpired between Wickham and me two years ago, Elizabeth knew enough to immediately turn protective. She abandoned the wineglasses in favour of taking my arm and quickly leading me back inside. The crowds were a comfort as witnesses to deter Wickham from trying anything else, and I felt my heart rate slow back down and my lungs stop heaving. My heightened state of alert faded, giving way to a realisation of what had just happened.

Wickham was threatening me again. He had threatened Kitty. If I hadn't removed myself from the situation, I had no idea how he was planning for it to end.

I stumbled over my own feet as it all hit me, Elizabeth having to support my weight for a moment to stop me falling.

"As soon as we find Darcy, we are taking you back to the house," she assured me. "No one is going to hurt you, Georgiana."

I wished it was only me I had to worry about.

His dance with Kitty complete, Darcy was to be found in the corner of the room, drink in hand as he talked with Mr. Bingley and Jane. Elizabeth made straight for them, not stopping to apologise to the people she practically elbowed out of the way to get us there precious seconds sooner.

Mr. Bingley was best positioned to see our approach and must have said something to Darcy, who turned, ready to greet us. His face went from joyful to concerned with just one glance.

"Georgiana? Your face is as white as a sheet," he said, taking a step closer and lowering his voice to avoid attracting attention. "Are you unwell?"

"Can we leave?" I begged.

Mr. and Mrs. Bingley were already looking at me with confusion that edged closer towards pity with each moment, and I didn't want anyone else to adopt the same expression. My entire experience with evenings of merriment was that they never turned out particularly merry at all. Indeed, so far they were proving to be some of the worst evenings of my life—moments of intimacy with Kitty Bennet notwithstanding.

"What happened?" Darcy pushed.

His eyes darted around the ballroom, looking for what had unsettled me. I hoped, for Wickham's sake, he had not come inside. I doubted Darcy would treat him kindly. It was tempting to consider not saying anything specific, but I knew Darcy was going to want an explanation, especially after the weak one I'd given at Pemberley. The quickest way to make an escape would be by telling the truth. Before I had to, Elizabeth cut in.

"George Wickham is here."

My brother's face immediately turned stony. He examined me carefully, as if expecting to find physical injuries. But, other than an ache in my knuckles, I was unharmed.

"Did he hurt you?" Darcy asked.

I shook my head. "Please, I just want to leave."

"Of course."

He took my arm and strode towards the exit with similar disregard for anyone in his way as his wife. Usually the attitude had me rolling my eyes, but I'd never been more grateful for my brother's defensive nature. If someone had interrupted my escape from that ball, I would've broken down. Excepting, of course, for one person.

Kitty appeared just before we reached the doors, reaching out to touch my arm to get my attention.

"George?" she asked, the concern in her voice making it clear she knew something was wrong. "What's happened?"

Darcy tried to ignore her and keep moving, but my feet had stopped and, short of dragging me along behind him, he had no choice but to stop, too. I twisted my spare arm to take Kitty's hand, squeezing tight. We desperately needed to talk. She had to know what Wickham had threatened, even if he had no proof beyond a dance countless other people had witnessed and that was not, in and of itself, worthy of scandal. First, I needed to get as far away from the assembly hall as possible.

"Wickham," I explained quickly.

It was enough. The fire in Kitty's eyes burned bright enough to rival Darcy's, and her grip on my fingers was almost painful.

"I'll kill him," she mumbled, so full of rage it tightened her jaw.

Despite everything that had happened, I couldn't help but smile fondly at her protective instinct. Between her, Darcy, and Elizabeth, I felt almost safe, even knowing Wickham was probably still close.

"I'm fine," I assured her, just to quell her bloodlust. "But I'm leaving."

"Then so am I," she declared.

I couldn't quite interpret the look Darcy gave us, but he said nothing as, with me sandwiched between him and Kitty, we finally left the ball.

Once we were outside and Darcy had called for the carriage, he, in a way entirely devoid of subtlety, tried to look around for Wickham. A few revellers were getting some air, but there was no red coat amongst them.

"Take Georgiana home," Darcy instructed Elizabeth. "I believe I have a disagreement to settle with Wickham. I should have done it long ago."

His implication was clear: He meant to challenge Wickham to a duel. From the way Kitty still clutched my arm, he already had an enthusiastic second, but I wasn't willing to let anyone fight on my behalf. Duels were fought with lethal weapons, and with that came lethal consequences. Everyone had heard tales of women left widowed and children left fatherless. I was already an orphan; I would not risk losing my brother. Before I could voice my distress, someone else was voicing theirs.

"No," Elizabeth said, her voice firm and unyielding. I'd never seen anyone order my brother around like that. "That is not what she needs."

"No duels," I managed. "He's a soldier. He'll kill you."

Darcy laughed darkly. "He's a terrible soldier. I'd kill him."

"And you do not want that blood on your hands, no matter how awful a person he is," Elizabeth reasoned, gripping my brother's arm tightly and steering him away towards the carriage. "He is not worth it."

In any other situation, it would be amusing to see my brother marched around in such a way, but given the evening's events, I opted to focus on the relief that Darcy seemed to have surrendered his desire to fight at the will of his wife.

Kitty tugged me after Elizabeth and Darcy, not letting go until she had given me her hand to help me up into the carriage.

"Would you permit *me* to challenge him to a duel?" she whispered in my ear as she settled next to me on the bench.

I poked her in the ribs. "Absolutely not," I hissed.

She was likely speaking in jest, but I wasn't willing to take the risk that she'd be mad enough to try and someone would be mad enough to let her. Darcy might have had confidence in his abilities with a gun, but I knew Kitty had never fired one, let alone had any idea how to accurately aim. She would be sure to lose, and I refused to lose her. I rested my head on her shoulder, too wrung out to care about the audience sitting facing us.

Elizabeth had only a fond smile for me, but Darcy's features had settled into a frown. Whether because of Wickham or because of how close I was cuddling up to Kitty, I wasn't sure, but I couldn't be persuaded to move. I was in no mood to give up the comfort her proximity brought me. Kitty didn't seem keen to deny me it, either, laying her head against mine. A blonde curl tickled the side of my nose.

I stripped off my gloves and stuffed them into my reticule, pleased when Kitty did the same without me having to say a word. She slipped her hand into mine, the familiar gesture reassuring. What Darcy might have to say seemed insignificant in comparison with the motion of Kitty tracing gentle circles over my bruised knuckles.

"What did he say to you?" Darcy asked, fury lingering beneath his words. "You cannot go anywhere with him, you—"

"I know!" I protested. I hated that the lie I'd told made me look so foolish in his eyes. "I wouldn't."

"You have done so once before," he pushed. "I need your word that you have no intention of meeting him, of contacting him in any way, of—"

"Darcy," Elizabeth interrupted him sharply. "Stop."

"She is *my* responsibility, Elizabeth. My younger sister," he argued. "I am in charge of keeping her safe."

I hated that he was talking about me like I wasn't there. I hated that he thought me so easily tricked and misguided. I hated that I was lying to him by omission, never telling him about Kitty, or about Helena. So I finally told him a kernel of the truth.

"I know he never loved me!" I interrupted the

arguing. "I knew exactly what he wanted. He was only ever after my dowry, and I *knew* that."

Both Elizabeth and Darcy turned to me, confused.

"What haven't you told me?" my brother asked, his eyes narrowed.

There was no sense in telling another lie. I was going to tie myself entirely up in knots if I tried to lay out yet another version of events, one which had to be closer to the truth yet not veer too close to candour. Now that he was watching closely for falsehoods, Darcy would be able to see them. No matter where it left me once told, I had little option but to lay out the true events.

I let go of Kitty, shifting along the bench to put some distance between us. I was ready to tell the truth about myself, but I didn't know for sure if she would be happy to be included in that story. That was up to her. My own lies, however, were finally ready to be unravelled.

Chapter Sixteen

"Mr. Wickham was in Ramsgate when we summered there from London. I do not know if that was an accident or if he orchestrated it that way, but he secured invitations to some of the same events I attended. His intentions were clear, but I had no interest. He is not... I do not... I did not want a match."

Elizabeth was watching me patiently, encouragingly, but I could see the speed of Darcy's thoughts racing behind his eyes. He was desperate to interrupt with questions, but I hoped he would let me get through what I needed to say.

"There was a ball. It was nothing important, just a small affair, but there was another girl there that I was friendly with." I left out Helena's name. She had achieved the life she'd always wanted, with a titled husband and a baby, and I wasn't willing to compromise that. "Partway through the evening we left the ball and found a room and…"

I looked at the floor, focusing on the frayed wear at the end of my dancing slipper ribbon. I could not watch Darcy's face as I admitted to this. What I might see there had the power to break me entirely.

"And Wickham interrupted us a few minutes later. He caught us in an intimate moment. I had kissed her." I was almost whispering the words, but I knew from Darcy's quick inhale of breath that he had heard me. "She already had high prospects, and Wickham knew that, so he threatened me with his knowledge of the encounter. I was to elope with him, to allow him access to my dowry, or he would use the scandal to cast a shadow over the Darcy family name and he would ruin the other girl's impending marriage.

I had a choice, and I made what I thought was the right decision for everyone."

Kitty's fingers were twitching beside me, but I couldn't take them. Not unless I wanted to force this relationship into the light, too.

"Did you know?" Darcy said, his voice so measured and low that I couldn't detect an emotion in it.

I looked up and found him directing his question to Elizabeth. She shook her head.

"I had no idea." She was watching me carefully, tears collected in the corners of her eyes. "I'm so sorry, Georgiana."

"Why didn't you tell me the truth?" Darcy directed that same flat tone to me.

Fear. Frances. Concern that he would look at me exactly like this, like he no longer recognised me.

I cast my eyes back down to the floor, unable to give him a satisfactory answer. I didn't continue my story any further, not wanting to bring Kitty into it. Elizabeth had all the information to continue the thread in her own mind. Darcy could have drawn together the clues to a likely conclusion and guessed at Kitty's role, but I didn't offer it up. I was not in the business of laying bare other people's secrets, and I didn't know what Kitty wanted to say. Sitting beside me in the carriage, she added nothing.

I had spoken for the entirety of the journey home, twisting my fingers into complicated knots. When we pulled into the drive of Longbourn House, Darcy sat for an endlessly long, painfully silent moment, before leaving the carriage and heading for the house.

"I think he just needs time to process. I'll speak to him," Elizabeth assured me, a stable hand on my knee. "That was incredibly brave."

Then she was gone, too. Kitty wasted no time before pulling me into a hug, and I gratefully sank into the contact.

"What do you think he'll do?" she asked.

I could only shrug. This was unlike anything I'd ever presented my brother with before. He'd dealt with me being an easily led child, or so he thought, but I was wilful in this version I was now asking him to accept. I had made dangerous decisions to protect a girl I was fond of, and I knew, with Kitty's hand in mine, I would do it again without a second thought.

As grateful as I was for the privacy of the carriage, it was far from the most comfortable place to pass time if other options were available. Kitty and I soon vacated it in favour of her bedroom. I didn't feel much like maintaining my distance, so I climbed into Kitty's bed while she was stripping down to her chemise. When she turned and found me curled up under the blankets, she laughed.

"Excuse me," she said, mock scandal in her voice. "I do believe that's my bed you're in."

"My mistake." I made no attempt to move. "I don't suppose you'd be willing to share?"

"If I must," Kitty said with a long-suffering sigh. She sat on the edge of the bed, combing through my hair with her fingers. "Are you all right? He didn't hurt you, did he?"

I shook my head, leaning into her touch. With her to ground me, Wickham felt a million miles away.

"It was just more threats," I told her. "He wanted me to... to act as his mistress."

The earlier fury in Kitty's eyes returned just as brightly.

"Yet you wouldn't let me kill him?" she all but growled. "He is married to my sister, and you want nothing to do with him and—"

I took her hands, stroking my thumbs over them gently to calm her down.

"I punched him," I reassured her, startling a laugh out of her.

"Excellent," she announced, flopping down beside me on the bed. "He deserves it. I hope you broke his nose."

I thought she was rather overestimating how much damage I was capable of causing him, but I was going to take it as a compliment. Kitty settled beside me, tucking her face against my neck and wrapping an arm around my waist. It felt nice. Safe. I was loath to ruin the tableau by revealing that Wickham's threats had not been made against me alone, but she deserved to know.

I told her everything he had said, how he'd watched us dance and drawn invasive but ultimately true conclusions, and threatened to reveal that knowledge. It seemed doubtful he would make good on the threat. It would earn him nothing from me but Darcy's ire and would ruin the reputation of Wickham's wife's sister, which would not be in his interest. I explained that to Kitty, hoping to mitigate any anxieties she might have, but she just held me closer.

"Let him tell people," she said. "I don't care."

"They could keep us apart," I warned her. "We have no power here."

"Elizabeth knows. She's on our side. And Mary," Kitty pointed out, because I'd told her about that, too, hoping to balance out the bad news with the good.

"But they are not the ones who can make the decision to send us to an asylum," I reminded her.

"You think that's what Darcy will do?" Kitty asked, playing with the ribbons around my wrist.

"He sent away a maid for having relations with another woman," I said, my words almost whispered in my reticence to admit the man I looked up to most had done something I disapproved of so fervently. "It was the first thing he did after our father died. I dread to think what happened to her, with nowhere to go."

My hands were shaking. Kitty took them in her own and squeezed tight.

"He would never do that to you," she said with enough conviction I could almost believe her.

I hoped she was right, but women had been sent away for far less by people they had once trusted. No one, except perhaps Elizabeth, would even disagree with Darcy if that was what he decided. I could only hope his love for his wife outweighed any newfound hatred he might have for me.

Whatever my brother chose to do, I hoped he wouldn't enact it until morning. No one had yet come rushing into the room to drag Kitty and me apart, so I was optimistic we had at least until then.

Trying to ignore the feeling of doom in the pit of my stomach, I curled closer around Kitty and closed my eyes. Her hair was soft against my cheek and her body warm through her chemise. It was enough to help me forget Wickham's threats and Darcy's silence.

When I awoke the next morning to find I hadn't been wrenched away from Kitty's side, I let myself believe it was all going to end happily. Perhaps if Darcy could not accept what I had said, he could at least forget it. Life could go on as normal, with everyone pretending nothing had changed.

Neither Darcy nor Elizabeth made an appearance at breakfast. I couldn't stomach much. I just about managed to nibble at a crust of bread liberally layered with jam. Kitty ate enough for both of us, either unconcerned by the way our future hung in the balance, or turning to toast and slices of cold ham to comfort her fears.

Once she'd relented in her attempt to eat her parents out of house and home, she disappeared in search of Lydia. Kitty wanted to find out what she knew, to press her for information on why Wickham was in Meryton and how long he planned to stay. She never expressly said it, but I was almost certain she also wanted to know what, if anything, Wickham had told Lydia of the night before.

Preferring to stay far out of the way of any members of the Wickham family, I retired to the study. Not ten minutes after I'd settled down with a book, the door was pushed open to reveal Mary. She sat herself down opposite me, sliding the chessboard into the centre of the desk without needing to ask.

"Did you enjoy last night?" she asked, lining up her pawns.

I thought I could hear a tone of teasing in her voice. Perhaps she imagined it had been an evening of dancing with Kitty, secret brushes of fingers and stolen moments. I would have loved it to have been nothing but that, but I didn't much feel like admitting to the dismal truth, either.

"Yes," I said, focusing on how it had been before Wickham's unwelcome entrance.

I doubted I was all that convincing, but Mary seemed happy to believe the lie, or at least keen to swap chatter for chess. We were halfway through a game when a knock came at the door. Mary called out for the person to enter, likely assuming that it was Kitty again. Instead, Darcy walked inside.

His hands were behind his back, his posture oddly formal for a familial setting. Mary took one look at his demeanour and slipped out the door before being asked.

"I've made some enquiries," Darcy said, not taking the vacated seat. "Wickham is staying at an inn in town. While I cannot reasonably request him to take his leave without formally declaring a duel with set terms, I can move you somewhere safer."

"To Pemberley?" I guessed.

I didn't hate the idea of going home. Kitty might prefer to stay in Longbourn until things settled with her father's condition, but I knew her feelings now. I could write to her, and she to me, and she could travel north again as soon as she was able. It sounded ideal, especially if it meant I could avoid Wickham.

"No," Darcy said, stopping my thoughts in their tracks. "Elizabeth will be remaining here, and I with her. Given... recent circumstances, it does not seem prudent to send you anywhere without a guardian."

It was unclear if *recent circumstances* meant my injury in the gardens and my encounter with Wickham, or my admission of my past with Helena and my closeness with Kitty. I clenched my teeth, now much less certain I was going to like this plan.

"I am sending you to Rosings, to stay with our aunt. She has been requesting your presence there for some time, and it seems like the most fitting place for you until I return to Pemberley," Darcy declared. "George Wickham will not know where to find you, and would not be allowed on the property even if he did. It is where you will be safest."

He did not leave much room for argument, but I refused to let that dissuade me.

"No," I protested. "I will be fine at Pemberley. Ruth will be there, and Emma. You trust the staff there, do you not?"

"This is not up for debate, Georgiana. I am in charge of your well-being, and this is my decision. You will stay with your aunt and do as she says for the duration of your time there."

Lady Catherine de Bourgh might have been my aunt, but she was far from a welcoming figure. Owing to the fact she vehemently disapproved of my brother's decision to marry "beneath him," both Darcy and I had enjoyed limited contact with her for the past year.

This felt like a clear message. Darcy wasn't going to acknowledge what I'd told him, what he had to suspect was going on, but he did expect me to fix it. Lady Catherine wanted nothing more than to see me married, and with me at Rosings, I was sure she would speak of nothing else.

"Please don't do this," I all but begged. "You don't need to."

"Emma is packing your things. The carriage departs within the hour."

Darcy turned and left the study without another word, leaving me stunned and broken.

I wanted him to listen to me. All I needed was one chance to sit down and explain that I understood this was difficult to comprehend, that it made things complicated, but also that it wasn't something I could control.

Even if they married me off to a man, I would never be able to love him. It wasn't fair on me or on the gentleman unlucky enough to be paired with me. Far from a dutiful wife eager to give him plenty of children, he would get a lovesick, distracted ghost of a woman.

If I had only an hour before I was forced to leave, I needed to find Kitty. I refused to repeat the past and leave her with no explanation due to an older sibling's orders. She needed to know exactly where I was going and why.

I found both Kitty and Lydia in the kitchen. Lydia was perched on the table, eating her way through a bowl of candied almonds. Kitty had been sitting beside her but immediately slid down and took a step towards me when I walked in.

"Is everything all right?" she asked, primed for bad news. Or perhaps the expression on my face gave it away.

"We were actually in the middle of talking," Lydia said, flicking her eyes between me and the door in a clear suggestion I should walk back out of it.

Kitty ignored her, taking my hand as concern built up in her eyes.

"George?" she pushed.

I shifted my grip so I could clutch at her fingers.

"Can we go somewhere?" I asked, unwilling to cry in front of Lydia but unable to stop the tears prickling at the corners of my eyes.

Kitty nodded, tugging me out of the kitchen and through the house until we were safely behind her bedroom door.

"She knew Wickham was coming," Kitty said. "Apparently he convinced her it would be a nice surprise. Although I'm not sure anyone found it nice. I don't think he's told her anything about what happened last night. She likes to pretend to play coy, but she cannot resist the latest gossip. If she knew, she would be talking about it."

I listened to Kitty talk, revelling in the way she played with my fingers seemingly without even knowing she was doing it. I'd grown used to being in such close proximity to her, and it started to occur to me just how much I was going to miss her. Taking a few steps forward,

I wrapped my arms around her and tucked my face against the curve of her neck. Kitty hugged me close reflexively, her words trailing off.

"Can you tell me what's wrong?" she asked, her palms smoothing over my back. "Whatever it is, I'll fix it. I just need to know."

Her confidence and determination hit me hard in the chest, and the tears I'd feared would fall made tracks down my cheeks. When my knees threatened to buckle and I swayed against her, Kitty led me to her bed and sat me on the mattress. I clung to her embarrassingly tightly, but I knew how soon I would have to let her go. Instead of pushing me to answer, she held me and let me cry. When I finally pulled myself away a few inches from her, she nudged my chin up so she could look into my eyes.

"Is this about last night?" she asked.

There wasn't an ounce of judgement in her gaze. If I was crying over seeing Wickham the night before, she would have accepted that without thinking less of me. But I had to shake my head.

I explained everything Darcy had told me. Kitty's face fell the second she heard I was leaving, but she let me talk through everything I had to offer her. I tried to make it sound more positive than I felt: This was only temporary. Once Darcy and Elizabeth were back at Pemberley, I would get to go home.

"At least you'll be far away from Wickham," Kitty pointed out, which was the sole upside to Rosings. Lady Catherine wouldn't let a man like George Wickham within ten miles of the grounds. "Do you think Darcy and Elizabeth will let me visit again, when you're back at Pemberley?"

"I hope so," I said with a sigh, pressing a kiss to her hair. I couldn't imagine not being allowed to see her ever again. "I can't tell how my brother truly feels about what I said. But I will see you again. This will not be the last time."

I sounded more confident than I felt, but I needed at least one of us to believe it. Emma had already cleared my things out of the room, so I knew we didn't have long left until I had to leave. After I scribbled down Lady Catherine's address, I curled up in Kitty's arms and relaxed into the way she stroked my hair.

It was a childish response, but I didn't know what else to do. Pemberley was legally Darcy's. If he didn't want me there, I had no right to reside there. Nor could I stay at Longbourn unless the Bennets were willing to house me, and I knew they would bow to Darcy's wishes to have me leave—especially if they knew about my relationship with their daughter. That left me homeless. As bitter and single-minded as my aunt could be, staying at Rosings was a fate better than attempting to depend on the kindness of strangers and a purse full of pin money that would get me only so far.

"It's just temporary," Kitty whispered. "You'll be all right. We'll be all right."

I let myself believe her, if only to stop another round of tears from falling.

Chapter Seventeen

The journey to Rosings was miserable for all parties involved. I alternated between staring out the window and staring down at a mostly blank piece of paper, hoping for inspiration to strike. I had Darcy's name at the top, but the perfect words that would persuade him to let me reside anywhere other than Rosings eluded me.

Emma had to endure my pitiful attempts at conversation. She tried to persuade me to engage, but I lacked the enthusiasm for anything but moping. Eventually she gave up and we sat in silence.

It was dark when we turned onto the long road that led to Rosings Park. It had been years since I'd visited my aunt, and those stays had resulted in few happy memories. I still remembered being made to play the piano endlessly, until I could perform whole sonatas by heart without making a mistake. It had turned me off practise for weeks afterwards.

With the late hour, I'd hoped to avoid my aunt entirely for the evening. Neither she nor my cousin seemed likely candidates to stay up into the night. But rather than being ushered straight to our bedrooms, Emma and I were shown to a drawing room which lived in my memory predominantly for its overstuffed seating and terrifying oil paintings. The olive-green walls with their gilded moulding were not particularly inviting, instead giving off the distinct air of ostentatiousness.

While it seemed my cousin Anne had not been forced to welcome us, her mother stood proudly in the centre of the room, dressed for visitors. Emma had the luxury of staying in the shadows while I stepped forwards to greet my aunt.

"Miss Darcy," she greeted me, with a slight nod.

I dipped into a deep curtsey, almost at risk of toppling over, but I still remembered her telling me my bow was not sincere enough and forcing me to hold the position beside her while she wrote several letters. My legs had ached for days afterwards, and I doubted she would take my fall off a wall as an excuse not to do the same thing again.

"Lady Catherine," I greeted her. "Thank you for taking me in at such short notice."

They weren't the words I wanted to say, but I knew I would only be damning myself if I spoke honestly about how much I didn't want to be there.

"Yes, well, it has been an inconvenience to my staff, but arrangements had to be made," she said, every bit as haughty as I remembered. "And I have been insisting that your brother release you into my care for years. Particularly after the choices he has made recently. Really you should have been sent here the moment your father died. You and Anne could have received the same education. It is a pity you are so far behind. I will do my best, but I cannot work miracles."

Part of me wanted to reply in Greek. Then in Latin, French, Spanish, and Italian, just to prove there was nothing lacking in my education. But a larger part of me was committed to self-preservation. I had no allies here the way I did at Pemberley and Longbourn. The only person I was going to be able to trust within the walls of Rosings was Emma, and she had even less power than I did. There was no choice but to swallow the injustice of my aunt's words and my despondency that Darcy would choose to send me somewhere he knew I hated.

"Yes, ma'am," I said. "Thank you."

The part of my education that taught me to be obedient was far from dormant. Even if my time living with Darcy and Elizabeth had encouraged me to carry myself as an equal, and time with Kitty had eroded the finer points of my deportment training, I was still Georgiana Darcy, and I knew exactly what behaviour was expected of me. The trouble was, I much preferred being Kitty's George.

Despite clearly revelling in holding court, Lady Catherine stayed only long enough to look me despairingly up and down and instruct me to make myself more presentable for breakfast in the morning. Once she'd swept out of the room, I finally let myself breathe.

"Ready for bed?" Emma asked, stepping forwards from where she'd been holding perfectly still at the edge of the room.

I nodded, allowing myself to be led upstairs to a room lacking all my favourite things: no piano, no chessboard, no stack of books. No Kitty. Even when I was tucked under the sheets, my toes heated by the residual echo of a warming pan, I knew sleep would take its time to come.

It was the kind of night most productively spent in the library, ideally with Kitty at my side. Rosings had such a room, but I wasn't confident I could find it, especially in the dark, and I doubted I would be particularly welcome there, even during the daylight hours. There was only one book in the bags I'd brought with me, and I climbed out of bed to dig around for it in my valise.

The Disposition of an English Lady came everywhere with me, so I'd taken it to Meryton without a second thought. Between my initial confusion over Kitty's feelings and my contentment once things had settled, the book had not even come out of my bag. Now, left alone at

Rosings, I craved its familiarity. I had memorised every word inside with how much I'd read and reread it over the years, but it was still a comfort to hold the volume knowing my mother had done the same.

I couldn't help but wonder whether she'd agree with my aunt in thinking that I was uneducated and conducted myself poorly. I found it hard to imagine her disapproving of Darcy's marriage to Elizabeth in the same way Lady Catherine did, not when they were both so clearly in love and all the happier for it. My mother existed for me only in my head, conjured out of the pages of this book, but I could not imagine her to be cruel.

Despite my best effort, I had strayed far from every rule in the book. I wanted desperately to believe that my mother would understand, but she'd found the rules important enough to underline and annotate, her writing cramped into the margins. They mattered to her, perhaps in a way that would eclipse the way Kitty mattered to me. The question would never be answered, so I doubted my guilt over the matter would ever fully subside. I was not the woman my mother would want me to be.

Setting the book down on the table beside

my bed, I curled up underneath the blankets and waited for my exhaustion to overwhelm me, my fingers knotted around Kitty's ribbons at my wrist.

I tried to reassure myself that this was not what my forever looked like, but I knew it could be. If Darcy never let me move back to Pemberley, this was all I had. It was not an asylum like I had feared, but it wasn't much better. My aunt seemed to take so much joy in the power she got from being unattached to any man, but her sole aim was nevertheless to see me shackled to an eligible suitor I did not love. The incongruity was bitter and biting. She seemed happiest unmatched, but unwilling to consider that I might be, too.

The tears that fell onto my pillow were silent but heavy, and hot with suppressed anger.

Breakfast at Rosings was far more formal than at either Pemberley or Longbourn House. I had taken Lady Catherine's words to heart and implored Emma to help me look my best. Walking around in a chemise and an old coat with my hair loose around my shoulders was not an option unless I wanted to invite abject criticism. I needed to do what I could to make this stay bearable. When I was shown into the dining room to find Anne de Bourgh already dressed to receive visitors, I knew I had made the right choice.

"Miss de Bourgh," I greeted her, as formally as I had addressed her mother the night before. "I hope you are well?"

I had never known her to be well. Despite being cousins, we had socialised little together when I had been younger, owing to Anne's weak constitution. It was, on occasion, hard to tell how much of her sickness was genuine and how much was a figment of Lady Catherine's imagination, but the result was the same. Anne spent much of her life resting, unable to travel or go to balls or even hold a stimulating conversation.

It was no secret that my aunt had hoped for Anne to marry Darcy. Financially, it would have been a most convenient arrangement, but I never could imagine this pale, fragile girl as my brother's wife, and nor, I was sure, could he. She shared too many of my features—the dark hair, the harsh jaw, the thick brows.

Marrying Anne was a notion Darcy had never

entertained, but Lady Catherine seemed to blame Elizabeth solely as the reason her plan could now never come to pass. Unless, of course, she was hoping for the current Mrs. Darcy's death.

Anne's own opinions of a potential marriage to my brother had never been clear to me, but her smile when she saw me suggested she did not entirely share her mother's newly intensified disdain for the Darcy name.

"Miss Darcy! I was delighted to hear you'll be staying at Rosings," she said, beaming up at me. It brought some colour to her cheeks, reviving her complexion.

"Your mother was very kind to take me in," I said, focusing on graciousness rather than my anger at being sent away.

"What brings you here at such short notice?"

Explaining Kitty was out of the question, but I could have at least vaguely sketched out the circumstances with Wickham. I would not be the first woman to flee a county to avoid the pursuits of an unrelenting man. Still, I didn't seek to embarrass Lydia for the poor behaviour of her husband and wasn't sure I could tell the story without being talked out of anonymity. So I opted for a carefully constructed lie.

Over toast and jam, I explained the crowded nature of Longbourn and how, in the Bennets' hour of uncertainty regarding the fate of the head of their household, an extra visitor was unnecessary strain. Anne listened intently, eyes wide as she nodded at each line. It was hardly a daring tale of adventure, but she seemed so desperate for a new story or two that she was willing to entirely invest in mine. I almost felt bad for not giving her the vastly more eventful truth. I avoided the questions on her tongue only by the arrival of Lady Catherine.

She swept into the room with a demeanour carefully constructed to silence conversations. Anne and I were both on our feet immediately, heads inclined in place of the curtsies the table prevented.

"Sit," Lady Catherine ordered, but only to Anne. When she turned to me, her lips pursed as if she'd tasted something sour. "Turn."

She waved me away from the table and gestured for me to spin. Feeling like I was being judged for my presentation at court rather than over cold cuts and warm bread, I did as I was asked. For a long moment, there was silence—until my aunt finally spoke.

"Passable," she said, with no note of confidence. "Except this."

When she reached out and grabbed at my wrist, I thought perhaps she was going to find fault with my nails, but when I looked down, I realised it was Kitty's ribbons. I snatched my arm back, holding it behind my back in protective instinct.

"It's fine," I protested.

Lady Catherine's only tell for anger was a slight flaring of the nostrils, but I still felt her discontent in waves.

"You are far beyond the age of childish trinkets," she admonished. "Ribbons are for dresses, bonnets, and hair decorations, not for playthings and distractions."

It was clear she wasn't going to let up until I took them off. With Anne staring intently at her bread, I picked at the knot I'd tied in the ribbons and carefully unwound them from my wrist. My aunt held her hand outstretched, palm up, expecting me to surrender them to her. Nothing on earth could have persuaded me to give them up.

"I will return them to Emma," I lied, "for use in my hair."

Lady Catherine's fingers curled in one at a time, elongating her dissatisfaction, but she didn't protest any further. The second her attention was instead focused on Anne, I tucked the ribbons into the top of my bodice, planning to hide them alongside Kitty's letter in my bag. I would not risk losing them.

Breakfast continued, for me, in dutiful silence. Lady Catherine believed young women should speak only when spoken to, and all her further comments prompted only Anne for a response. It suited me perfectly fine, leaving me with time to listen and observe. Beyond enquiries into Anne's health, the conversation was awfully bland. Not only was there none of Kitty's gossip and revelry in scandal, there was equally nothing of any thoughtfulness. I never thought I would find myself so specifically missing Darcy asking me my opinions on the current political situation on the Continent, but I was desperate for news of the wider world. Doubtless Lady Catherine did not think reading newspapers a fitting activity for a young woman seeking a husband.

Once the table had been cleared, Lady Catherine rose from her chair and finally seemed to remember my presence.

"I will have one of the maids set you up with some needlepoint in the front parlour," she said. "If I am to prepare you to be an acceptable wife, I must at least first see that you are capable of embroidering your linens."

I could already tell her she was going to be disappointed. My sewing was functional, but rarely pretty. If the linens needed mending with fast, sturdy stitches, then I didn't doubt my capabilities would be perfectly adequate, but scrolled initials and decorative flowers never came out quite as planned. A lack of innate skill and several years of lapsed practise were going to do nothing to endear me to her.

"Actually, I was hoping to see the library?" I asked, by no means confident of any results.

"The pertinent books will be brought to you," my aunt said, dismissing the request with a wave of her hand.

The books she deemed pertinent were likely far from the ones I would have chosen for myself. Sermons and etiquette guides were all perfectly suited to certain situations, but my current desire for escape and distraction were likely to go unfulfilled. I had never longed more for free roam of Pemberley's library.

"Might I at least take a walk beforehand?" I tried. "I have not had time to properly settle in, and I should like to settle my thoughts."

Lady Catherine's eyes narrowed, no doubt suspicious that I sought only to delay my needlework. While amongst my aims, it was secondary to my need to breathe for a little while. I forced a demure look of deference while I was scrutinised, until my aunt sighed and waved me away. It was as close as I was going to get to permission, and I quickly made my exit before it could be revoked.

Chapter Eighteen

I had not visited Rosings Park in quite some time, but I still remembered the grounds fondly. While the house was austere and often unfriendly, the gardens held happier memories of long walks and peaceful escape. Beyond the manicured pathways and orchard, I sought out the woodland.

Lady Catherine had imposed no limits on the length of my walk, neither in duration nor distance, and it was a lapse of judgement I was happy to exploit. I didn't doubt that my excursion would soon be called to an end, but if I was beyond the landscaped boundaries of the gardens, I was going to be much harder to find and bring back.

In my haste to gain a little freedom, I had neglected to seek out proper footwear for traipsing through the woods, but my time spent with Kitty had me used to unfamiliar terrain underfoot. Be it the gardens of Pemberley, the forest at Longbourn, or the paths of Rosings, I was starting to find myself rather enjoying being able to feel pebbles and branches through thin soles.

The commonality of woodland eased my unhappiness. As I put Rosings behind me and allowed myself to get lost amongst the trees, I could have been anywhere. It was easy to pretend I was only minutes from my home of books and musical instruments in Pemberley, or that Kitty was just behind a tree, waiting to jump out and surprise me with a kiss. I let nature guide me through the fantasy, taking the paths that the trees seemed to gesture to with the bend of a limb or dip of a branch.

Despite the innate musicality of the woods as distant birds chirped to one another and the breeze rustled branches high above my head, there was a kind of natural stillness that made it quite possible to believe yourself alone. It was only when I pushed my way through a denser collection of branches that I realised I wasn't the only person there. A woman in a dark grey day dress and apron was kneeling on the ground, picking a few fallen chestnuts to add to a basket already half full with glossy brown shells. When she looked up and saw me, she rose to her feet and revealed the noticeable sign of late pregnancy under the fabric of her dress.

"Oh!" I couldn't help my surprise. It was rare to see a woman so far along in her condition out and about, but she seemed happy to be on her feet.

"Miss Darcy," she greeted me, nodding her head politely.

I blinked at her, confused by her immediate use of my name. In my surprise, I had forgone the polite greeting and apology for my intrusion that I should have voiced. She seemed to know me, yet I could not place her amongst those I had previously met on visits to my aunt.

"I'm sorry, I don't… Have we met?" I asked, hoping I was causing her no offence.

"I'm afraid I have not had that pleasure, but you look just like your brother, and I heard this morning that you had come to stay," she said with a smile. "My name is Charlotte."

I dipped into a curtsey to greet her properly. It was rare for a woman of standing to introduce herself with only her given name, but it would be impolite to correct her on her own introduction, and I had already been rude enough. Some days I was tempted to omit my surname, too, when I didn't want the weight of its gravitas.

"Please, allow me to carry that," I insisted, gesturing to the basket. Women in a delicate way were encouraged to rest often. They certainly were not supposed to be collecting chestnuts from the forest floor. "Forgive me, but ought you not to be in bed? If you are acquainted with my aunt, she would no doubt be happy to lend you some assistance until you are delivered, if you need it."

Charlotte laughed fondly and simply bent down to add another handful of nuts to the basket, seemingly completely unimpeded.

"Thank you, but I am relieved to still find myself able to take the air. This will not be my first child, and I am quite capable of staying on my feet," she assured me, with an easy confidence I found myself entirely unable to argue with. "But I would happily welcome the company for my walk home, if you wished to extend your walk as far as the parsonage."

"Mrs. Collins!" I said almost gleefully, once I realised exactly who I was speaking to—for only Mr. Collins's wife could be before me. "Elizabeth speaks of you fondly."

Charlotte's smile fell a little at the use of her married name but was much revived at the mention of Elizabeth.

"Please," she said, "you must call me Charlotte. Any friend of Elizabeth's is a friend of mine, thus her sister-in-law must be as dear as a sister to me. She writes equally fondly of you in her letters."

Charlotte Collins was at the heart of many of the stories Elizabeth told about Longbourn and her childhood. Although Charlotte had married a man who had once first proposed to, and been rejected by, Elizabeth, her letters were some of Elizabeth's favourite to receive. Only letters from Charlotte and from any of her four sisters would Elizabeth drop everything to read immediately. Charlotte was, by all reports, a kind and hardworking woman who was willing to fight for what the world would not easily grant her.

Meeting her after hearing so much prior felt a little like meeting a character from a much-loved book.

I was delighted to walk alongside Charlotte as she led the way back to her home. She did not ask about my sudden appearance at Rosings, instead focusing on how she planned to roast the chestnuts she'd collected, and how roasted sweet chestnuts used to be a favourite of Elizabeth's. Charlotte seemed pleased when I informed her that they still were, and that I had since acquired the taste for them, too.

The parsonage was entirely new to me, but it was clear it was Charlotte's domain. She led me around to a door at the back of the cottage and showed me through to a small kitchen. A maid stirred a pot on the stove, turning quickly and hurrying forwards to take the basket from Charlotte.

"Mr. Collins has been looking for you, ma'am," she said.

Charlotte's mask slipped for only a moment, an almost imperceptible frown. It was quickly covered by a serene smile and a nod.

"Please inform him I am entertaining a guest for a little while, and will find him when I am free to do so," she said, and I realised I was a tool she was using to delay that meeting. If she needed distance that much, I was happy to help her provide it.

Charlotte left me in the front parlour for a few minutes before reappearing with a baby girl who sat happily on her knee, burbling a little as if she wanted to join in with the conversation but had not yet mastered the fine art of speech.

"This is Catherine," Charlotte said, introducing me to the little girl. "Named after your aunt, of course. My husband wouldn't have it any other way."

I laughed. "There seem to be an awful lot of Catherines in my life at the moment; what is one more?"

"Beyond this little one and your aunt?"

There was clearly a question behind Charlotte's words, fuelled by genuine, innocent curiosity. If she was good friends with Elizabeth, I could only assume that she was at least passably acquainted with the rest of the Bennet family.

"Catherine Bennet?" I offered.

With any luck, my cheeks appeared less red to her than they felt to me. Simply saying Kitty's name brought to mind her smile and her curls, and it was enough to remind me how completely in love with her I was.

Charlotte lit up at the name, recognising it instantly. When she realised I knew more of the Bennets than just Elizabeth and that I had, until recently, been staying with them, she was keen to hear updates on how they were all doing. She spoke so fondly of Meryton that it was clear at least part of her heart was still there. I was as forthcoming with the information she wanted as I could be, until she asked why it was that I'd left the Bennets to stay with my aunt. I didn't want to dwell on thoughts of Wickham, instead opting to cite the overcrowding of the Bennet house as the reason for my departure. It was either an underwhelming topic for Charlotte, or she could sense my reticence to talk about it, because she swiftly moved the conversation back to happier subjects. I could talk about Kitty endlessly.

"You are fond of Miss Bennet?" she asked when I paused to take a breath.

I bit my tongue in my haste to shut my mouth. I had said too much, been too indiscreet. The opportunity to speak freely about Kitty had simply been overwhelming, but I barely knew Charlotte.

"They are a kind family," I said, keeping my words measured and careful. "I have enjoyed getting to know them all, Kitty included, since my brother married Elizabeth. I...I enjoy her company."

"I used to be able to talk as much about Elizabeth as you do about Kitty," Charlotte said wistfully. "It seems a lifetime ago, before all this." She gestured to the parsonage around her.

"You married rather late, did you not?" I asked, before I realised how dreadfully rude it sounded, my eyes widening with horror. "Forgive me; I did not mean to offend."

"I take no offence," Charlotte assured me. "It is hardly a secret."

"Some of the girls I knew in London spoke of waiting to marry like it was the most shameful thing, but it only seems sensible to take time to find someone you truly want to marry, rather than rushing into things," I said.

It was a line I'd been testing out in my mind. I did believe it, but I was also hoping it would buy me time when people started to ask too many questions about my own unwedded state.

Charlotte's smile didn't quite meet her eyes.

"There is certainly no shame in waiting for

someone you love. What hurts most is finding that love and it still being out of reach. I suspect you might know what that feels like as well as I do. Sometimes I wonder what my life would have looked like if I had not been forced into this choice."

I blinked at her, trying to find a sensible way to interpret what she was saying. She could not be suggesting what I thought she was. There was no possibility that she could be trying to tell me that we shared an affection for other women. But her smile was small and almost nervous, and she carried the tension in her shoulders of having revealed *something*. I wanted to press her on it, to confirm or deny my wild hopes, but baby Catherine began to cry and Charlotte hurried to sooth her. As she bounced her daughter in her arms, I repeated Charlotte's words to myself so I could overanalyse them later.

Both Charlotte and I benefitted from my time spent in her home, each hiding from a family member we wished to avoid, but I couldn't stay there forever. There was no doubt Lady

Catherine was already seeking to bring me back and subject me to a daylong lecture of how best to attract a husband, and I had already delayed its commencement by a handful of hours. Not to mention how I'd lied about simply taking a walk in the garden.

Reluctant to let me go, Charlotte had me promise to pay her another visit. It was an easy assurance to make—the warmth of the parsonage was far preferable to the cold grandeur of Rosings. I left her with a curtsey and baby Catherine with a tap on the nose to make her giggle, and walked myself home.

As I made my way up the driveway towards the house, I knew my absence had certainly not gone unnoticed. There was an unknown carriage parked in front of the house, with a family crest painted on the side that I could not place. When the front door opened to reveal my aunt, her arms crossed and face pinched, there was a man beside her I didn't recognise. From a distance I assumed him to be a member of the household staff, but as I got closer, it became obvious from the cut of his clothing and the tilt of his chin that he thought far too highly of himself for that. This had to be the owner of the carriage.

"Miss Darcy," Lady Catherine said, disappointment dripping from my name.

The entire walk back had been spent planning how best to approach this moment, and I quickly deployed the tactic I had settled on, despite the unexpected additional audience. Sweeping into a deep curtsey, I ducked my head so she couldn't read any insincerity in my eyes as I spun the events of my morning into something that was not entirely a lie, but fell short of an accurate truth.

"My apologies, Lady Catherine. I lost track of time. I encountered Mrs. Collins in the forest, and she needed some assistance carrying a basket, owing to her condition."

I held my breath, hoping my aunt was at least tolerably fond enough of Charlotte to deem such an excursion worthwhile. My aunt had been as absent from our conversations in the parsonage as the topic of Wickham had been. There was a long silence before I got a reply.

"Why had you ventured into the woods in the first place?" Lady Catherine asked.

"I took a wrong turn," I explained, well aware it made me sound entirely foolish to not have realised I was wandering from manicured gardens to freely growing woodland. Better foolish than insolent, if I wanted my time at Rosings to be bearable. "It has been so long since I visited, and I thought I remembered the pathways far better than I really do."

Lady Catherine studied me for longer than I could comfortably stand still, and I fought the urge to fidget under her scrupulous gaze. When she finally spoke, it was a relief to my tense muscles.

"Your poor timekeeping has kept Lord Salter waiting," she said, gesturing to the man who stepped forwards to look down at me.

He had to be twenty years my senior, grey wisps dappling his sideburns and his hair, before he covered it with the top hat he'd been holding. There was something snide in his features as he straightened his jacket and then addressed me like I was lucky to have his attention.

"Indeed it has," he said, shaping the words as insults. Then he turned back to my aunt. "She needs work. More than you led me to believe."

"She has been poorly raised, my lord, but now that she is in my care, we will soon see improvement."

I was speechless, trying to make sense of

the conversation in a way that didn't revolt me. Before I had time to say anything, Lord Salter tipped his hat to Lady Catherine.

"See to it. I can give you one month; then I will look for someone more suitable elsewhere," he said, before striding towards his carriage.

Rather than offer me any explanation, my aunt continued with her chastising.

"Poor timekeeping is unacceptable for a woman running a household. How can you expect punctuality from your staff if you are not there to enforce it?"

"Who was that?" I asked, finally finding my tongue again.

"The Viscount Salter," she said, as if I should already have known. "His family owns a large amount of land that will one day pass to him. They are influential and well-bred and are exactly the kind of connection you need to make to redeem your family name after the ill-conceived and woeful match your brother doomed you with. You ought to count yourself lucky that I have managed to convince him you will make a suitable wife. Although after today's poor judgement on your behalf, it will be a much more difficult task."

I wanted to protest her defamation of Darcy and Elizabeth, but her mentions of marriage shocked the fight out of me.

"But I do not know him," I said weakly. *I do not love him*, I held back. Love was not a prerequisite for a marriage, but to be promised to a total stranger was another matter.

I could not be married in England without my brother's consent, and I doubted Lord Salter would be expecting elopement at Gretna Green, but if Lady Catherine arranged the match and had it announced publicly, it would be as good as sealed. I could not get out of it without blackening the Darcy name.

"Why should it matter whether you know him?" Lady Catherine asked. "It is a sensible match. We have work to do."

Her words felt like the signing of a death warrant, but as far as she knew my only crime was being born a woman. Even without knowing anything of the shape of my heart or of Kitty, she would still subject me to a future of her choosing. Perhaps she had forgotten how it felt to be a powerless young woman all but sold to the highest bidder, or maybe she remembered perfectly and felt it had earned her the right to force me into the same fate.

I was not in control of this chess game; I was a pawn at the mercy of the player, and that meant I had only one option. Pawns could be promoted if they lasted in the game long enough to make it to the far side of the board, gaining the same status as the queen, who could move as she chose. It was a game of endurance, but perhaps it was still one I could play to win. All I had to do was survive.

It was difficult to say whether my first week at Rosings would have been more tolerable had I not disappeared for so much of that first morning. Lady Catherine tested me on every possible facet of my being that she saw any potential need to be honed to please Lord Salter. In the more studious aspects, I passed with flying colours. My French was impeccable, and my Italian almost as faultless. My piano was as practised as any governess could hope for, and my imperfections on the harp likely only discernible to a trained ear. The things I enjoyed, I excelled at.

The same could not be said for that which I found less to my taste. I had never been one for embroidery, and my attempt at a sprig of bluebells came out entirely unrecognisable. My drawing was adequate but lacking any real refinement, and it turned out I could remember dance steps only with Kitty to lead me across the floor.

I was, as a sum total of my parts, a disappointment. Lady Catherine kept ruthless notes on the aspects of me that most displeased her, creating a list of things to address. Not only was I expected to practise my skills in the things I most disliked, but I also had to endure an endless tirade of small corrections to every one of my mannerisms to which she took offence. I spoke incorrectly; I sat incorrectly; I held my fork incorrectly. I couldn't help but feel that any man who judged his potential wife on how she ate peas wasn't the kind of man anyone should be marrying.

Kitty did not give a damn how I spoke or sat or handled cutlery. She liked that I could be so absorbed in a book that I forgot the world around me. She did not care how well I could embellish a handkerchief with flowers. I could impress her just as easily with Latin or Greek as I could with a lopsided drawing of a vase. Those were the thoughts I relied on every night when I slumped against my pillows, exhausted from hours of deportment training that saw me walking up and down the portrait gallery with my chin parallel to the floor. The people who mattered most cared least about what was "proper."

There had been no more talk of Lord Salter, but I knew what I was being trained for now. I was being shaped to please him, and it made me feel sick to my stomach. The idea that Darcy might approve of the match was too upsetting to dwell on, but it nevertheless lurked at the back of my thoughts. I could only hope he came to Rosings to collect me before the one-month deadline was met, and that he valued my happiness more than my reputation.

Chapter Nineteen

Mornings were nothing to look forward to. I would spend a largely sleepless night trying to fight the urge to seek out the library, knowing it was not even the library I truly wanted to visit, and then spend a painfully formal breakfast trying not to fall asleep in my food while I conducted cordial conversations about the weather with my cousin. Then the lessons of the day would begin.

Lady Catherine had me sewing a sampler to improve my abilities with a needle. It was the sort of exercise usually carried out by children a decade younger, having them follow faintly pencilled lines to stitch out the alphabet and several decorative borders. It was slow work that, even with the use of a thimble, left my fingers pitted and sore. I hated the fact that the practise was helping. My *M* was far more orderly than my *A* had been.

While I sewed, my aunt kept close watch over me. She seemed concerned I might disappear again if she took her eyes off me, and it would be a lie to say the thought had not crossed my mind. I found myself using more force than necessary to stab through the cheap canvas she'd supplied me with in time with the scratch of her pen against paper as she wrote out a letter.

The arrival of the footman was a welcome distraction. While Lady Catherine took a break from her writing and her observations, I, too, could take a break from my sewing. Charles carried with him a silver tray atop which sat three letters. The top two he handed over to my aunt, but when she expectantly waited for the third, he hesitated.

"This arrived for Miss Darcy," he said, holding up a small letter on cream-coloured notepaper.

I recognised Kitty's handwriting immediately,

her looping script my favourite form of my name. It was all I could manage to restrain myself from knocking the footman over in my haste to read the letter's contents, but I tempered my excitement and waited patiently to be handed it.

Lady Catherine put out her hand before Charles could take one step.

"Give that to me," she ordered, and he was in no place to refuse. I couldn't blame him for it—it wasn't as if he knew how important that letter was to me and what damaging words it could possibly contain. Kitty's last letter to me would have caused irrepressible scandal if it had fallen into the wrong hands. It still would, in the unthinkable situation of it being discovered in the lining of my travelling bag.

"Who knows you are staying here?" she asked me.

My mouth was dry with worry, and I had to swallow before I could compose a coherent response.

"Miss Catherine Bennet, I believe," I said, as if the name meant little more to me than my sister-in-law's sister. A passing acquaintance.

As much as the name pleased me to say, Lady

Catherine was horrified by its very mention in her house.

"A Bennet? I think not. It is bad enough that your brother has lowered the reputation of this family by forming an attachment to one of their daughters. I will not have you associating with such people. You ought to be seeking highborn friends. What would Lord Salter think?"

I don't care what Lord Salter thinks.

Kitty is not merely my friend.

Every word was true, but none of it said aloud would be wise.

"Yes, Lady Catherine." The words tasted bitter, but I knew they were necessary. "If I could have the letter, I will write back and insist the correspondence ends."

I had every intention of doing exactly that. As keen as I was to hear from Kitty—indeed, it was the only thing that could make my seclusion at Rosings tolerable—it would only put us both in danger.

"I think your failure to reply will accomplish that perfectly fine," Lady Catherine said, every word clipped.

She had no intention of handing over the

letter. Her fingers crushed the paper as she tightened her grip, and I felt anger course through me. Kitty's words deserved to be treated with care, and that was before I even knew for certain what words they were.

Letting my aunt read that letter was out of the question. The moment she started peeling at the wax seal Kitty had stamped on the back, I lurched forward, pulling it out of her grip. In her surprise, she didn't have time to snatch it away. I wanted to hide it down my bodice so I could read it in secret later, but the confusion on Lady Catherine's face melted into stony anger, and I knew that wasn't an option.

"Miss Darcy," she shrieked, indignant at my lack of decorum.

I desperately needed to know what Kitty had written. Nothing would improve my mood more. I wanted to settle down in a comfortable chair with a plate of gingerbread and a new candle, the perfect atmosphere for a letter that would feel like home. But Lady Catherine wouldn't allow me to keep it, and I wouldn't allow her to take it, so I had only one other choice. Even ripping it up wouldn't be enough, simply creating a puzzle to reconstitute.

Dashing across the room before Lady Catherine could stop me, I reached the fireplace and opened my fist, the letter falling from my fingers and into the flames. The heat took it instantly, melting the wax seal and turning the paper to embers and ashes. I'd never get to read it, but nor would anyone else. It was the only way to keep both Kitty and me safe.

There was silence in the room. Charles had stepped back to hide in the shadows, but I wasn't quite as lucky. My aunt took two steps towards me, raised her hand, and struck me hard across the face.

"Insolent girl," she seethed. "You ought to be glad your parents aren't alive to see the disgrace you've become."

The words hurt more than the slap, even as pain radiated out from my cheek. I'd never known my mother and had increasingly distant memories of my father, but Darcy remembered both of them with clarity and fondness. Never once had he suggested I conducted myself in a way contrary to their wishes. Though I supposed his thoughts on the subject could easily have changed, given what he knew now.

Weighing up my options, I elected to flee the

room. Unlike the comfort of Pemberley, no corner of Rosings felt safe. The closest I could get was the bedroom I'd been allocated. It didn't have endless books or shell-encrusted walls or a piano propped open in the corner, but it did have a door I could close between me and the rest of the household. It took everything I had not to slam it.

Lady Catherine was not the type to give chase. I didn't doubt she was raging at whoever happened to be nearby, and I felt guilty for being the reason they were subjected to her fury, but I was safe at least until our paths crossed again. I considered planning out a strategy to avoid that circumstance altogether, but this was her house and my stay had no agreed end date.

Pulling my valise out from under the bed, I ripped apart the lining in the corner, held by a few loose stitches to secure the hiding place. Tucked inside were Kitty's ribbons and a well-worn letter, sent only a few weeks ago. It felt like so much longer. I ran my fingers over the silky surface of the hair ribbons for a moment, before pulling out the letter Kitty had sent me after she'd first kissed me.

I read it again and again until my eyes glazed

over, unable to focus any longer. I studied the words until I knew them by rote, and memorised every blotch of ink or faded character until the image was printed firmly on my heart. Then, with shaking hands and tears threatening to fall, I crossed my room and knelt beside the fire.

It was too dangerous to keep it. Lady Catherine had made it clear she harboured no trust for me, thinking me unfit to receive my own letters. Should she find this one amongst my possessions, she would read it, and should she read it, both Kitty and I were doomed to a fate unknown but unfriendly.

Pressing my lips to the soft paper, I clung to it one final time before I released it into the flames. The heat teased my fingertips, but I let them linger a moment too long before snatching them back. It felt right that this hurt physically, for it was tearing my heart apart.

I tried to take comfort in the fact I still had the ribbons. Nothing gave them away as Kitty's. The only thing suspicious about them was how hidden away they were. I knew they would be safer left in plain sight, so I relocated them alongside my own hair ribbons in the drawer of my dressing table. It felt like madness to store them so openly and irreverently, but it was for the best.

When everything was done, I slumped onto the end of the bed, feeling more alone than ever. I missed Elizabeth and Darcy. I missed Kitty. The only ally I had near Rosings was Charlotte, and I didn't think it likely I would be granted leave to visit her anytime soon. Especially not after my most recent outburst.

I sat there, waiting for the repercussions of my actions to find their way to me. The knock that sounded at the door almost a full hour after I burned the first letter still managed to make me jump. I considered climbing to my feet and standing demurely to show my regret, but I wasn't feeling particularly regretful. More than anything, I just felt even more lonely than before. I wished I could have read Kitty's words and, even if I had been the one to destroy them, it was my aunt who had left me with no other choice. I would not stand piously in deference.

Regardless of my lack of greeting, the door to my bedroom was pushed open anyway. I looked up to find Anne standing in the doorway. She seemed more tentative than vengeful, but I didn't doubt she was paying me a visit only at Lady Catherine's request. She was no one I could tell anything remotely approaching the truth to.

"Is everything all right?" Anne asked, taking a seat next to me on the bed. "My mother is worried about you."

I laughed bitterly, unconvinced. "She is angry."

Anne could have denied it, but after a moment she corrected herself.

"I am worried about you," she said quietly. "You are not…"

I was not refined. I was not well-behaved. I was not polite. I was not following a single rule of etiquette despite a rigorous upbringing that rivalled Anne's. Any ending would have been accurate, but she was kinder than my imagination seemed willing to give her credit for.

"You are not happy here," she eventually finished. "Is there anything I can do?"

"I do not want to be here," I admitted.

Anne nodded slowly. My confession was obvious, but I wasn't willing to say anything more. I would not gamble with Kitty's safety, and I was afraid if I started talking, I would say too much. Rather than asking why, Anne sat with me in a silence that began awkward but slowly turned comforting. It was broken only after several minutes.

"I can get a letter to someone, if you need to send one," Anne offered. "She does not check my post."

If I wasn't so afraid of Lady Catherine suspecting something and reading Anne's letters, too, or of Anne herself learning too much, I would have jumped at the chance to communicate with Kitty, but I still could not bear the risk. I thanked Anne all the same and forced a smile I hoped did not seem as weak as it felt. She rose from the bed and squeezed my shoulder.

"I will tell her you are feeling unwell," she promised. "That ought to give you some peace for a little while, and she may be a little more understanding of your outburst if you blame it on a fever. I would certainly advise you to keep your distance until her mood has had time to recover. Perhaps I will see you for breakfast tomorrow?"

"Thank you," I said, genuinely appreciative of her attempts to help. I did not doubt she was risking her mother's wrath if she was found to be comforting me.

After Anne took her leave, I followed her advice and confined myself to my room. She had seemingly made good on her promise to convey my state of ill health as food was brought to me and I was offered hot soup and tea. All I wanted to do was read Kitty's original letter, but when I raked through the ash in the fireplace, not a single scrap of her writing remained. It was better this way, but it still tore my heart apart.

Without a chessboard or piano or library to pass the time, I found myself reading through *The Disposition of an English Lady*. Every page talked of a woman's duty to her husband, how she ought to conduct herself to please and complement him.

It was not news to me that there was no mention of a woman taking a wife, for I knew the idea was practically unthinkable to almost everyone, but even living alone seemed out of reach of the author's conceptualisations. To be married and unhappy was a greater fate than to be happily a spinster, it seemed, and to happily spend one's life with another woman was beyond even imagination.

I thought of Charlotte's words. She had been forced to make a choice, but if it was a choice, then she could picture another option, a version that wouldn't have ended with her married to

William Collins in a parsonage in Hunsford. A version that sounded like it might not have featured a man at all. If she could imagine that, I wanted her to teach me. I couldn't see a way to being able to be with Kitty, but if there was one, then I had to know. I just needed to get back to Charlotte, and for that I had to appease my aunt.

I descended to breakfast the following morning expecting fire and brimstone. A restless night had left me tired enough that Anne's story of me having a fever could easily have been true. Regardless, I had dressed impeccably, ensuring not a single hair on my head was out of place and no wrinkle dared crease my skirts. There was already enough about me for Lady Catherine to criticise without providing her with further stones to throw.

Rather than exploding at me, my aunt sat silently through breakfast. It was worse this way. An icy surface that hid turbulent waters was more dangerous than the waters alone, lulling you into a false sense of safety. I refused to be deceived, staying on guard for what I knew for sure would be coming. When she finally spoke, I did not even flinch.

"I have been considering an apt punishment for your actions yesterday," she said calmly as she set her teacup down on the table with a delicate clink of china. "It occurred to me that perhaps you are not deserving of my tuition, but after much thought and no small degree of graciousness on my behalf, I believe I owe it to your mother to do my best to turn you from any erroneous path you have begun down. There's still good blood in you. It would be remiss of me to already consider you a lost cause."

"I don't understand," I said, barely louder than a whisper.

"My nephew clearly allowed your education to continue improperly after it was left to him, but there's no reason some further lessons won't be able to undo the damage and shape you into a becoming young woman, ready to make this advantageous match to Lord Salter and be worthy of your lineage."

She made it sound like we were descendants of royalty. The best thing about my brother had never been the surname on his calling cards or the money in his accounts but the loyalty and patience he showed the people he cared for. I hoped no one truly believed that the best thing about me was my parentage. Kitty's delight at the languages I spoke, the chess games I could always best her at, and the music I played made me feel like a person worth valuing, but not because of my name.

It seemed clear Lady Catherine would not be giving up. Part of me had hoped that perhaps she would decide me not worth the trouble and refuse to allow me to remain at Rosings, but instead I was to remain even more firmly under her thumb. I expressed gratitude I did not feel in an attempt not to make things worse. I needed her to trust me again.

Once breakfast was cleared away, I took my place in the drawing room and picked up the embroidery I'd abandoned at the first sight of Kitty's letter the day before. I kept my head down, stabbing the needle through the fabric with more force than was strictly necessary. It made my stitches even more uneven and poorly tensioned, but it was an effective channel for my anger.

Chapter Twenty

I did everything as Lady Catherine dictated. She told me daily how much more work was needed on my deportment, mannerisms, and general countenance before Lord Salter would consider me a suitable wife, but the month's deadline he had set was fast wearing out. I did not have long to find a chance to return to the parsonage and speak to Charlotte again.

I still prayed for a letter from Darcy summoning me home, and spent every night considering writing to him myself. I began three different attempts, burning each one. It was impossible to explain myself without revealing far too much for a letter Lady Catherine was sure to read, and even if I could explain myself, I had no guarantee he would come to my aid.

I endured endless sewing practise, dance lessons, and etiquette refinement. The things I would have most enjoyed practising, I already excelled at, and my time at music practise or speaking another language was restricted in favour of the skills I struggled with.

Occasionally I was allowed to sit at the piano, and I revelled in the chance to feel like myself again. I dutifully played through some popular airs and reels before I let my fingers carry me into Kitty's sonata, the music wrapping itself around me in a comforting embrace of memory and feeling and promise. I could imagine Kitty next to me, pressed too close and almost getting in the way but so, so welcome.

"What is that?" Lady Catherine said, her words clipped. "Who is the composer?"

"I am, ma'am," I admitted, ending the melody abruptly. My fingers rested on the keys, the final notes allowed to play out in their entirety.

"You will play sensible music," my aunt insisted. "Not nonsense you make up yourself."

I wanted to protest that it was sensible music, that I had not simply made it up but carefully crafted it to perfectly reflect the person I held most dear, but I knew arguing would get me nowhere.

"Yes, ma'am," I said, starting a simple piece I knew she would recognise and approve of.

It was slowly killing me to be so obedient. I had never taken issue with it before, happily doing as my father or my governesses or my brother asked. They had never had any reason to cut me off from the things I enjoyed or force me through arduous afternoons of things I did not. I had never truly realised the degree of freedom I had in being able to pursue that which truly interested me.

Lady Catherine's opinion of me appeared to change little, despite my best attempts to do her bidding. I expected it likely had something to do with my lack of success in my attempts. My dancing was still clumsy and my needlework unrefined. I received just as much derision and disappointment, but, slowly, a level of trust began to settle in.

I was no longer watched for every second of the day, and my aunt could be persuaded to allow me to go for walks in the gardens. I made sure not to step one foot off the landscaped paths and to return exactly at the time I was instructed. Eventually, three weeks after the arrival of Kitty's letter, I pleaded my case. I stressed that my dancing was suffering due to my lack of stamina and that building up endurance with some strenuous walking would have me showing much improvement in my lessons.

Insisting I was not to be unchaperoned, Lady Catherine allowed me to leave the house with Emma accompanying me. She seemed just as likely to get lost in the woods, but I didn't raise the issue. I was too thrilled at the very prospect of time away from Rosings. As soon as we started off down the drive, I was practically running.

"Slow down," Emma said, laughing. "I was not aware I'd agreed to a race."

I forced myself to slow a little, quashing the impatient urge to drag my feet in protest.

"My apologies," I said. "It's just nice to have a little freedom."

"So where are we heading to in such a hurry?

Is there an admirer waiting?" Emma probed, genuine curiosity in her voice.

"Only a friend."

Charlotte was not expecting me and was likely in the final stages of her pregnancy. She had every right to refuse visitors, especially the visit of someone who was all but a stranger, but I had to try to see her.

I carefully retraced the path I'd taken home last time until it brought me to the parsonage. Against Emma's best wishes, I couldn't help the spring in my step that carried me forwards at a quickened pace.

There was an anxious wait as Charlotte's maid disappeared to enquire whether I was welcome, but soon I was shown into the parlour, where Charlotte was settled on a sofa. Her dress draped loosely over her pregnant stomach, and a blanket covered her knees.

"Forgive me for not standing to greet you," she said. "Only it takes me far too long to get up and down these days, and I would barely be on my feet before it was time for you to leave."

I wanted to tell her that was perfectly understandable, to acknowledge that by even being out of bed, she was far excelling the usual activities of most women waiting to be delivered. Instead, safely out of the oppressive walls of Rosings, however temporarily, I wilted onto the sofa opposite Charlotte. The tears I had spent three weeks holding back fell in rivers, and my hands shook as I tried to brush them away. Despite her pregnancy, Charlotte was beside me in seconds.

"What's wrong?" she asked. "Are you in pain?"

I shook aside my overwrought emotions and helped her to sit beside me.

"I can only offer my apologies," I said through sniffles. "I should not have come here only to cry all over your upholstery."

"Better here than at Rosings," Charlotte said diplomatically. "Our furnishings are far less expensive. Now, tell me, what has happened up there that has chased you here?"

Against my better judgement and without all my faculties securely in place, I told her.

"My aunt intends to marry me to a Lord Salter and is determined to shape me into a suitable wife for him, but I have no desire to be married and I just want to go *home*. Kitty sent me a letter, and it was the one thing that might have raised my spirits but I just couldn't let my aunt read it so I had to burn it and now I will never know what it said because I cannot talk to her and I miss her and…"

I was revealing far too much, but I had bottled it up within me for far too long, and I struggled to restrain even the most sensitive details.

Charlotte took in every word. She held my hand and let me ramble until I stuttered to a stop. It was only once my brain caught up with everything I had been saying that I panicked, my eyes going wide. I held my breath, hoping I had been right in my suspicions.

"I…I don't…It is not…" I began, but there was no way to take back words already spoken, and trying to correct myself with more rambling would only make things look worse. At least Charlotte didn't look scandalised. Then she started to talk.

"I married out of necessity. I was risking spinsterhood and could not put the burden on my family to continue supporting me for the rest of my life. There was no fortune set aside for me," she said, with a very direct look. "All women have to make a choice. I made mine and now I live with it. It is perhaps better than any realistic alternative, but I will not pretend it to be the life of my dreams."

She shifted to get comfortable again, but I sensed she wasn't finished with her advice. Desperate for guiding wisdom, I didn't say a word.

"You are more lucky than you realise. Your choices are more free than I could ever imagine. Choose wisely. If you have someone you hold dear, don't let go of her. You are not the first young woman to be swayed by curls, flushed cheeks, and delicate features," she said, leaving me little room to misinterpret.

What she was proposing still seemed so impossible. The notion that Kitty was a choice I could make outside the safety of a daydream was overwhelming.

"I... I'm not sure I know how," I whispered.

Charlotte squeezed my hand tightly.

"Have you ever heard of Lady Eleanor Butler and Miss Sarah Ponsonby?" she asked. "Or perhaps you may know them as the Ladies of Llangollen?"

I sifted through all the information I could recall ever reading, searching for a memory of the names but coming up short. When I shook my head, Charlotte offered me a soft smile.

"Lady Butler and Miss Ponsonby are two women who have made a home together in a cottage outside Llangollen. I am not saying it is common or that it is easy, but it *is* possible. They live in peace and attract interest from writers, and from the queen herself, but that interest is rarely negative—merely curious. I doubt they can be the only pair who manages to live quite happily that way. All others presumably enjoy more anonymity. Perhaps that kind of life could be something to pursue."

What Charlotte was describing sounded perfect. Just Kitty and me undisturbed in a cottage. A few more tears tracked down my cheeks, and Charlotte pulled out a neatly folded handkerchief to pat them dry.

"Think very hard about the life you are willing to live, Miss Darcy," she said. "If you truly could be happy with things the way your aunt would have them, then by all means, take the trodden path. But if not, please remember you do deserve to be happy. And you might be one of the few people in a position to get what you deserve."

The words stayed with me for the rest of the visit and the entire walk back to Rosings. Emma's tentative enquiries into my changed demeanour went unanswered as I turned the very idea of Charlotte's suggestion over in my hands like a tangible object. The more I considered it, the more I couldn't imagine my life any other way. If it was conceivable for me to live with Kitty in a cottage, unbothered and unpersecuted, I didn't want anything else. I had to see her, to find out if she wanted the same thing. I would not wait around for one final week to see if Lord Salter would deign to take me as his bride.

Writing to Kitty was still too dangerous, and it wasn't a message I trusted on the lips of anyone else who had the means to travel to Longbourn. If I wanted to ask her, I would have to go myself.

Lady Catherine would never allow it, of course, but if I didn't ask, she had no chance to refuse me. I had pin money. I could catch Royal Mail coaches or hire carriages to get me to Longbourn. From there, Kitty would have a plan. She dreamt so much of travel that I was certain she would know where best for us to escape to. All I had to do was get to her and put the rest of my life in the palms of her hands.

It was a terrifying concept in more ways than one. Even the journey of getting to her was dangerous, but it felt no more perilous than staying at Rosings and facing a life married to Lord Salter, who had looked at me the way Wickham often had. I could not let myself end up his bride, and if I stayed I would have no choice. The decision was already made.

I waited until nightfall, and not a minute longer. As soon as Emma had retired for the night and I knew I would no longer be disturbed, I pushed aside my covers and redressed in the warmest clothes I had with me.

I didn't have much to pack. If I was to leave alone, as I knew I had to, everything would need to go in my valise. There were to be no chests of gowns or bulky hatboxes. Instead I stuffed in my most practical dresses with no regard for proper packing technique, tucking other essentials into every gap I could find. Shawls, a reticule, and my second-most-reliable pair of boots all found a home. My most reliable pair were tied tightly on my feet.

There was little with me at Rosings that held any sentimental value, but I made sure to collect Kitty's hair ribbons and wind them back around my wrist. I would not leave them for Lady Catherine to dispose of in a fit of rage when she noted my absence, which seemed a not unlikely series of events. *The Disposition of an English Lady* also found a home in my bag. I whispered an apology to my mother for my actions as I tucked it inside, hoping she would have understood what I needed to do.

With my valise packed so generously it was a trial to pull the buckles tight, I was almost ready to go.

My brother's coat had been tucked away in a drawer in the hope of my aunt not finding it and disapproving of me having it. I rubbed my thumb over the worn velvet and tarnished buttons before pushing my arms into the sleeves, the silky lining gliding over my arms. It was the first time I would ever wear the coat out of the house, but I found it was easier to hold my shoulders back and keep my chin up with it on. Besides, it was certainly warmer than any of my spencers. There was certainly a chance it would get me some strange looks as I travelled, but I was already going to be a woman travelling alone, so such looks were to be expected. At least this way I could be comfortable while people stared at me.

I left my room with no second glance or goodbye. There were no fond memories there.

I was going to be in need of something to cut through the darkness for a walk as far as the nearest town. Rosings still didn't feel familiar to me, but I knew the way to the kitchens, where I hoped there would be some spare candles. Creeping through the corridors like a spectre, I eased open the kitchen door and searched through every drawer. Each creak of wood felt like a cannon firing in the silence of the house, but eventually my fingers landed on the cool wax of a supply of taper candles. I took three, keeping one to light before I left the house and stuffing two into my coat pockets.

There was nothing standing in the way of my leaving anymore, and I felt thrillingly lighter as I turned on the ball of my foot. The spin turned into a stumble as I was greeted not with an open door but instead the figure of Anne, holding a candlestick of her own.

"What are you doing?" she asked, tiredness clinging to the end of each word.

"Please, say nothing," I begged.

Anne took note of my bag, and her eyes widened as she realised I was not simply in search of some late-night sustenance.

"Where are you going? Will you be back?" she asked.

"No," I admitted. "Please let me go."

Chewing at her bottom lip, Anne eventually nodded. She stepped aside so there was nothing between me and my way out.

"Stay safe," she insisted. "And write to me, whenever you get where you're going."

I nodded my agreement, but the notion was empty. I had no protests of a closer relationship with my cousin. She had proved herself endlessly more agreeable than her mother, but I still could not trust a letter sent to Rosings not to make its way into my aunt's hands. She would have read Kitty's letters to me, so I did not doubt she would be eager to read my letters to Anne in the instance of my disappearance. I would be tracked down in no time.

Leaving all of Rosings behind, Anne included, I all but ran towards the rest of my life.

Chapter Twenty-One

It was a cold walk to town, even with my coat, but I had a purse full of pin money I'd never had much need or inclination to spend, so it was easy to pay my way to Longbourn. I failed to see the process of travelling in the golden-hued light I knew Kitty did, but knowing she was at the end of the journey made it easier to endure the cramped corner of a shared coach and the endless rocking of the wheels.

The sun rose and set over my travels, leaving me facing an exhaustion staved off with small pockets of sleep where I could catch them. When I made it to Meryton, if not for the tiredness setting in, I would have walked the entire way to Longbourn House, but I didn't trust my feet not to stumble.

For the right price, I managed to persuade a carriage driver to take me out to the Bennets' residence despite the late hour. I bid him to stop and wait a few hundred yards away so the sound of the horses' hooves and wheels on gravel would not wake anyone. The last portion of my journey was completed on foot, taking me right to a place I felt I had not seen in years.

I looked up at the house and realised there was a hole in my plan. There was no way for me to get inside without waking someone, and I needed there to be no notice of my visit to anyone but Kitty. Any member of the household staff who woke would feel obligated to tell their master or mistress, and the Bennets or any of their guests would likely try to stop us. I was already asking Kitty for something completely mad. A dissenting voice could easily be all it took to talk us both out of it.

If I could not go through the house, the only option I was left with was Kitty's window. I knew exactly which one it was and crept around the outside of the house until I could get a good view of it to appraise the situation. Climbing the brickwork felt like the most apt idea if I was aiming to recreate the events of a novel, but I knew I would not make it one foot off the ground before falling. If, by some miracle, I made it any higher, the fall would only hurt more. I was in no hurry to injure my leg again.

Shouting would wake the entire household, so I opted for something a little more subtle and collected a handful of pebbles. They were, I hoped, small enough that there was no risk of them breaking the window, but heavy enough that they would hit with enough force to alert Kitty to my presence.

All my first attempts hit brickwork. Chess and piano had not given me much of an arm for throwing, and the motion felt strange and unwieldy. Correcting the mistakes of each previous throw, I adjusted my aim and finally made contact with the glass. The soft clink wasn't so loud I worried I'd wake anyone else, but did leave me concerned it wouldn't be enough to even wake Kitty. I had known her to sleep through a lot more. Desperation kept me going, unwilling to surrender my only viable option to get past this stage of the plan.

Once five or six stones had bounced off the glass, I saw movement behind the window. It opened inwards just before I could let go of the next stone, revealing a sleepy-eyed and very confused Kitty. Her hair was covered by a nightcap, and she was fighting back a yawn, but my heart still leapt in my chest. As soon as she realised the identity of the fool beneath her window, she leant forwards, gripping the windowsill as her eyes widened in surprise. I quickly held my finger to my lips, urging her to be quiet. After all of this, I didn't want her waking the staff with a shout. I gestured for her to come down to meet me, and she nodded, immediately disappearing.

The seconds before Kitty came flying out of the door felt longer than the entire journey from Rosings to Longbourn House, but eventually she was in my arms, holding me so tightly it was a chore to breathe. I still did not want her to let go. She repeated my name under her breath like a prayer, hugging me close for a full minute before pulling back to press kisses across my face.

"I missed you," she whispered, resting her forehead against mine.

"I missed you, too," I whispered back.

"What are you doing here? And so late?" she asked.

It took me a moment to answer, my faculties much distracted by the feel of her palm against the back of my neck and the depth of her eyes. The dim light might have denied me the full spectrum of shades of blue in them, but the spectrum of emotion was as plain as under the brightest sun. Once I had shifted past the confusion and surprise, the relief and love and joy sang through.

"Run away with me."

I had meant it to be a question, but it came out as far more of a request. There was no context, no explanation, and yet Kitty's response was immediate.

"Anywhere," she vowed, punctuating the word with another kiss.

I could tell she thought me less than serious.

"I mean it," I insisted. "I cannot imagine a fate worse than being tied to a man I could never love. My heart is no longer my own to give away."

Her smile was teasing as she laced her hand with mine.

"Is it mine?" she asked.

There were no reservations.

"Yes."

I could taste Kitty's delight in the curve of her lips when she kissed me again, but as soon as she pulled away, my words seemed to settle in her mind and her face fell.

"They have found you a suitor?" she asked, her fingers tightening around mine.

"Yes," I admitted, "and I'd rather take my chances starting anew than be married to him."

The shiver that ran down my back was born half of the chill of the night, and half of the idea of being married off to Lord Salter to further the prospects of the family name, or to cover the tracks of my sins.

Kitty chewed on her bottom lip, her eyes overcast with a shade of deep thought. I didn't push the request to run away. If she wanted to stay, I would never force her to leave a family I knew she loved.

"Where would we go?" she asked.

I dampened down my excitement at the realisation she was truly considering my madcap request. For the first time since leaving Rosings, my entire plan felt real. It felt possible. The answer to her question mattered deeply, as the truth of it all was that I had no real destination in mind. It should have been the first thing I considered before I had taken one step away from Rosings, but getting away had always felt more important than where I ended up. I just wanted to go somewhere that felt safe, but with Kitty standing in front of me, I realised that was not a place, but a person.

Choosing my words carefully, I crafted the perfect utopia.

"Somewhere they have never heard of a Bennet or a Darcy."

The idea was intoxicating. Kitty would be free of the expectations set by her sisters. I would never have to worry about bringing shame on my family name. There had to be somewhere we could settle where people would look the other way and pretend they didn't see how dear Kitty was to me. Charlotte's story of the Ladies of Llangollen played itself over and over in my mind, like a novice practising scales at the piano. It was all I could think of. It was everything I wanted.

"That sounds perfect," Kitty said softly. "Are you truly serious about this?"

When I nodded, she pressed a kiss to the back of my hand. Then she turned back to look at

Longbourn. I knew what she was feeling because it was the same thing I felt when I imagined never calling Pemberley my home again. She would be leaving behind so many memories, so many of her things that we wouldn't be able to take with us, and her entire family. The idea of asking her to come with me started to feel selfish and ludicrous. Only then Kitty put her back to the house and focused solely on me.

"All right," she said with a decisive nod. "I want to go with you. Can you wait here for a minute while I pack a bag? Do you not have anything with you at all?"

I explained the waiting coach and promised to stay out of sight while Kitty gathered some things. As I leant against the side of the house, pulling my coat close around myself to keep warm, I tried to stave off concerns that Kitty wouldn't come back. With a little distance to develop some clarity, it was inconceivable she would still think this a good idea.

But Kitty did come back. She had changed out of her nightwear and wrapped herself in a pelisse, with a valise over her arm. There was no hint of hesitation as she took my hand and we walked, together, away from Longbourn House.

It was clear Kitty was tired. She rubbed at her eyes with her spare hand and fought back yawns the entire walk to the carriage. Even when we were sitting inside and no longer needed to put energy into walking, she let her head slump onto my shoulder as if too exhausted to hold it up herself. It was understandable. I had woken her up in the middle of the night.

The carriage driver needed directions, and I was at a loss. I was finding it easier to keep my eyes open than Kitty was, but I still struggled when it came to trying to think sensibly. Choosing a place to settle for the rest of our lives wasn't something either of us could do in the state we were in. Instead I nudged Kitty into giving the name of a town to the north that would have an inn. We would just have to hope that it was far enough away that no one from Longbourn would find us there before we could make a proper escape the next morning.

"We will need to be awake and moving again before anyone realises you're gone," I said to Kitty.

"I left a note," she said through another yawn. "I didn't say why I was leaving or who with, but I reassured them I would be safe and that there was no need to look for me. I promised them this was no foolish scheme. I can only hope they believe me."

I could not help but laugh.

"After everything that happened with Lydia, they will start looking for you the moment they realise you have left." I pressed a kiss to her temple. "You are too precious to simply let slip away like that. I know Elizabeth would not allow it."

"Elizabeth isn't there. My father has regained some of his strength, and no one is quite so worried about him, so she and Mr. Darcy returned to Pemberley late last week."

Her words stung more than she could have imagined. Darcy said he'd let me return to Pemberley once he was back there himself, yet they had continued to leave me in Rosings. It felt like proof that he never wanted much to do with me again. I knew now that I was making the right decision. Anger bubbled in my stomach, but I tamped it down. It was nothing I needed to dwell on.

Chapter Twenty-Two

The inn we found ourselves at was modest but comfortable enough for what was left of the night. While the innkeeper was far from pleased to be awoken at such a late hour to grant us a room, a generous tip turned his spirits, and he promised us a breakfast before we left. I did not mention that I hoped we would be long gone before he was awake to cook it.

We were shown up the stairs by a disgruntled maid who lit a candle in the room and wordlessly headed for the door and, no doubt, her bed. I stopped her just before she could leave and pressed a coin into her hand for her troubles. The notion seemed to surprise her, but she nodded a shallow curtsey and wished me a good night.

I was going to need to start curbing the instinct to be generous. As bad as I felt inconveniencing people, my pin money was not an unlimited fund. My purse already felt a little lighter, and this was now all the money I had in the world. Until we could find a way to earn more, we needed to rely on it for our shelter, our transport, and our sustenance. For now, however, I would have paid every penny I had for a handful of hours in Kitty's company.

Ducking to return the purse to my valise, I turned to find Kitty with her ear against the door. When she was convinced that the maid who had shown us to the room was gone, she slid across the lock, testing the doorknob to ensure it held firm. I knew it was a sensible idea. We were two young women staying alone in an unfamiliar place with any number of potentially unsavoury characters just rooms away. Yet it still felt significant. Deliberate. Satisfied with the security of the door, Kitty turned, resting back against the door with pious innocence on her face.

"If we've learnt anything, it's that there is no

friend to vice quite as firm as a locked door," she said.

I felt my cheeks heat up with a violent blush, but I couldn't argue with her words. More than enough people had interrupted me when I'd been seeking a moment alone with a pretty girl.

For someone who had been fighting sleep in the carriage, Kitty was now very awake. I reached for her automatically, wanting her close after the distance that had been between us. And she had no protests, crawling onto the bed next to me and wriggling close until her body was pressed against the side of mine. I thought she was going to kiss my lips, but instead she dropped her kiss to the tip of my nose, then the space between my eyebrows, then my temple.

"Kitty!" I tried to stifle my laughter as she pressed further kisses across my cheeks and forehead.

"Yes?" she asked angelically.

There was so much I wanted to say to her, and I had no idea where to start, so instead I just reached for her and pulled her into an embrace, hiding my face against the curve of her neck. It was the calmest I'd felt in weeks, and I knew I'd be able to fall asleep within moments the second

I let myself go, but I could feel how restless Kitty still was. I nudged her gently in the ribs to prompt her to share what was on her mind. If she wanted to go back to her family, I'd understand.

"If one of us were a man, we could go to Gretna Green," Kitty said with a heavy sigh.

It thrilled me to know she had desires to marry me, but shot me through the heart with a reminder that we would never get that chance.

"If one of us were a man, we would not be running in the first place," I reminded her.

"True," she allowed. "Although I am glad neither of us is a man. I think you might not love me if I were, and I love you most exactly as you are."

"Oh, and what am I?" I teased.

She tickled my waist for my impertinence at seeking compliments, easily overpowering my half-hearted attempts to push her fingers away. When we had both had our fill of giggles and breathless protests, she collapsed beside me, studying me carefully in the candlelight.

"Quiet brilliance," she said, sweeping an escaping curl behind my ear. "That's what you are, George."

I blushed, but did not argue. It seemed far more important to return the sentiment.

"And you are bold adventure," I whispered, kissing her softly.

I wrapped my arm around her waist and pulled her in, feeling her relax as she settled her cheek against my shoulder and breathed against my neck. It almost didn't matter where we were going the next morning, as long as she was with me. But if we wanted any kind of real freedom, we needed to be beyond the reach of our families. We needed a plan.

The moment we were in was perfect, but the future would sneak up on us whether we liked it or not, and it was wise to be prepared. Especially since it wasn't going to be easy.

I knew how I wanted it to look. Kitty and me living together, unburdened and unbothered, the picture of the marriage we could never truly have. I knew of only one couple who had achieved it, and for that they seemed almost mythical to me. Only they weren't. They were real and alive and, according to Charlotte, used to visitors.

"Kitty, those atlases you read—have you ever noted Llangollen?" I asked, sitting up straight so quickly she fell against the pillow with an indignant whine.

She pushed herself up to look at me, seemingly sceptical of my mental state.

"It's in Wales," she said, a little wary. "Why?"

I told her everything I knew about Eleanor Butler and Sarah Ponsonby. It was woefully little, but even what I could recall from that morning in Charlotte's parlour lit a fire in Kitty's eyes, one stoked by hope.

"Maybe that's where we should go. Llangollen," I finished. "We could ask them how they have managed it. Even if we go abroad it will still not be easy, so I think we might be in much need of their advice."

Kitty grinned, taking my hands and squeezing tight.

"I have never been to Wales," she said, "but I am very glad to be going with you."

That settled it, then.

I fell asleep with the potential for a future worth living warm and secure in my heart. With Kitty tucked beside me, her breath against my neck and her fingers hooked around mine, I struggled to think of a single regret.

We left before the sun had even started to rise. I was keen to put as much distance between us and

Longbourn as possible, especially with a destination in mind. Kitty's knowledge of the country's geography came in useful as we secured ourselves passage to Llangollen. Thankfully it came at a price less than the coins I had in my purse, but only just.

I had plenty of questions for the Ladies of Llangollen, but near the top of the list was money—how did they afford their life together when no one was willing to pay a woman what they paid a man, or even let them do the same work? It was the biggest barrier to having the future I wanted, and I was hoping they could share their secrets.

We boarded a Royal Mail coach with four other passengers, who mercifully seemed to have little interest in us. An older woman and her male servant spoke neither a word to each other, nor to anyone else. The other couple seemed to be a husband and wife, perhaps newly married. They were cheerful and talkative, but were interested only in each other. I watched the woman embroider a handkerchief, her face pinching when a rocky turn in the road caused her needle to slip and prick her skin. Regardless of the less-than-ideal situation, she made quick work of a delicate, scrolling pattern as a monogram took shape beneath her fingers.

"I don't know how to embroider," I whispered to Kitty. "At least, not well."

She turned to look at me, confusion heavy in her eyes, before the corner of her lip quirked up.

"It's good to know you're not perfect," she said with a grin. "Why do you mention it?"

"No, I mean...I cannot neatly mend clothing or embroider linens."

"You think I care about embroidered linens?" Kitty asked. "I ran away with you in the middle of the night, without a linen or a handkerchief or even a needle in my bag. I care about *you*, George. And if we suddenly find ourselves in dire need of embroidery or mending, I think you will find me quite adept with the skill."

It had not occurred to me that my deficiencies would be solved with Kitty's talents, even though it should have done. She matched me perfectly. I told her as much in a low whisper, careful that the words not be overheard by any of the other passengers, and I knew from the look in her eyes that she wanted to kiss me. It was undeniably an expression mirrored in my own features, but it was too dangerous a risk. Instead Kitty reached for my fingers and looped them with her own, hiding them within the tucks and folds of our skirts. That was as good as we could get until we found ourselves another locked door.

The Royal Mail coaches took us as far as Llangollen, changing horses and speeding away as we were left staring up at hills carpeted with thick forests. Buildings were few and far between, all in the shadow of the ruins of a once large building clinging to the tallest peak. Dark and ominous, it stood in a bleak reminder of whatever had felled it. I shifted closer to Kitty, unsettled by the feelings of stepping into one of my books. None of them ever ended well for people like us, after all.

Llangollen's coaching inn was nothing ornate, but seemed respectable enough. A room there would no doubt be beyond the few coins I had left in the bottom of my purse, so it was all I could do to hope that the ladies Charlotte had spoken of would be kind enough to let us stay, at least for one night. I quashed every fear I had of them slamming the door in our face and channelled the anxious energy bouncing around inside me into something useful. The boy who had helped turn over the horses had walked them around behind the inn and, before I could stop myself, I hurried after him with Kitty in tow.

"Excuse me," I called as soon as I saw him across the yard, brushing down one of the horses. "Do you know this town well?"

The ostler raised one eyebrow in surprise at the sight of two young women who had both forgotten to pack a hairbrush and were in desperate need of a good night's sleep, but he didn't stop what he was doing.

"You could say that, miss. Lived here my whole life."

The rhythmic sweep of the currycomb across the horse's back was an accompaniment to the lilt of his accent, a strong Welsh tone that I'd never heard so prominently before. I should have expected it, but the notion of how far we'd truly travelled struck me silent long enough for the ostler to clear his throat.

"Can I help you with something?"

Silently pleading he wasn't going to ask for money in exchange for information, I nodded.

"Do you know of Lady Eleanor Butler and Miss Sarah Ponsonby?" I asked.

It didn't take a verbal response to convey his answer. Both his eyebrows raised this time as he looked between Kitty and me, sceptical and appraising. I tried my best to give nothing away, glad I had not given in to the urge to hold Kitty's hand. Clenching my jaw and squaring my shoulders, I stared back at him, daring him to accuse us of something. Thankfully he seemed to think better of it.

"Aye, I know of them," he said.

"We don't have any money." Kitty stepped up beside me. "We can't pay you. We just... have come a long way."

Every word of it was honest, but it was still a risk to say it. She wasn't admitting to anything, but the unspoken truth was sitting just underneath each word. We could still deny it all, but we weren't hiding like perhaps we should have been. I could guess where Kitty's courage came from, because I felt it, too. No one knew us here. We weren't a Darcy and a Bennet to this boy; we were just two wayward girls out of their depth.

The ostler took too long to consider his

options, still brushing out the horse's coat as he looked at us the way I looked at a chessboard. Deciding we would be best off seeking help elsewhere, I turned and grabbed Kitty's arm, ready to hurry both of us away before he could form too accurate a mental picture and get us into trouble.

"Wait," he called before we could get more than a few feet. "You go off walking ling-di-long, and you'll end up at the castle before you find Plas Newydd."

I ignored the first of the expressions I didn't understand in favour of the second.

"Before we find where?" I asked, unable to keep the excitement out of my voice.

With a long-suffering sigh, the ostler finally put down the comb and stepped away from the horse with a soft pat to the side of its neck. He ushered us to the road the coach had travelled and pointed out the route we needed to take to get where we wanted to go. Plas Newydd, home of the Ladies of Llangollen. Once we'd repeated the directions back to him and he seemed happy he wasn't sending us off to go missing in the Welsh countryside, he nodded approvingly.

"Don't get lost," he ordered. "And tell Sioned that Llew sends his regards."

Not wanting to test the limits of his patience, I didn't ask who Sioned was. Instead Kitty and I both thanked him as effusively as we were able, but Llew seemed more interested in returning to the horses than in listening to what we had to say. He waved us off with a faraway goodbye and headed back into the yard, leaving just Kitty and me and the road ahead. From his directions, it wasn't far. I turned to her, my smile shaky but genuine.

"Shall we?" I asked.

She laced her fingers with mine, and we took the first step together.

Chapter Twenty-Three

Plas Newydd was like no house I'd ever seen before. It sat beyond an ornate and immaculately maintained garden, clearly someone's pride and joy, and rose up into a large white-brick cottage. Dark wooden panels adorned the walls, the kind of carvings more suited for the interior of a church than a house in rural Wales. The stained-glass panels fitted into the windows did little to assuage the grandeur.

It was almost enough to inspire me to turn around and ask Llew how long we'd have to wait for the next postal coach out of town, but we had gotten this far. I needed to see how the story ended. There was still a chance for a happy ending, and I wasn't willing to sacrifice it until I had tried my very best to hunt it out.

"Ready?" Kitty asked.

"I think so," I whispered back, half afraid we were already being watched from the other side of those elaborate windows.

We wove our way down the garden paths until we reached the front door. Kitty went to pull her hand away from mine, but I held firm. If there was one doorstep we could grace hand in hand, it was this one, and I wanted to take the opportunity while we could. Our entire future was reliant on being honest about who we were and why we were there. With my other hand, I reached up and rapped the door knocker against a door that matched the rest of the ecclesiastical woodwork.

My heart sat in my mouth as we waited for a response, leaving no room for words. I gripped Kitty's hand so tightly I felt the strain in my fingers, but I couldn't let go. She was too important.

Eventually, the door swung open to reveal a short woman with her hair tucked up into a white cap. A faded apron covered a much-mended dress. This was Sioned—I didn't need to wait to be told. The resemblance to the young ostler was clear.

"Good evening, ma'am," I said with a shallow curtsey, aware the sun was fast starting to set. "Llew sends his regards," I offered before she could greet us, hoping the name would encourage a little kindness.

Scepticism ran in the family as strongly as sharp chins and grey eyes. Just as Llew had, Sioned raised an eyebrow.

"And how'd you know my little brother? What trouble's he been getting himself into now?" she asked, her accent just as strong.

"He only gave us directions," Kitty explained. "We were hoping it would be possible to see Lady Butler and Miss Ponsonby?"

She stepped a little closer to me, her skirts brushing against mine. The movement drew Sioned's attention to our interlocked hands, and she sighed, the sound soft and affectionate.

"Come in," she said, stepping aside to usher us into a cosy hall, dark wood panelling on every wall. "With those accents, you've come a long way."

She led us down a corridor lined with more

of the intricate carvings, similar to those outside. They'd been affixed to the wall in a sort of patchwork, leaving no bare space uncovered. Unable to stop myself, I reached out and ran my fingertips over the topography of the ridges and valleys. They seemed to tell stories, cracked and gouged and clearly on at least their second life, but still beautiful.

Sioned stopped in front of a door that almost blended into the panelling and knocked. At the approval of a distant voice inside, she showed us into a library that could rival Pemberley's. Shelves covered every inch of the walls, with books lined up in rows and then crammed into every other available space. I couldn't help my gasp, too focused on the literature to note the woman sitting in an armchair beside a crackling fire until she started talking.

"I was not aware we were expecting guests," she said, setting aside a book and getting to her feet.

I thought it likely she was at least seventy, but she wore her age too well for it to be easy to pinpoint. Her hair was powdered and arranged in a style long out of fashion, and her black riding habit seemed an odd outfit for an evening reading beside the fire, but it suited her. Despite her confusion, her face was welcoming, more inquisitive than angry at the disturbance.

When I had planned this all out in my head, I had never quite gotten this far, or ventured into so much detail as how I would explain our predicament to the Ladies of Llangollen. Panicking only slightly, I dipped into the deepest curtsey I'd ever managed, pulling Kitty down with me by virtue of her fingers still being locked with mine.

"Lady Butler, this is..." Sioned trailed off as all three of us realised Kitty and I had never actually introduced ourselves.

"Kitty Bennet, ma'am," Kitty said quickly.

"Georgiana Darcy," I added.

"Miss Bennet, Miss Darcy, this is Lady Eleanor Butler," Sioned said smoothly, settling back into her rhythm of introductions. "And Sappho."

At its name, the small black dog, sleeping so soundly in front of the fire that I hadn't even noticed it was there, raised its head. We were granted one cursory head tilt before it once again settled down to doze.

Lady Butler walked over to us, taking in the sight of her two uninvited guests. She showed no surprise or confusion at our linked hands, simply nodding at us before turning to Sioned.

"I think you'd better fetch Sarah. And bring our guests something hot and something sweet."

Five minutes later we were settled on a sofa beside the fire, each with tea and round, sultana-dotted sweet breads. Lady Butler had returned to her original chair, with Miss Ponsonby beside her. Sarah Ponsonby was perhaps ten years younger than her partner, her face showing the same signs of a happy and graceful aging, only in slightly finer lines. Sappho had settled on her feet, snoring gently as Kitty and I explained why we'd come all this way.

To start with, we were coy about it. As we told the story in tandem, we used euphemism and hints, but it soon fell apart. If we could not truthfully tell them of the predicament we were in, we had no chance of earning any useful advice to get us out of it. So I went back to the start and revealed everything, from Helena to Wickham to Kitty. London to Pemberley to Meryton to Rosings Park, and finally to Llangollen. Kitty's and my story was already well travelled, and we'd yet to even really begin.

Lady Butler and Miss Ponsonby listened as we

unloaded everything, but they said little until we reached the end. They shared a look with each other that formed a conduit for more words than I could interpret. Eventually Lady Butler set down her teacup and turned back to Kitty and me.

"You are very brave, girls," she said, her accent distinctly Irish amongst the Welsh we'd heard from Llew and Sioned. "I won't underplay the dangerous position you put yourselves in getting here, because I'm sure once you have fully let reality come back to you, you will realise that, but you ought not to forget that your courage saw you safely through. We are happy to have you visit, but I cannot help but wonder exactly what you are seeking."

Kitty and I shared a look of our own.

"I think I wanted to know you were real," I admitted softly. "A friend spoke of you, and it seemed...like a dream. This"—I gestured to the room, the couple before me, the life they'd made—"is more than I ever thought possible for someone who feels the way I do."

Lady Butler reached for Miss Ponsonby's hand, and I felt my heart grow in my chest. I wanted that. I wanted all of it. In forty years I wanted to be sitting in front of a crackling fire, surrounded by books, with Kitty's hand still in mine. And this was the first proof I'd ever had that the image in my head could happen. Tears collected in the corners of my eyes, and I discreetly tried to dab them away. Considering Miss Ponsonby reached over to hand me a handkerchief, I was not as subtle as I'd hoped.

"I will not sit here and tell you it has been easy," Lady Butler said, "but I can assure you with all certainty that every moment has been worth it."

Kitty dropped her head onto my shoulder, shuffling a little closer. We didn't need to pretend here. More tears spilt from my eyes, falling into my lap and soaking into my skirts before I could mop them off my cheeks.

"We wanted advice on how to manage all this," Kitty added. "What do you say to people? Does everyone know the truth, or do you still have to hide it? How do you make money to live off?"

"Perhaps," Miss Ponsonby said kindly, "those kinds of questions are best suited for the morning. Your trip here has not been a short one, and I don't doubt you could use the rest. I'll have

Sioned make you up a bed, and we can discuss everything you want to know tomorrow."

She left the room with Sappho at her heels, kissing Lady Butler on the cheek as she passed her chair. The exchange filled my heart so full with hope it could burst. Lady Butler watched her partner go.

"I will tell you one thing tonight, girls," she said. "The secret to this kind of happiness is to find someone who makes it all worth it. If you've done that, you are already at least halfway there."

I looked at Kitty, whose eyes were only slightly less tear-filled than mine. She kissed the back of my hand, lingering and fierce, and I knew for sure I had found someone who made it all worth it.

We slept soundly at Plas Newydd. The house was characterful and homely and full of people I felt I could trust more than any other strangers I'd ever met. Between its welcoming walls and Kitty's warm embrace, I felt none of the anxiety of inns or the coldness of Rosings. If I thought too much about the uncertainty of the future or the worry we had no doubt inspired in Darcy and Elizabeth, I knew my tranquillity would quickly fade, but I pushed it aside until birds were chirping outside the window and the sun was casting blue-and-green shapes onto the floor through the stained glass.

Breakfast was thick-cut ham and freshly baked bread, served with tea and more of the same round cakes as the night before. They weren't quite Ruth's gingerbread, but I helped myself to two, wondering how we were ever going to repay the kindness of our hosts. By the time the meal was finished I had Sappho sitting beside my chair, begging for scraps with wide, soulful eyes as if she hadn't been fed in a week. Based on her owners' affection for her, I highly doubted she'd been starved. When I managed to resist her charms she quickly moved on to Kitty, who caved within moments and sneaked her a sliver of ham. My affectionate eye roll was entirely unpreventable.

We settled in the library again after the table was cleared. It seemed to be Lady Butler and Miss Ponsonby's preferred room in the house, and I certainly could not blame them for that. It had the same atmosphere as Pemberley's library, a place that had become only more entrenched in my heart since Kitty had come into my life. The possibilities of the stories in all the books that surrounded us were rivalled only by the possibility on show in front of our very eyes.

Lady Butler and Miss Ponsonby kept their promise of answering our questions, but first they started by sharing their own story in exchange for the one Kitty and I had told the night before. Hand in hand, they told of meeting in Ireland and growing close to each other. Threats of unwanted marriages or, failing that, sequestration in a nunnery, encouraged them to leave their families. It was a familiar story.

I thought that might be it, one simple tale of fleeing Ireland and settling in Llangollen, but it had not gone quite so smoothly. Once found by their families, there were attempts to talk them out of their plans. It was only afterwards that they moved to Llangollen and eventually settled in Plas Newydd. When I heard they survived on begrudgingly given money from their families, I felt my stomach drop like stone.

It made sense there was no secret form of income they could share knowledge of, of course. I had been foolishly hoping there would be a way to replenish the money in my purse without ever needing to contact my family again. I didn't want to face them, couldn't bear the idea of Darcy hating me. Not for this. But it seemed like the only way. Charlotte had said I was one of the few people who might be able to live the way I wanted, but only because of who my family was.

"Do you think your families would support you at all?" Miss Ponsonby asked, not noticing how quiet I'd gone.

"My family has money," I admitted softly. "I just don't know if I can ask for it. My brother will be angry that I ran away, and he is the one who separated me from Kitty and sent me to an aunt who wants nothing more than to find me a husband."

Kitty's arms were around me before I could fall apart.

"He loves you," she promised me, and I desperately wanted to believe that could still be true.

"Even if he is uneasy with the life you choose, to deny you money would be to prefer to see you starve," Lady Butler said. "That is a rather extreme position for a man to take when it comes to his sister, no?"

I hid my face against Kitty's shoulder, not

wanting to face the question of to what extent I'd disappointed Darcy.

"Perhaps you should think it over for a few days," Miss Ponsonby suggested. "You are welcome to stay here while you make plans, whatever those are."

So began four idyllic days in the Welsh countryside, in the company of two women who lived a life I thought possible only in my imagination. I learnt Lady Butler had been raised in a convent in France and delighted in having lengthy conversations with her in fast French that our partners struggled to follow. Kitty took to accompanying Miss Ponsonby on long walks with Sappho, returning to regale me with tales of the Welsh hillsides and explorations of the castle ruins atop the hill. I chose to explore Plas Newydd, thrilled by the discovery of both a piano and a chessboard, which combined were enough to keep me endlessly entertained.

I preferred the library out of all the rooms available to us, but Lady Butler did, too. It took a little convincing for me to fully believe that I was welcome there even when she was already comfortably situated with a book. The quiet company as we both sat and read was a pleasant way to spend an hour.

Plas Newydd's library provided an infinite choice of new reading material, but I couldn't help but settle down on the second afternoon with *The Disposition of an English Lady*, reading over the same words I'd long since memorised and trying to find a way to reinterpret them to make it so that I hadn't broken almost every rule.

"My dear," Lady Butler said gently from across the room, "whatever on earth is in that book that's got you so upset? Is it one from our collection?"

I hadn't realised how hard I'd been biting at my lip, or how much I'd screwed up my face in my concentration. Closing the cover of the book, I fought to regain my composure before answering her.

"It was my mother's etiquette guide," I explained, stroking my thumb over the soft leather binding. Then, because I knew I ought to explain the strong response I had shown to it, I admitted, "I don't think she would approve of the woman I've become."

There was a soft thud as Lady Butler closed

her book and another as she set it down on the table.

"How young were you when you lost her?" she asked.

"Not quite two years old," I said, my throat a little tighter at having to talk about her passing.

"Then there is no sense in imagining the worst, child," she said, getting up from her chair and moving to sit beside me on the sofa. She took my hand in hers, squeezing it reassuringly. "Whatever she may have wanted for you at the age of two, it would have changed and grown as you did. Any mother with compassion wants only the best for their daughter, and I have seen you with Miss Bennet. I do not believe there could be anything better for you than that."

The corners of my smile met the tears tracking down my cheeks, but I brushed the latter away and forced a nod. There was every chance my mother would have been horrified by my actions, but that did not exclude the possibility that she might have welcomed Kitty with open arms if she'd known how much she meant to me. I could not bring my mother back and I would never know for certain, but perhaps dwelling on an imagined negativity was doing her a disservice.

"I daresay I am a little older than your mother would have been, and I know my approval is not what you're seeking, but I want you to know you have it," Lady Butler assured me. "I was educated by the church, and my family are Irish nobility, and regardless of everything I was taught, I still believe the both of us ought to be free to reside in the company of the people we love the most, and who return that affection. Do not underestimate the ability of someone to rise above prejudices they may have been taught, not when it concerns the ones they care about."

Unable to help myself, I threw my arms around Lady Butler. She was kind enough to return the embrace, squeezing me tight until I was ready to let go. I dried my eyes and looked down at the etiquette guide in my lap. The books I had been prescribed by my governesses did not capture my own thoughts, so perhaps even if my mother had been taught from it, it did not represent an accurate catalogue of her opinions. Perhaps she would not have minded the woman I had become. Perhaps she would even have been proud.

On the third evening at Plas Newydd, I found the harpsichord. It was tucked into the back corner of a drawing room that was usually ignored in favour of the library, and I lifted the lid to find the underside delicately decorated with flowers. Sitting at the bench, I let my fingers rest over the keys, not pressing down—I didn't have permission to play it—just reassured by the familiar position of my arms and my hands.

"You can play it; they wouldn't mind."

The voice from the door made me jump, my fingers landing on the keys and plucking a tuneless melody before I snatched them away. Sioned stood in the doorway, an apron tied over her dress and a dusting brush in hand.

"Sorry, I did not mean to intrude," I said, getting to my feet and shutting the lid of the instrument.

"You're not," she assured me. "The only reason it's in here is because Miss Ponsonby prefers the piano. You're as welcome to play this one as you are that."

I should not have given in as easily as I did, but I was so keen to play Kitty's melody on the instrument that suited it best that Sioned's encouragement was all it took. I gave her a grateful smile and sat myself back down, readying the instrument before the melody poured out of my fingers. It was better than I'd ever played it, smooth and confident and exactly as it sounded in my mind. Even when a hand on my shoulder made me jump halfway through. I looked over to see Kitty nudging me aside so she could join me on the bench. Glad to make room for her, I didn't break the melody as I slid along and pressed a kiss to her temple. When I finished it, she knocked her shoulder softly into mine.

"It's still beautiful," she said. "Just like its composer."

I turned my face into her hair to hide my smile, kissing the crown of her head through the curls.

"I wrote it for you," I admitted. "I started working on it before I met you, but I could never get it to sound right. And then I did meet you, and it became clear that you were what it was missing. So I rewrote it to sound like you do when you laugh or smile or talk endlessly about the Continent. It's yours."

Kitty was quiet for a long moment, long enough for me to worry that perhaps I had offended her. When I gathered together the courage to shift away and look, I found tears in her eyes. She reached for me, stopping me getting too far, and rested her forehead against mine.

"I love you so deeply I forget there was a time before I felt this way," she said, the words whispered and sacred and mine. "You are the best thing to ever happen to me."

"And you to me," I replied, kissing her softly before wrapping her into an embrace I did not intend on breaking anytime soon.

It was easy to forget this was only a temporary pause in our journey and we soon needed to move on. When everything felt so safe and so freeing, I never wanted to focus on leaving, but when we reached our fourth morning in Wales, Lady Butler joined me in the library and broached the subject as gently as she could.

"I don't wish you to think we're trying to hurry you out, but have you thought about your plans for the future?"

The question shattered my serenity. I had curled up by the fire, Darcy's old coat around my shoulders and one of Kitty's hair ribbons pulling my curls out of my face, not putting on any kind of act or obeying any kind of rules from the pages of an etiquette guide. Plas Newydd was not the kind of place where such things were necessary, but idyllic as it was within the house's walls, time outside did not stop.

I closed my book—*Candide, ou l'Optimisme* in Voltaire's original French—and gave Lady Butler my full attention. She was right that I needed to face up to reality. We had already overstayed our welcome.

"Kitty wishes to travel," I said, because I had promised her she would get to and I intended to make good on my word.

Clearly I was not as convincing to Lady Butler as I sounded to my own ears.

"And do you?" she pushed.

That was not quite so easy to answer. There was plenty to keep me occupied overseas, so many books I had no access to in England, and sites to be visited. Besides, someone had to keep Kitty out of trouble and translate for her when she tied herself in linguistic knots. Not to mention the increased level of difficulty it would bring to the notion of either of our families finding us and dragging us home. Still, something about the idea of having no true home left me uneasy.

"I would give her the world if I could, but

travelling the Continent with her seems likely to be as close as I can get," I said, deciding to focus on Kitty rather than myself.

"Certainly only one of you knows how to sit still. Do you truly want a life constantly on the move? Travelling can easily become running."

"We do not have the money for a home," I said.

"You do not have the money to travel, either," she reminded me. "Have you given some thought to contacting your brother?"

Candide was suddenly fascinating to me. I kept my gaze on the volume in my lap, tracing the edge of the binding with my thumb as I blatantly ignored the question. Lady Butler let me suffer in the silence for only a few moments before she broke it with a change of subject.

"Do you read poetry, my child?"

"I read everything," I said, grateful to be allowed to focus on books.

She got up and headed directly for a shelf near the fireplace, knowing exactly which volume she was reaching for without having to search. When she handed it over to me, I surrendered the familiar comfort of *Candide* and reached for the soft brown leather-bound book she held out. I noted the name in gold tooling down the spine: SAPPHO. Before I could ask, Lady Butler was answering.

"The dog is named after her. She was an ancient Grecian poetess, and I daresay you may find you have something in common with her inclinations."

The sparkle in her eye said everything her words did not. Instinctively, I tightened my grip on the book as if someone might take it away from me. She could not truly mean I was holding a published account of someone like us. Like a woman possessed, I frantically turned the pages, desperate to read the words inside. Lady Butler left me to it with a gentle squeeze of the shoulder, allowing me to get lost in the book.

I read the volume cover to cover, over and over again until I had memorised every word. I wanted to be sure I understood it truly and had internalised every possible interpretation of this poetry that seemed to echo in my heart. I quickly learnt it was an English translation from the original Greek, which the library sadly seemed to lack, so I appeased myself by attempting to translate the fragments back to Greek in my mind as I read, wondering exactly which words Sappho had chosen to describe how the sight of a beautiful woman left her awestruck.

I was entirely unaware how much time had passed until Lady Butler returned, but when she disturbed my reading again, the sun was beginning to set through the windows and I suddenly found myself aching from sitting in one position for too long, and my stomach twisting from the lack of a midday meal. I had noticed she was there only when she moved to stand directly in front of me, blocking the light by which I was reading.

"We have guests," she said.

I blinked for a second, taking a moment to return from Sappho's ancient Greece to modern-day Wales, but once I had readjusted I jumped up. The library was where Lady Butler and Miss Ponsonby preferred to greet people, and I was monopolising a space that wasn't mine to begin with.

"Oh! I'm so sorry; I can move. I'll just—"

"They are here to see you," she said, cutting me off. "And I would greatly advise that you speak with them, my dear. I have never seen two people so relieved to be assured of someone's well-being."

Darcy and Elizabeth. It had to be. No one else would come all this way. I hugged the book to my chest, unsure I was willing to lose everything I'd gained since arriving at Plas Newydd. I finally felt like I understood myself fully, like I truly deserved a happy ending, and I didn't know if Darcy would try to talk me out of that.

"Did you write to him?" I asked, a bitter taste of betrayal on the back of my tongue.

"No, I promise you we did not. They both seem rather frantic to see you. I don't doubt they have been looking for you from the moment you disappeared," Lady Butler explained, and I believed her.

They had come all the way to Wales. They were looking for us. Surely it would be easier to let us disappear on our own if Darcy truly meant to disown me for my sins. I had to believe that wasn't what this was.

"I have no reason to think this will go poorly," Lady Butler said, "but you have my word that, if it does, you will not be alone. We will not see either of you suffer if your families cannot even manage begrudging financial support and nothing else."

She swept me into a hug, her grip surprisingly

strong for a woman who often took a cane with her when she left the house. Her powdered hair tickled my nose, but I still clung to her for several extra moments until I felt ready to face my brother.

"Shall I have them shown in?" she asked, stepping back to look at me. I didn't even hide the fact I was hugging the volume of Sappho's poetry to my chest.

"All right," I said quietly, closing my eyes and nodding as I prepared myself for whatever was about to happen.

Chapter Twenty-Four

"Mr. and Mrs. Darcy, miss," Sioned said, introducing them with a curtsey as if this was a perfectly ordinary call.

Darcy and Elizabeth both stood in the doorway, staring at me as if they could not believe what their own eyes were showing them. It felt like years since I had seen them, so much so that it was startling for them to be looking exactly as they had when I'd left Longbourn House. I brushed my hands awkwardly over my skirts. Lady Butler has assured me she would fetch

Kitty back from her usual walk, but until then, I was alone in this.

"Good afternoon," I said weakly, unsure where else to begin.

My brother took three long strides across the room. For a moment I expected him to strike me like Lady Catherine had done for burning Kitty's letter, but instead he pulled me into a hug, crushing me tightly in his arms. I just stood there, too surprised to return the gesture.

I tried to get the words out once Darcy had stepped away, but Elizabeth swiftly took his place, wrapping me up in her own embrace just as firmly. There were ten dozen questions filed away behind their eyes, but I began talking before they could start asking them. I'd decided what I was going to say only in the moments after Lady Butler had left the room.

"I would like the money Father left for me. I won't... It will never be needed for a dowry, and I should like to have it. I plan to travel and shall need funds. You need not try to look for me." My voice was shaking, and I had to hide my hands behind my back so their trembling was less evident. "I would also like your word that Emma will be provided with assistance in locating another position. She shouldn't have to suffer because I ran away."

Elizabeth and Darcy both looked at me like they were listening but not actually hearing. It was as if they'd seen a ghost, rather than a tired, unkempt seventeen-year-old girl with no idea what was about to become of the rest of her life.

"Are you all right?" Elizabeth asked. "We went to Rosings as soon as we heard you had left, and we spoke to Charlotte. She thought you might be here."

"Yes, we are perfectly all right," I assured her.

Underneath the tiredness and unkemptness, I felt more like myself than I had in a long time. Certainly I had not been this all right since I had left Longbourn. My nerves at having to stand before them both and wait for judgement would fade, and I would be left with a lifetime with Kitty, and nothing could be more right than that.

"We?" Elizabeth asked.

Her confusion made it clear they thought I was alone. If they'd left Pemberley as soon as they received word from Rosings, they would have missed any subsequent message from Longbourn. They didn't even know Kitty had left home.

"Kitty is here," I explained. "She is safe, I promise. Only out for a walk. They have gone to fetch her back."

Elizabeth's eyes went wide as she raced through several emotions in quick succession, from fear to worry to relief. Her experience with Lydia's abscondence with the intention of marrying Wickham had no doubt left her practised in the art of sisterly concern.

Darcy opened his mouth but closed it before any words could come out, his teeth clicking together. I wasn't sure if there was anger amongst the emotions in his eyes, all of them too muddled to tease apart. Once he did find the words, they rushed out in a series of questions, each one latching on to the coattails of the one before it.

"Why did you run? You cannot be serious in meaning to leave again? When will you return?"

Each one was a barely restrained demand, but I knew he wouldn't like my true response to any of them. In an attempt to reduce his anger, I opted to answer only one.

"I'm not sure it would be wise for me to ever return," I said quietly, focusing on the books on the shelves behind him so I didn't need to meet his eyes. Even so, I heard Elizabeth's quick intake of breath. Darcy remained completely silent. "It is for the best," I tried to explain. "I am in love with Catherine Bennet."

I risked raising my gaze and found Elizabeth smiling softly at me, seemingly proud and almost encouraging. It was perhaps the closest I would come to earning the blessing of Kitty's family. Darcy was not smiling. His brow was furrowed in deep concentration as if he couldn't find a way to reconcile what I was telling him with how he understood the world to be.

"As I understand it, women often form close female friendships. It's—"

"No," I said, cutting him off. I would not let him explain this away in the most palatable way. "I feel it here." I put my hand over my heart. I didn't tell him how every word ever written about love paled in comparison with the way Kitty's smile made my whole chest contract, but I hoped he could still at least try to understand.

"It is Kitty you plan to... travel with?" Elizabeth asked tentatively.

Before I could speak for her, Kitty's voice sounded in the doorway.

"Yes," she said, stepping into the room.

I could not blame her for joining the conversation as soon as she'd arrived. It was never enjoyable to listen to people speak about you without being able to add your own voice.

Elizabeth rushed across the room to drag Kitty into a tight embrace.

"I cannot believe you thought this was a good idea," Elizabeth chastised, pulling away to look her younger sister in the eyes like she was a disobedient child. "After what Lydia put us all through. With Father still recovering!"

"I left a letter," Kitty said, her voice meek as if she was well aware what a weak comfort that would be for her parents when they found her gone. She ducked her head, clearly feeling shame.

I fervently hoped Elizabeth had not talked her out of our plans. I would not stop Kitty from going home, but I was certain that, if she did, she would not be permitted to leave again to go gallivanting across the Continent with me. Even if her parents did not know the depth of our feelings for each other, we were still intending to hop from country to country with little regard for the proper way of things, completely unchaperoned.

Kitty wrung her fingers together, a little

overwhelmed by the attention. She crossed the room to stand close to me and tucked one of her hands behind her back. The request evident, I took it in my own and squeezed, letting her know I would not let go. If Elizabeth or Darcy noticed, neither of them mentioned it.

"Have you thought this through, Georgiana? This is not... It's not like you," Darcy said.

I held my head high. "This is what I want," I promised him, certain. "I will not lie about who I am anymore."

"What if we found you a husband who was prepared to... look the other way? You need some kind of stability, and there are no guarantees I will be here to protect you forever," Darcy said. I could tell he was attempting to reason with me, but I was not much in favour of changing my mind.

"I don't want a husband," I said, fiercely enough that I hoped he would see how unwavering I was on the matter. I had seen the life Charlotte lived and, while she made it work as best she could, I knew I wasn't that strong. The lie would eat me alive, and she'd been right—I had another option. I had seen it with my own eyes, and I wanted nothing else.

"I don't care if it's more difficult or if people disapprove or that I can never properly marry Kitty," I insisted. "I'm willing to leave, to go to another country if that's what it takes. I have no desire to bring shame on our family, but I will not live a lie. If you grant me my money, I will settle as far away from Pemberley, and London, as I can. You need not ever hear from me again. There is no need to send me away like you did Frances. I'll do it myself."

"Frances?" Darcy asked, his brow furrowed with confusion.

The name that was constantly in my thoughts meant nothing to him. My jaw tightened, anger coursing through me on her behalf.

"Our chambermaid. You sent her away when she was caught with a maid from another household. It was the first thing you did, after Father died. Even before his funeral," I explained, forcing him to remember.

Darcy clearly struggled to grasp at a memory I would never be able to forget, but I watched realisation take over his features, and he latched on to it. He shook his head and I waited for his excuses, but they weren't quite what I expected.

"No, I... It was the last thing Father did. He

gave the order before he died and... I let it happen. I regretted it then, if you'll believe me, and I regret it much more so now, but I was newly head of the family and had so much to worry about, and even through the veil of death, I didn't know how to argue with our father," he said, his head bowed. "I apologise."

I was not the one his apology should have been directed to, and there was no telling what had become of Frances in the five years since she'd been sent away. Still, I accepted his words with a nod, knowing he intended them to excuse not the action of expelling Frances from Pemberley, but for the years of doubt it had grown in me.

"It has been plaguing me for years," I told him, because he had to know.

Darcy's eyes creased with sadness, aging him five years instantly. I refocused on the floor, hating to see that I'd upset him. The wood grain of the floorboards was starting to go blurry in my vision when Elizabeth spoke up, her words aimed at Darcy.

"If you lose her like this, you are the only one who will carry the blame," she said. "I will not forgive you."

She crossed her arms and fixed my brother

with a stare, and I had never loved her more. I knew without question that her support wasn't only because it was her sister I loved. She would have done the same thing regardless of who had captured my heart.

Darcy looked away from his wife's gaze and towards the door. For a moment I thought he was inclined to walk out of it but, after a second to gather himself and clench his jaw, he managed a stiff nod to Elizabeth. Then he turned to me.

"Forgive me; I cannot help but be protective of you, after everything that has happened," he said. His words seemed oddly heavy, like emotion was weighing them down and making them harder to get out. "I suppose it is time I acknowledge you are no longer a child and that my protection is, perhaps, unwarranted."

The hope building in my throat threatened to choke me, and Kitty's grip on my hand was degrees away from crushing bones. I squeezed back just as tightly. The contact kept me tethered as Darcy continued to talk.

"I regret that I cannot make life easier for you, but there are, of course, certain things I have no power over. I cannot change the law, nor do I have any sway over what constitutes customary practise in wider society. But within Pemberley's walls, you need not ever know fear. It is your home, Georgiana. That has not and will not change."

"And Kitty?" I asked, my heart threatening to beat out of my chest.

Darcy turned his attention to her, and I felt her recoil against my side, but there was no animosity in his eyes. Instead he seemed wary, looking at her like he was sizing up her worth. For all my instincts to stand in front of Kitty, it was exactly how Darcy would have assessed a potential suitor. Silently, I dared him to say anything about how she had no money of her own and no prospects to come into any. He had married her sister and could not claim he was anything other than perfectly happy with that arrangement.

"Miss Bennet is welcome at Pemberley whenever she likes, so long as you are happy to receive her. You may, of course, also visit her in Meryton. If the two of you are still…" He appeared to struggle for the right phrasing, but quickly clutched at something. "Committed to each other in a year or so, we can consider a more permanent arrangement. You are still young, Georgiana, even if you are not the child you once were. I just want you to come home."

I let go of Kitty's hand to surge forwards and throw my arms around my brother, resisting the urge to cry into his shirt. He startled for a second but reached up to pat my back.

"I was so worried about you," he muttered, so low I likely wasn't even meant to hear it. Then, a little louder: "I apologise for sending you to Rosings. I truly believed it was the safest place for you, in light of the predicament with Wickham. It was a decision made in panic, and I knew Lady Catherine would never have allowed him near you. I was trying to buy some time. It was never meant to be a punishment, but Elizabeth has talked some sense into me, and I can see that it may have come across as one. It was my mistake."

I hugged him tighter, turning my head to offer Elizabeth my thanks for her support. When I saw she was preoccupied, brushing away Kitty's tears and sharing her smile, I fought back my own grin. I knew how much it meant to Kitty to have her family's approval, even if she pretended it didn't. As soon as she stepped away, I gave Elizabeth a hug of my own.

"I'm sorry I could not stop you ending up there in the first place," she whispered.

I shook my head, unwilling to accept an apology that wasn't necessary. "You have done so much. Thank you."

While Elizabeth and I embraced, Darcy and Kitty stood awkwardly. I stepped away and retook my place at Kitty's side.

"Would you be all right with settling at Pemberley?" I asked her. "I know you want to see the world."

"I do want to travel," she admitted, "but I am more than happy to have somewhere to call home, too. And I know you love it there. It is hard to travel with a piano."

I laughed, tears in my eyes, and just had to kiss her cheek. Had we been without audience, it would have been her lips. She would still get to see the world, I would make sure of it, but we would be travelling rather than running.

Trying hard not to watch us, Elizabeth gripped Darcy's arm tightly enough to relay a clear message. He cleared his throat and straightened his spine.

"It is good to see you safe, Miss Bennet," he said formally with a single, curt nod.

It was the kind of acknowledgement a man would give his sister's suitor, even if it could have been delivered with significantly more warmth. He was trying, and I loved him for it.

Kitty's response was carefully considered, taking a few moments longer than an instinctive reply. She lifted her own chin so her posture was just as formal, and held out her hand. It was a bold gesture, one usually only shared between men of the same standing, and my brother would have had every right to refuse. Instead he took her hand, almost successful in masking his amusement.

"Thank you, Mr. Darcy." Kitty shook his hand with a little bob of a curtsey she had learnt too thoroughly to omit.

"I hope you will treat my sister with the courtesy and respect she deserves," Darcy said. "She means a great deal to me."

"And to me," Kitty said boldly, squaring her jaw and tilting up her chin even higher. "I trusted you with my sister, Mr. Darcy. Perhaps you could trust me with yours."

Elizabeth was hiding her grin about as well as I was, biting down hard on her lower lip. My brother raised an eyebrow, no doubt surprised by

Kitty's audacity, but I caught the slightest quirk at the corner of his mouth.

"Duly noted," he said, inclining his head to her before turning his attention back to include me. "The two of you should also know that you have nothing to fear from George Wickham."

For a moment, my veins ran cold and my eyes went wide. He said it with such certainty that I had to look to Elizabeth for confirmation that there was no blood on my brother's hands. That she was still willing to hold one in her own eased my fears a little, as did her small smile and shake of the head.

"How so?" I asked, still tentative.

"I have reached an agreement with him. It was what delayed me writing to you to call you back to Pemberley. I wanted to be sure I could offer you true safety. For every year he makes no attempt to see you, speak to you, or speak of you, I will pay him a small sum, granted only at the close of that year. A fee for good behaviour, to ensure upon it, rather than a bribe he can run away with," Darcy explained.

It was not a settlement I could really argue with, but neither was it one I particularly liked.

"You should not have to pay him!" Kitty

protested, echoing my own thoughts. "We have not done anything wrong."

"No," Darcy agreed. "You have not. But no cost is too great to buy your safety, and if this is the price for him to truly leave you both alone, then I will gladly pay it without complaint. I make no promises regarding my actions if he fails to keep his word, however."

His voice was dark, and I shuddered at the implication. I hoped it would never come to that but, while I truly hated the idea of violence on my behalf, I was encouraged by the notion that my brother still wished to protect me.

"Now, if you'll excuse us for a minute, I believe I ought to beg some writing material from your kind hostesses so we can send some letters to explain where the two of you got to, before we end up with a search party trying to track you down," he said.

The second he and Elizabeth left the library, I slumped down into a chair, my legs unable to hold me up for much longer. His talk of letter writing had me keen to write my own letters to Charlotte, to explain where I had gone and share stories of Llangollen, and to my cousin, to express my gratitude for letting me leave, but they would have to wait. I was too preoccupied with the realisation that I would get to see Pemberley again. I could beg gingerbread off Ruth and tell Emma of my wild adventures. I could play my harp and my piano and blow the dust off my chess set. I could choose a book from the library and settle down to read with Kitty's head resting in my lap. I had told myself I'd never see the house again, and I needed to undo every single one of the goodbyes I'd said to it in my mind.

"George?" Kitty said, skimming her fingers over my cheek to draw my attention up to her. "Is everything all right?"

I surged up to pull her into a hug, then kissed her without a hint of hesitation. I was so giddy I felt I could explode with it, and I spun her around, the soles of her shoes barely skimming the floorboards.

"Put me down!" She laughed, both her hands on my cheeks as she kissed me back.

Even when I stopped bearing any of her weight, she still swayed against me, clinging to me. Although I was now safe in the knowledge no one would ever make me let go of her, I still struggled to do it willingly. Kitty Bennet was born to stand in my embrace and I in hers. It felt like we had finally righted an imbalance in the universe. From the look of absolute wonder in Kitty's eyes, she felt it, too.

Epilogue

Open books covered the library floor, a patchwork of texts and images that Kitty was poring over. She flitted from one volume to the next, pulling the smaller books into her lap as she interrogated the pages for information, as if she hadn't read them all dozens of times already during the five months she'd officially called Pemberley home.

"Do you think we can visit Greece?" she asked, looking up from a map she'd folded out of an atlas.

"I think we can visit Greece next time," I said with a laugh.

In order to stay out of the way of Kitty's apparent plan to open every travel-related book within Pemberley's library, I'd settled myself on one of the armchairs with a battered copy of *Robinson Crusoe*. Exchanging the atlas for a book of watercolour landscapes, she picked her way across the sea of paper and climbed unceremoniously into my lap. I protested, sacrificing my place in my novel in order to keep ahold of her, but couldn't keep the fondness out of my complaints.

"Look how beautiful it is," she said, gesturing down to the image in the book.

"Extremely beautiful," I agreed, not looking away from her face as I tucked a curl behind her ear, "but we're only going as far as Switzerland. It's a two-month trip, love. If we go to Greece, we'll miss the birth of our niece or nephew."

Kitty huffed, resting her head on my shoulder. We'd been over our travel plans countless times, but her excitement still got the better of her. This trip was a short one, planned to take us back to Llangollen for a visit, and then to give Kitty a taste of the Continent. We were due back before Elizabeth gave birth. A proper journey could come later—if Kitty wanted to go to Greece, I'd take her there.

"Elizabeth and Jane are making me look bad," Kitty said with a sigh. "Married to successful men and now Lizzy's going to be a mother. At least Mary's still at home, or I don't think I'd ever hear the end of it."

I pressed my lips to her temple in a silent reassurance. She promised me that her future featured me and only me, that she'd never marry regardless of how much her mother might insist, but I knew she wasn't quite like me. She could love a man. The fact she chose to stay with me in the face of her family's potential disapproval was a blessing I did not take lightly.

"Considering Mary still assures me in her letters that she can dream up no worse torture than receiving suitors, I daresay you're safe for a little longer," I said.

Since returning to Pemberley, I'd found myself with more than a few new letter-writing commitments. My letters to Mary had begun rather formally, but now I wrote to her as easily as if she were my own sister, exchanging book recommendations and chess tips between Pemberley and Longbourn. I had started writing to

Charlotte immediately, filling page after page with details of Plas Newydd and its inhabitants.

Lady Catherine had firmly decided that my brother and I were beyond help, and other than a lengthy letter to Darcy detailing my failings, it seemed perhaps we were both finally free of her. Still, I sent Charlotte letters for Anne, trusting her to pass them on without my aunt getting the chance to read them.

Obviously keen to forge a connection with the Salter family, Lady Catherine had apparently presented her own daughter as an alternative bride. Anne confided in me that she'd never before pretended to be as weak and sickly as when she first met Lord Salter as a suitor. He had never returned. The letters were more contact than I'd had with Anne for years, but she was far more agreeable than her mother and, amid our lengthy exchanges, I could see the beginning of a shy friendship.

Then there were, of course, letters to Lady Butler and Miss Ponsonby, in which I still expressed my gratitude and appreciation for their kindness, and assured them of my brother's continued support of Kitty and me.

The most important letters, however, were

those I was sending all over the country, trying, perhaps in vain, to find Frances. With Darcy's help, I was attempting to track her down to confirm that she was safe. If she needed money, he had promised we could provide it. If she still wanted a job after all these years, she was welcome back. I had gotten far enough to know she was not welcome with her family anymore, but there were still leads to exhaust, and I would not let the matter rest until I had followed each and every one. I desperately hoped she had built herself a comfortable life alongside the girl with whom she'd been caught.

Kitty kissed my jaw, trailing her fingertip over the inside of my elbow to spark shivers up and down my arm. She knew how best to try to talk me into something.

"It will be hard for Mother to play matchmaker if I'm in Greece."

There was a tone of sweet persuasion to Kitty's voice, her eyes sparking with hope. If we hadn't already promised Elizabeth and Darcy we'd be there to help them with their newborn child, it would have been all too easy to give in.

"Next time," I assured her. "We can spend as much time in Greece as you like."

"You know," Kitty began, innocently, "Sappho was Greek."

I felt myself blush, even though I had been the one to show Kitty the scraps of her poetry that survived. A well-loved copy had been delivered courtesy of one Charlotte Collins after I'd told her all about Llangollen in my letters, and Elizabeth had ensured it was rebound in a deep red leather and gilded with silver foil. I'd only ever treasured one book quite as much in my life, and I kept it next to *The Disposition of an English Lady* in the drawer beside my bed.

I'd let Kitty read the English translations herself, and recited her the original Greek. It felt like the closest I might ever get to seeing a published account of how it felt. How I felt. There were those who tried to argue Sappho felt no love for women, but I understood what I read. The original texts, free from any translator's attempts to adjust the meaning, did not lie.

"I am aware," I said, tracing my thumb over Kitty's cheekbone. "Is that why you want to go to Greece?"

"I want to go everywhere," Kitty whispered, "as long as it's with you."

She turned her face to kiss my palm, and

when she looked back at me, she had made her eyes wide and pleading. I braced myself for what I knew was coming.

"Speaking of places we could go together, Elizabeth and Darcy are holding a ball tonight," she said, as if anyone in the house had spoken of anything else in the past few days. The request for my attendance was unspoken but so blatant I could not ignore it.

"Kitty…" I sighed, resting my head against her shoulder.

We had the freedom to be ourselves at Pemberley under normal circumstances, but we couldn't do that when it was full of other people. No matter how supportive Elizabeth and Darcy were, there was no guarantee their friends would grant us the same courtesy. Everything had changed, but at the same time nothing had changed. I still could not be Kitty's partner in public.

"Please? It's no fun at all without you," Kitty begged, and it was so hard to argue with her when she was pressing kisses to my hair and running her fingers up and down my arm. I wasn't even sure she knew what exactly she was doing. "Besides, it will be the last one before we leave, so whatever happens, we can escape to the

Continent afterwards. And I promise to keep you away from any walls you could fall off."

I couldn't help my burst of laughter. "Okay," I relented. "I'll go."

At least it meant an evening of seeing Kitty happy. She leant forwards to press her lips to my temple, then trailed kisses down across my cheekbone. I let my eyes flutter closed, still giddy with the fact we could do this in the middle of the day, in a communal area of the house.

When Kitty moved to kiss my smiling lips, she shifted in my lap and I felt the book of Grecian landscapes slide over her skirts, heading for the floor. Before it could bounce onto the hardwood and destroy its spine, I grabbed it and tucked it beside *Robinson Crusoe* where it was safe. She was lucky I loved her more than books.

Despite Emma's skilled needlework and best attempts, there had been no saving my pink dress after its unfortunate encounter with the garden wall. When I told her I would be going to the ball that evening after all, I expected to be wearing an older dress that had been languishing in a chest with no events to be seen at. I hadn't minded the idea, but instead Emma's smile had been knowing and indulgent.

"I think I have just the thing for you to wear," she said, evidently part of a conspiracy.

The dress she retrieved was a soft lilac, with embroidered white vines trailing around the hem. It had more of the old Grecian style that most dresses were starting to move away from, but the colour was subtle and romantic, just far enough away from white for it not to be seen as outdated.

"Whose dress is this?" I asked. I hadn't bought a new one in months, not since before I met Kitty.

"Yours," Emma admitted. "I told Mr. Darcy that I couldn't mend the one that got damaged, and he insisted it was to be replaced. The design was mostly Mrs. Darcy's input. They wanted it to be kept a secret until you felt ready to go to a ball, so you wouldn't feel you had to go just to wear it."

"It's beautiful," I said. It was understated and quiet, but elegant enough to give me that extra spark of confidence I needed to walk into a room full of veritable strangers.

"And I do believe I have the perfect feather in a matching shade of—"

"No!" I laughed. "Still no feathers."

Emma held up her hands in defeat, before ushering me over to sit down so she could start attempting to persuade my hair into respectability. She smiled at me in the mirror, squeezing my shoulder.

"Miss Bennet won't be able to take her eyes off you," she whispered.

I ducked my head so I didn't have to watch my cheeks flush. I still wasn't used to anyone being so openly approving of my relationship with Kitty. Emma had taken it all in her stride when I had told her the entire story, and she had become one of my most enthusiastic supporters. If she hadn't, I suspected my brother might have seen to it that she was seeking new employment.

Emma's work was, as always, perfect. My hair was tamed and out of the way; my cheeks and lips were darkened with just enough rouge to make someone doubt themselves if they thought it was there, but enough to bring colour to my face. She was meticulously twisting a curl back into place when someone knocked on the door. I expected Elizabeth to be standing there, or perhaps Kitty.

Instead, when Emma swung open the door, my brother waited in the doorway.

"Some of the guests have started to arrive," he said. "If you're ready to go downstairs, I thought you may be desirous of an escort. I am told I have rather a repellent effect on presumptuous men wishing to try their luck with my sister."

My reply came almost too fast. "Yes. Please."

No doubt my latent fear was clear to Darcy, but he was good enough not to mention it directly. Instead he waited patiently while Emma fussed with my dress, brushing off invisible pieces of fluff and rearranging the drapes of my skirt as if I wouldn't disturb them with the first step I took. Eventually she squeezed my hands and took a step back.

"Come back safe tonight," she ordered, as if I weren't simply going downstairs in my own house. There was something serious in her eyes.

"She will," Darcy said, both firm and reassuring. "I'll make sure of it."

Considering the outcomes of the last two balls I'd attended, the level of concern from them both seemed fair.

Darcy held out his arm, and I gratefully took it, holding on just a little too tight.

"No one will say a word to you that you don't want to hear," he assured me as he led me through Pemberley's corridors. "This is your home, and you are safe here."

They were such simple words, but they still meant so much, even though he'd been taking the opportunity to say them as often as possible. I relaxed my grip on Darcy's arm, not wanting to repay him by cutting off the circulation to his hand. I focused on his words as the noise of the ball got louder.

Everything was very much the same as at the last ball I'd attended at Pemberley, before my whole life had changed. The same musicians in the corner, the same guests, the same reassuring smile from Elizabeth as she hurried over the moment she saw us enter the room. The same Kitty, beaming to see me and shining in a light green dress. She rushed past Elizabeth, taking my hand as soon as she was close enough.

"You look beautiful," she said, her eyes not leaving mine.

Darcy cleared his throat, and Kitty took half a step back so she could look up at him. There was no fear in her eyes as she nodded her head respectfully in greeting.

"I'll look after her," she promised him.

Darcy smiled. "I know. If you want to leave, then you need not feel like you have to stay for the benefit of Elizabeth and me, but go upstairs rather than outside this time, please."

He let go of my arm and I quickly took Kitty's, my gloves sliding over the bare skin of the crook of her elbow. Her skirts brushed against mine. It was easy to forget the rest of the room was even there, but Elizabeth started talking to me and I had to wrench my gaze from her sister to have any hope of listening.

"I'm glad the dress suits you," Elizabeth said, taking my place at Darcy's side. "You look lovely."

"Thank you, both of you. You didn't need to replace the one I ruined. It was my fault."

"Nonsense," Elizabeth clucked, a little of her mother coming through. "It was an accident, and you needn't be punished for it. This dress was the least we could do."

I hugged her quickly before relinquishing both her and my brother to the room. As the hosts, they were in high demand as conversational partners in a way Kitty and I were blessedly not. Even as they moved away to talk to another couple, Darcy kept an eye on me. It once might have annoyed me to be so closely watched, but when I caught sight of James Honeyfield across the room, I was grateful for my brother's caution. I refused to be forced into dancing with eligible bachelors to obey ridiculous etiquette guides that did not even recognise the potential existence of the love I felt for the girl beside me.

"Dance with me?" Kitty asked, gesturing to the dance floor. A dance floor full of men facing opposite women.

I wanted to be able to say yes. I was in my own home, and I should have been able to take her hand and walk to the centre of the floor with my head held high, but I still couldn't. Darcy and Elizabeth might not have protested, but the room was full of people whose reaction could not be counted upon. I loved my brother too much to damn the reputation of our family name quite so boldly in our own home.

"We can't," I told Kitty sadly. "I want to, but it's not sensible."

I rested my forehead against her temple for a long moment, squeezing my eyes closed and wishing I could kiss her.

"No," Kitty said abruptly.

She stepped away from me but grabbed my

hand to pull me after her across the room, back towards Elizabeth and Darcy. I wasn't sure exactly what she was protesting, and my surprise didn't give the me chance to ask before she was depositing me next to Darcy and dragging Elizabeth a little further away to whisper frantically in her ear. They were talking about me, that much was clear, with Kitty's little gestures in my direction and then towards the rest of the room. Darcy asked me the same questions I had with a raise of one eyebrow, but all I could do was shake my head. Kitty could still be an enigma to me if she wanted to.

Whatever she was hearing, Elizabeth was focused on it intently. She listened and whispered her own questions back, nodding slowly for a moment when Kitty rested her case and returned to my side.

"What are you doing?" I asked her.

"Finding a compromise," she replied.

She grabbed my hand and took a candle out of its holder before leading me back over towards Elizabeth. I was confused but too curious to protest as the four of us slipped out of the room.

Kitty knew where we were going, taking us all upstairs and into a rarely used drawing room above the ball. She appraised it with her arms crossed for a moment before nodding and crossing to throw open the windows. Darcy and Elizabeth seemed to catch on, with Darcy helping with the last few windows as Elizabeth took the candle to light those scattered around the perimeter of the room. The chandelier remained unlit, but there was enough of a glow to chase away the shadows and illuminate the space. It reminded me of the library late at night.

The music from downstairs drifted through the open windows, wrapping around me and finally providing the answer to Kitty's plot. We could dance together here.

"You are welcome downstairs, whether you want to dance or just stand and watch, but we understand if you would prefer fewer eyes," Elizabeth said, gesturing to the expansive floor that was all ours.

I surged forwards to give Elizabeth a hug, whispering my thanks into the sleeve of her dress. Kitty took my place as soon as I was done, squeezing her sister tightly.

"I mean it. You can come downstairs if you'd prefer," Elizabeth said. "Please don't think you have been banished up here."

"No, I know," I promised her.

The offer meant the world to me, but so did the opportunity to dance with Kitty without worrying what anyone else might be saying. Elizabeth and Darcy left arm in arm, leaving Kitty and me in blissful solitude. The first thing Kitty did was kiss me.

"Now will you dance with me?" she asked, her lips barely removed from my own.

I nodded, the movement turning into another kiss as someone announced the start of the next dance from the room below. We could just about make out the voice calling the steps, but half of them were useless to us anyway. With only two of us on the impromptu dance floor, we had to improvise every time there was a direction to swap partners. Halfway through, both Kitty and I were breathless more from stifled laughter than exertion.

The next time I passed near Kitty, she caught me and held me close, wrapping her arms around my waist to keep me there.

"This isn't the step," I protested, but neither of us were convinced by my objection.

Kitty just hummed, resting her forehead against mine and pulling me even closer. If we did this downstairs, we'd cause a scandal—any couple would—but up here with no one to comment on what we did, I had no arguments. We swayed gently with the music, not really dancing but letting it carry us on a slow, aimless path across the floor.

"My quiet brilliance," Kitty whispered.

"My bold adventure," I whispered back, pressing a kiss to her forehead.

She raised her chin to kiss me properly, the movement so instinctive that I could barely believe there was a time I thought it impossible. As we continued to drift in each other's arms, I thought of Lady Butler and Miss Ponsonby, I thought of Charlotte, I thought of Helena, and I knew that if this was what the rest of my life looked like, I would be happy. I had found the person who made it all worth it.

The End

Acknowledgments

Despite not being a particularly superstitious person, I felt it would be unwise to keep a list of people I'd need to thank at the end of this process while I was actually writing the book, just in case I jinxed its chances of publication. But now here it is, in your hands! Perhaps my concerns were well-placed, or maybe they had no influence whatsoever, but now I have to remember years' worth of people. If I forget anyone vital, it is absolutely my fault and in no way means I am not grateful for your support, I promise.

This book would never have gotten anywhere without the incredible support of my agent, Mike Whatnall. They unfailingly answer all my questions, no matter how minor, and all my emails, no matter how late I send them (the benefit of an eight-hour time difference) or how increasingly unhinged the subject lines are. Publishing is often a terrifying place, and Mike has made me feel infinitely less alone as I navigate it.

I am extremely grateful to Nikki Garcia for believing this story had potential and championing it so effectively. So many people have a hand in bringing a book to life, so I need to thank Andy Ball, Esther Reisberg, Sarah Chassé, Sarah Mondello, Su Wu, Erica Huang, Karina Granda, and anyone else at Little, Brown Books for Young Readers and beyond who was involved in the process. Particular thanks are due to Milena Blue Spruce, who held everything together and has understood and supported Georgiana's story the whole way through.

Before this book found success in the query trenches, it was a part of the SmoochPit mentorship programme. I am incredibly grateful to the organisers and to my mentor, Emery Lee, for helping set up this book for success.

The early seed of the idea that became this book was planted at a performance of a play called *Pride and Prejudice* (*sort of*), in which five women irreverently retell Jane Austen's iconic tale. Thank you to Isobel McArthur and the show's West End cast for proving just how gay this story can be. Go see the show, if you ever get the chance. It is the best tonic for any kind of melancholia.

Jane Austen herself is obviously dead so could not have stopped me writing this book even if she wanted to, but I hope very much that she would not have been too angry with how I've chosen to interpret her characters. She left Georgiana and Kitty unattended, with so much of their stories left untold, so I simply cannot be blamed for stealing them. But I do owe her my thanks for creating them in the first place, and for her delightful world in which I got to play.

Eleanor Butler and Sarah Ponsonby, the Ladies of Llangollen, were real people. They left Ireland to settle together in Wales in the late 1700s and lived as a couple at Plas Newydd for almost fifty years. Some historians will try to tell you they were just really good friends. Those historians are evidently ignoring the fact that Eleanor and Sarah had a series of dogs, all of which were named Sappho. The Ladies of Llangollen seemed like the perfect mentors for Georgiana and Kitty, and I hope they wouldn't have minded me putting their likenesses, their home, and their dog into the pages of this book.

Writing is often said to be a very solitary activity, which is true enough, but talking about your writing is a different pastime entirely, and one I often excel at. If I could have kept these characters inside my head, I wouldn't have had to write a whole book about them. Thank you to all my friends and family who asked how the book was going, even knowing it would mean they had to endure a monologue in response. So many people practically learnt a new language in order to understand the ins and outs of publishing and what on earth I was going on about. I'm grateful to everyone who let me witter on, and especially so to the people who actually listened and said they thought a sapphic sequel to *Pride and Prejudice* was a cool idea.

Particular thanks must go to Siobhan, who reassured me that I had not entirely made up all the music-related parts of this book, and to Kat, for the endless Discord messages and optimism. I can't wait until it's my turn to hold your debut book in my hands.

Questionable thanks must also go to Tilly, my cat. Without her, editing this book would have been a lot easier. Despite her efforts to repeatedly introduce a varied and nonsensical string of letters and punctuation into my manuscript at any given opportunity, I would not trade her presence for anything. Since I had to remove all of Tilly's suggested edits so my editor didn't start questioning my sanity, I'll include one here so she can see her work in print:

[g]vlok78;/.6//////

The next great voice of a generation, I'm sure you'll agree.

ERIN EDWARDS

is a lesbian with a love for all things literary, historical, and theatrical. By day, she can be found in an archive, attempting to decipher old handwriting and digging through boxes of hidden histories. By night, she's probably in a theater, waiting for the lights to go down and the magic to start. There is a fair chance she's already seen the show before. Erin grew up struggling to find enough queer fiction to fill a single shelf, and now she's committing to the cause of helping to fill endless bookcases with queer stories. She lives in London with a cat that is at least 85 percent fluff.

CELEBRATING 100 YEARS OF PUBLISHING

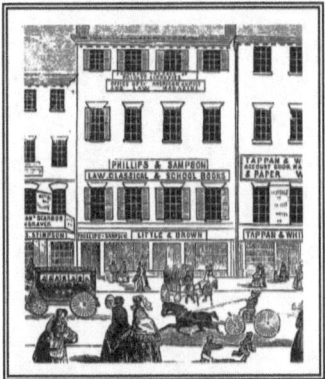

Dear Reader,

You may have noticed the words "Little, Brown and Company" on the title page of this book and wondered what they mean. Well, Charles C. Little and James Brown were the founders of this publishing house, and the "and Company" is all the editors, designers, marketers, publicists, salespeople, and more who help produce each book and bring it to readers like you. Little, Brown was founded in Boston, Massachusetts, in 1837, and some of its early publications included *The Writings of George Washington* and *The Works of Benjamin Franklin*. The catalog grew to feature works by Emily Dickinson and Louisa May Alcott, among many other notable authors. In 1926, recognizing that the literature we read when we are young has a deep and lasting influence and requires expert curation, the company appointed an editor to lead a dedicated children's department.

In 2026, Little, Brown Books for Young Readers celebrates one hundred years of excellence in publishing. Today, we are a division of Hachette Livre, the third-largest publisher in the world, and we are based in New York City. Our staff has grown from a team of two to more than one hundred people. And with the changes in technology, our books are read by more readers, in more ways, and in more countries than ever before. However, one thing has not changed: our commitment to providing a supportive home for all creators and superb stories for all readers. Thank you for being one of them.

Megan Tingley
Megan Tingley
President and Publisher

To learn more about Little, Brown's history,
authors, and books, please visit LBYR.com.

www.ingramcontent.com/pod-product-compliance
Lightning Source LLC
LaVergne TN
LVHW031535060526
838200LV00056B/4508